Fn Helen Harkins

from

Isabelle Strang

Other books by the same author

CECILY
AMANDA'S CHOICE
THE MAN WITHOUT A FACE
HEADS YOU WIN, TAILS I LOSE

Kilgaren

a novel by

Isabelle Holland

Weybright and Talley
New York

Copyright © 1974 by Isabelle Holland

All rights reserved, including the right
to reproduce this book, or parts thereof, in
any form, except for the inclusion of
brief quotations in a review.

Weybright and Talley
750 Third Avenue
New York, New York

Library of Congress Catalog Card Number: 74-75719
ISBN: 0-679-40121-0
Manufactured in the United States of America
Designed by Jacques Chazaud

FIRST PRINTING, APRIL 1974
SECOND PRINTING, APRIL 1974

 # 1

It all began—and ended—with Lady Margaret, who died before I was born. But of course I didn't know that when Jonathan, my half brother, wrote inviting me back to the island. He wrote to Mother who passed on the invitation with a rider of her own that she felt strongly I should accept it.

"After all," Mother said, "he's your brother. And he now owns all that property. Even he admits he should do something for you."

"I hate him and I'd rather be dead."

"How can you hate him when you don't even remember him?"

"I remember him very well. Too well."

"You were eight when you last saw him—if you call that remembering. Don't be ridiculous, Barbara!" Mother glanced into her dressing table mirror at me, looming gawkily behind her, and came to her real reason for urging me to go. "If you think you're going to tag along with Renaldo and me—that is, I mean, not that we wouldn't be happy to have you with us, for a while—"

"I liked it better the first way, Mother. At least it's honest." Renaldo is Mother's newest boyfriend and he has a thing about youth—his, not mine. A grown-up ugly duckling of a would-be stepdaughter is not something he likes to have in his general environment.

"It's not," Mother said, peering at her lovely face in the glass, "as though you made an effort to be congenial. Making sarcastic remarks and all but accusing Renaldo of being a fortune-hunter is hardly the best method of endearing yourself to him—or to me. Especially," she added drily, "as I don't have any money."

I had to admit Mother had me there. The household had been disastrously short of cash, minus now even the check that Father's estate had grudgingly sent for my expenses, and that stopped the day I was eighteen. As far as Father had been concerned, I had two strikes against me: I was a girl and I was Mother's daughter. He, and after his death his lawyers, paid to the letter of the divorce agreement, that is, until my eighteenth birthday—and that was it. I inherited nothing.

But still, and despite our (relative) poverty, there was something about Renaldo that made it hard for me to believe that he was one to count the world well lost for love. Perhaps it was the soft look that came into his liquid dark eyes whenever the topic of money or wealth came up. Or, to be fair, maybe it was because his poorly masked aversion to me made me willing to believe the worst of him. I decided not to argue that particular point.

"I'm not trying to endear myself to either of you. I just want to go to Rome. Once I'm there, I'll find a job and you won't see me again. I want to be around you and Renaldo as little as you want to have me around."

Mother looked up at me in the mirror in which she was now carefully applying her eyeliner. "Why Rome?"

Why indeed? Because Rome was where Nick was. Nick—on whom I had had a crush since I was fifteen and he was eighteen. Now, three years later, he had some kind of job at the U.S. Embassy in Rome, and although I didn't really think that I could make him (or anyone) fall in love with me, at least I'd be near him and maybe if I made myself very useful and helpful and devoted. . . .

"If you're thinking of Nick Caldwell, don't bother. From all I hear he's surrounded by a human wall of admiring lovelies in five languages. Just where do you think you'd fit in?"

It's one of Mother's least lovable qualities that she can usually read my mind. Not that it's difficult, at least as far as Nick is concerned. Going bright red whenever his name is mentioned is not the way to acquire a reputation for aloof indifference.

Mother glanced at my face again and put down her eyeliner. "Don't try, Barbara. You're not in his league. With his money and looks and connections he can pretty well take his pick, and has, from everything I hear, for the past year, up and down the *Via Veneto*. Do you really think you can compete with that? Although you may not believe it, I don't want to see you hurt."

Mother and I had never been what you could call friends. For one thing, although she had been given custody of me and I had always technically lived with her, I had seen almost as little of her as I had of my father since their separation when I was eight. Mother had brought me back to New York, had hired an apartment and a series of governesses to look after me and, the moment I was old enough, had sent me to boarding school. During all that time she had acquired one or two other husbands but not, as I finally learned, more money. We had moved to progressively smaller apartments. By the time she encountered Renaldo, the lease on the last and the smallest apartment had expired. Mother and Renaldo were about to leave for Rome where, Renaldo kept saying, they could stay in one or another of his family palazzos. Whether or not that was part of Renaldo's gift for hyperbole I didn't know. But it was certainly true that he had family and friends there and Mother knew a lot of the crowd that seemed to drift around that part of the world.

If it weren't for Nick nothing would have induced me to try, in Mother's words, to tag along with them. But ever since that ghastly summer I spent with the Caldwells after my first operation my heart belonged to Nick. Like many disfigured people I had a bottomless hunger for physical beauty and Nick, with his blond hair and handsome features and graceful, athletic body, filled that hunger as nothing and no one ever had. I had first seen him in the Caldwell's living room shortly after my bandages came off. He walked through the French windows, pausing as he came in from the light to the darkened room. From where I was sitting the sun seemed to surround him like an aura. I took one look and was lost.

Much good it did me.

The Caldwells had a big house on the north shore constantly filled with young people. It was Nick's younger sister, my classmate, who had invited me there when I had nowhere to go after the plastic surgery. I was shy and awkward and miserably self-conscious about my scars and infinitely preferred to be left alone. Most people took one embarrassed look and granted my wish. Nick would undoubtedly have done the same except that I turned out to have some skills he badly needed that summer. He was cramming for some exams in French and Italian and after traipsing around with Mother and her current husband during school holidays from one European watering place to another, I was fluent in both. His gratitude didn't go to such exorbitant lengths as taking me out or (for example) giving me a kiss—a little fantasy that flowed in and out of my mind like a happy dream. Towards the end of my stay there, when the scars and the scraping had started to heal and showed less, I peered in my looking glass each morning to see if such a tender and secret imagining had any chance of materializing. But I had always looked at things—including my face, especially my face—squarely. And I knew the fantasy would stay a fantasy. Still, it was all right. I was willing to admire him from afar, so to speak, and help him pass his exams, which he did.

He and I both went back to school. Since then I had had two more bouts with plastic surgery. The burns had been deep and the results neglected. Good plastic surgery is expensive. Until I was fourteen and the money suddenly and mysteriously materialized from Father's estate, Mother was too poor, she explained, to have it done properly, so nothing was done at all. I learned a lot of things in those years: That there are two kinds of people—those that stare fixedly at you in a sort of locked gaze and those who will look at anything—the sky, the floor, over your left or right shoulder—rather than your face.

I'd better explain here that I wasn't a monster. If it hadn't been for that terrible nursery fire when I was six, I might have been quite pretty, because I look like Mother—the same pale blonde hair, dark gray eyes and general conformity of features, and while inheriting anything else from Mother—brains or disposition, for example—would hardly have been signs of Divine Grace, there was no denying her beauty. But when I was six and we were still living on the island, a fire broke out in the east wing of the house where the nursery was located. What made it bad was that I had been locked in for some misdemeanor by my half brother, Jonathan. He was a lot older than I—nineteen years—and even then was a tyrant. So it was his fault that I was a mass of third-degree burns by the time they finally got me out. For years every time I looked in the mirror I was reminded of Jonathan, and muttered island curses against him, hoping for the worst to happen. But he went on, flourishing like the green bay tree, getting richer and richer and, when our father died, inheriting the land, the sugar plantation, and the whole island. And now he'd had the gall to write to Mother, suggesting that I return to the island and teach in the family-run elementary school there.

"He's demented," I said, as Mother, still applying makeup, tried to point out the advantages. "I'd never work for him. I'd—I'd go on Forty-second Street first. I'd walk the streets!"

"You wouldn't get very far. That's an extremely competitive and overcrowded profession. And you have to admit, Barbara, you're handicapped."

"It's nice of you to point it out. I thought all this plastic surgery was going to work miracles. Three operations and I'd step out of the shell—*Voilà*, a beauty! It sure hasn't worked out that way."

"Not miracles. An improvement. And it has. The scars are much less noticeable, and they're still fading. In a little while you should be almost—" She hunted around for a word.

"Normal?" I asked innocently.

Mother missed the sarcasm. "Yes. Normal. An average-looking girl." And she glanced at her own reflection in the mirror. She didn't mean to be offensive. I've accepted that. If you're an accredited beauty, a glance in a mirror is like breathing.

"No," I said.

"No what?"

"No. I will not go back to the island and work for Jonathan."

"Well, just what do you intend to do? Be a telephone operator? You don't even know typing and shorthand. And if, as you're always saying, you want to teach and help young children, then this is an ideal offer. To do this here in the United States you'd have to have at least four years of college plus a teacher's certificate. Why don't you go to the island school for a year and then come back to get your training? It's not as though Jonathan isn't going to pay you handsomely—plus your keep, since you'll live at Four Winds."

If the offer hadn't come from Jonathan I would have snapped at it. Everything Mother said was true. I had loved the island as a child, the Green Isle, I always called it to myself, with its lush tropical trees and foliage and mountains, and until that horrible fire and despite Jonathan's repressive presence, I'd been happy. I'd had a governess, of course, but I used to slip away either to ride one of the horses in the family stables that I was forbidden (by Jonathan) to ride, to climb some of the island's giant trees, or to play with the brown and coffee-colored and black children whose huts and little farms lay at the edge of the enormous plantation. For this, and when I was caught, I was soundly trounced (by Jonathan) on the excuse that I would probably catch one of the plagues or diseases that kept the infant mortality of the island rather high.

For a minute I wavered. Then I remembered how much I had loathed Jonathan and how he had ruined my life and how I had sworn that never again would I let him get any power over me. I shook my head.

Mother shrugged. "Suit yourself. But you're not coming to Rome with us. And I'm not going to give you the money to go by yourself, so unless you find it somewhere else, you're stuck."

It was no use asking Mother why she was so adamant about my not going with her and Renaldo to Rome. I knew, or thought I knew. Renaldo didn't want me and that meant Mother didn't want me. And if that sounds as if I were hiding a broken heart over my rebuffed affections, let me say again, the feeling between Mother and me was entirely mutual. But Nick was in Rome.

Despite my refusal I pondered the matter the next few days. I had, in my own savings account, one hundred and three dollars. That would not only not get me to Rome, it wouldn't buy me so much as a pasta when I got there.

Well, said the other side of my on-going internal argument, Nick can find you a job when you get there. After all, he owes you one. It was true. He did. But my pride didn't feel comfortable with that approach—especially when I considered the Lovelies Mother referred to. And it felt even less comfortable when I found in my room a day or so later one of those magazines filled with photographs of the jet set and the Beautiful People. It was lying, open, on my bed. And there, covering one whole page, was one Nicholas Caldwell IV, strolling along the *Via Veneto*, with one of the young Lovelies on his arm. And she was very lovely. The caption didn't help either. It said, in an Italian bursting with insinuations, that the young American, Nicholas Caldwell IV, could be seen here with his dear friend, his *chère amie* and so forth, Michaela Biancci, daughter of some Italian oil tycoon or other. They were seen together all the time, it said. And their friends were confidently awaiting an announcement, it said.

I sat down and stared at it.

This, I knew, would be all that was needed to get most girls on a plane by means fair or foul or with the aid of a stolen credit card. After that, things would take care of themselves.

But I was not most girls. I looked into the mirror. As I said, I was always a realist. Those scalded patches had disappeared. The puckered scars had been smoothed out. I had nice eyes and good bones. But I did not look, and never would look, like a young beauty with virgin (if you'll forgive the expression) unblemished skin. That being the case, even if I could scrounge up the fare, I would not go to Rome dependent on Nick for my next hundred lira. Having for twelve years been dependent on Mother and whoever her current husband happened to be for every movie ticket and ice cream soda, I knew what that—financial dependence—could be like.

I thought again about Jonathan and the job he was holding out and my oath never again to be in his power and going to Rome with some money in my pocket and a year's teaching experience under my belt. And I decided to reorder my priorities. That oath applied when I was small. I was now grown. *Vive la différence!* I looked again at the magazine. Then I closed it and went into Mother's room.

"Okay. You made your point."

Mother, who was putting things into a suitcase, turned around. "Then you'll go back to the island?"

For a minute I reflected that she seemed awfully eager to send me there. Then, because the depression instigated by that picture of Nick and his Lovely started to feel like a tidal wave, I decided it wasn't worth pushing the matter.

"Yes, I'll go. And if I join their pitiful little revolutionary movement and blow up Four Winds and Jonathan and the whole feudal mess, you can take all the credit."

"Barbara—!" Mother looked aghast. She didn't have much humor and if there was anything that really upset her metabolism it was the word "revolutionary." All the things and people she liked best would be the first to go in any revolution worthy of the name.

"Don't worry. I won't. At least, not till I leave. Which is what I intend to do in a year."

2

*T*wo weeks later, having helped to close the apartment and put the furniture in storage, I saw Mother and Renaldo off at Kennedy Airport. Then I took a taxi to another airline and boarded a slightly smaller plane to Jamaica. Jonathan had sent money (to Mother, not to me) to pay for my fare to Kilgaren Island which would include not only the flight to Jamaica but the hire for a private plane from there to the island, since the more usual means of transportation were infrequent and erratic.

There are several highly respectable airlines that go to Jamaica, but I didn't take any of them because they would have insisted that Sedgewick go with the luggage. And I couldn't permit that. Sedgewick would have cried his heart out and probably given everyone else a nervous breakdown. It was the realization that he would have to go in the hold to Italy that made it slightly easier for me to decide that between Nick's Young Lovely and me there was no real contest. So Sedgewick and I flew what was practically freight to Jamaica. But at least he could sit up on the seat next to me.

Since Sedgewick is to figure (however unintentionally) so largely in this story I had better explain how he and I found one another and why he was important to me. The last part is the easiest to answer: empathy. Sedgewick registered just about zero on everybody's Richter Scale. And with this I had, as the psychologists would say, total identification. He knew it, and I knew it, and we both knew that the other knew it. It was a powerful bond. Anthropomorphism, Mother once said, after she had heard someone use the word and looked it up in the dictionary.

Sedgewick is a mutt I picked up on Second Avenue, obviously a stray and one that had been on the losing side of many fights, not only with dogs, but with cars. I had noticed him once or twice in the neighborhood, going along on three legs at quite a surprising speed. He had a fourth leg but held it off the ground and must have done so for some time because he was as nimble with three as most dogs are with four. He was a dirt colored dog with dark red patches—some of which turned out to be skin disease—one and three quarter ears, and a thieving disposition. It was when he was being driven out of a deli at the end of a pole with wire things on it and yelping painfully that I took a hand. I've never been particularly impulsive but the next thing I knew the pole was in my own hand, its business end smashed up against the grocer who looked as though he was being attacked by a mad woman, as indeed he was, and an interested crowd had gathered. It was that that saved Sedgewick. I could see the police car coming to find out what was causing the hubbub. Before anybody knew it the wretched animal would be in the pound. I dropped the pole, heaved the filthy dog up into my arms, and ran as fast as I could around the corner.

"Do you know what almost happened to you?" I said to him, panting, as I put him down. "Let that be a lesson to you."

He raised himself unsteadily on his one good hind leg, whimpering a little, and tried to lick my hand and then my face. We proceeded towards my apartment, Sedgewick prancing ahead as though the whole thing had been arranged by Divine Authority.

Evidently the doorman to our apartment building didn't see it that way. "Out! Shoo! Get Away!," he said, advancing threateningly. "There's one of them nasty-looking strays following you, Miss Kilgaren. Let me call the ASPCA."

Sedgewick backed into my legs, making bold noises, but I could feel him trembling.

"He does not look nasty. He's mine. And I'm going to keep him."

"You know what the rules say, Miss Kilgaren. No dogs."

"And what about that Mrs. Van Derventer's poodle?"

"Miss! That poodle won the blue ribbon last year."

"That's discrimination. Come, Sedgewick!" And I stalked in.

Mercifully, Mother and Renaldo were away. By the time they got back, Sedgewick, the better for several baths, two visits to the vet and a nightly anointing of his sores with salve, was established.

"Why on earth did you call him Sedgewick?" Mother asked, appalled, when they returned.

"I think it suits him," I replied blandly. "I mean, he's so aristocratic-looking."

Mother gave me a darkling look. The older I got, the less she knew when I was joking. I waited to see if she would try to forbid my having him. She and I had been having one or two trials of strength lately (this was shortly before Renaldo decided they must live in Italy and Jonathan invited me to the island) and I was quite prepared to do battle, up to and including moving myself and Sedgewick out. But, a little to my surprise, she retreated.

"Which just goes to show," I told Sedgewick, when we were having morning coffee on my bed the following day, "that you never know your own strength, doesn't it? Have some muffin!" Since Sedgewick was used to an extremely varied diet out of garbage cans, English muffin with orange marmalade obviously struck him as ambrosia. He disposed of his half and looked hungrily at mine. I gave him half of my half. "I wouldn't admit this to Mother," I told him, "but your aristocracy is like your beauty—zilch. Like mine!" I added, because the thought was always there, "But you love me as I am, don't you?" Sedgewick rolled over ecstatically. His dirt color, when washed, had become off-white (more off than white. Pollution had had its permanent toll). His red patches, those that were real and not leprosy or mange, were liver-colored. He was plainly descended from a long line of curs. But he was living proof that kind hearts and virtue have nothing to do with coronets or Norman blood, because now, wherever I went, he followed, from room to room. When I had a bath he sat on the bath mat which now smelt more of dog and antiseptic ointment than it did of expensive talcum. And if anyone even raised a voice in my direction, his scruffy hair stood up with fury and he forgot his basic cowardice and became Tiger the Terrible.

We were great friends, Sedgewick and I.

We sat together in the small hired plane and looked down on the isosceles triangle that was Kilgaren Island growing rapidly larger beneath us. The long apex pointed northwest, an almost solid green cone that revealed itself, the lower we flew, as acres on acres of sugar cane, divided and crisscrossed by dirt roads. Near the tip, west by northwest, was the village, consisting of a paved, broader street, a steeple, a couple of buildings that stood out and, below that, a huddle of roofs.

But my eyes were not on the village. They were on the dark mass that lay towards the southeastern base, just south of the cane fields and immediately beneath the surprisingly high mountains behind. That was Four Winds, ancestral home of the Kilgarens.

I suppose at this point I had better explain about the Kilgaren family and its history, which is something between an albatross and a joke. The first Kilgaren, rather more than less of a pirate, took the island from a horde of less successful pirates in the name of her gracious Majesty Queen Elizabeth I. Having taken the island for the Queen, he then characteristically named it after himself. And perhaps because the queen was in a good humor, or more likely because she had a soft spot for his handsome arrogant face with its black hair and beaky nose (the portrait still hangs in the central hall of the house), she let him get away with it. And then, because his impudence and arrogance knew no bounds, he built a huge, even then outdated horror for himself and called it Kilgaren's Castle. It was the islanders who ignored such pretentiousness and renamed the house Four Winds, because its location and altitude enabled it to capture every breeze that blew across the island. The bungalows and shacks below might swelter in the midday heat. But not Winds, as even the family came to call it, especially after my great-grandfather pulled down the fake crenellations and built an equally bogus Victorian gothic in its place. So Kilgaren Island and Kilgaren Castle—the property deed still carried the absurd name—have remained for almost four centuries a family holding. Not, of course, without a spot of trouble here and there.

Probably because the island had almost nothing to be said for it except that it was, like George Leigh Mallory's mountain, there, the trouble never amounted to much. The island was tiny, altogether only about fourteen square miles. It had no treasure. It had no decent port. And although its soil was lava rich, there simply wasn't enough space to grow enough of anything for a really brisk export trade. The family sold a little sugar to the United States and a little to South America and rumbled a little rum to everywhere, and that was it.

Overlooking the Ulster origin of its pirate-founder, the family has always considered itself staunchly English. As with all such families, it developed its own customs, traditions and legends. The oldest and best observed was that Kilgaren men always returned to England for their schooling and their brides.

Father's first wife, Jonathan's mother, was the Lady Margaret Trelevyn. Ironically, it was this lady, descended from a family whose role in English history predated the Norman conquest, who gave the impetus and educational wherewithal to the island's minute and rather limp revolutionary movement. Unlike most of her predecessors on the island she did not, after presenting her husband with the requisite heir, return to England. (Life on a small Caribbean island that was not, when you came down to it, much more than a large sugar plantation, lacked social diversion.) But Lady Margaret got out of her tweeds and into her cottons and set about useful things like building a new and much better equipped school for the "natives," installing a free clinic, getting an extra doctor, and establishing one or two scholarships for the brighter graduates of the school. (Of course all English children on the island—the parson's, the doctor's and those of a handful of business and professional people—went back to England for school, just as Jonathan did.)

Her activities did not please everyone. No good would come of such Bolshie notions, warned the English and some Americans, sipping their drinks on the porch of the cricket club or in one another's houses. And of course they were right. Much of the recent trouble on the island that made even the New York papers—a strike or two and a couple of mini-riots—had been brewed by the pupils and graduates of that very school.

Part of Father's trouble after he first married Lady Margaret was that as other parts of the world started to grow sugar, the price the family was getting dropped and some of the markets fell away altogether. One outlet, the United States, was then in the midst of a major depression, and American orders were being cancelled right and left. Since almost all the family money was tied up in the crop this was a major crisis. Reluctantly, because no Kilgaren really liked being anywhere but on the island, Father started to make business trips to negotiate for new markets. That was when Lady Margaret made her moves. When he got back from his first trip she had started a school and installed a schoolmaster more than a little tainted by the London School of

Economics. After his third trip Father found a new clinic. When he returned from his fourth he learned that the first island newspaper had been launched. All of this was underwritten by Lady Margaret's personal fortune, which was considerable. And she was canny. If her husband had been there he could have prevented her beginning any of these enterprises. But even he, absolute monarch that he was, did not care to create a public issue out of closing them—not with his lack of cash and an urgent need to get out the biggest possible harvest. But he was not pleased, and if Lady Margaret had not, during his fifth absence, produced the much wanted heir he would—or so the island gossip went—have been the first Kilgaren to seek a divorce. But there Jonathan was when his father returned, and while, of course, he had known that Lady Margaret was pregnant (at last!) long before he left, his suspicion of her by that time was so great that he fully expected her to bring forth a girl. So when she did the proper thing and presented him with a son he forgave her her transgressions—that is, he forbore to close down the institutions that her money kept going. After her death from a tropical disease when Jonathan was six, he simply let them dwindle and die, replacing neither staff nor equipment.

Jonathan would have gone back to England to school at seven as did all the family males, but even the Kilgaren tradition had to bend to the exigencies of World War II and German submarines. So he was tutored on the island until he was nine. After that he went to England. When he was eighteen and at Oxford his Father astounded him and everyone else by breaking tradition and marrying an American—my mother. Once again the entire white population of the island (about forty-seven people not including The Family) said no good would come of it. And again, they were absolutely right.

Mother was the ambitious daughter of one of those New York blue-book families hanging on by their fingernails to the privileges they could no longer afford. Her tuition at an exclusive girls' boarding school and her coming out had been paid for by a wealthy godmother. She'd been out for about a year when she met Father at a party at Government House in Jamaica. Father, at that time, was more than twice Mother's age, but this was made up for by his distinguished good looks, his name, his island, his title and what appeared to be the trappings of wealth. It wasn't until after the wedding, when Mother had actually gone to live on Kilgaren, that she realized that the trappings were just trappings, that every penny the family owned was sunk in its island sugar crop.

I was born a year after they married, an event that, I gather, was looked on by both parents (but for entirely different reasons) as of no importance: my father because I was a girl and therefore not a back-up heir, and my mother because by this time the novelty of living on an oversized sugar plantation, cut off from everything she considered civilized by land, sea and air, had palled. Luckily for the family fortunes, unluckily for Mother's amusement, the Kilgaren men had never been nominal landlords (one of their ladies had said bitterly that the taint of Trade must run in their blood.) Kilgarens looked after their plantations, their trade and their interests. For their women it was frustrating and (with the exception of the indefatigable Lady Margaret) boring.

Mother's visits to New York became more frequent and longer. I don't remember this myself. I put it together afterwards out of servants' gossip. At the time she was simply a dim, glamorous figure who would periodically descend on the nursery. I thought she was splendid-looking, but I didn't think she had much to do with me or my life.

My nurse was Nemi. She was soft and kind and coffee-colored—and she drank. She wouldn't let me touch the bottles of dark rum out of which she took big nips all day long, but she would let me help her find places to hide them.

And then there was Jonathan, an increasingly powerful presence. I think, during the early years of my life, he was doing a lot of traveling for the estate. But then an old wound that Father had acquired at Anzio flared up. It became harder for him to get around, and he finally had to resort to a wheelchair. So Jonathan came home permanently and took over the actual running of the estate. As Father grew weaker Jonathan became, in all but name, master of Kilgaren.

I shivered a little in the toy-sized plane as the reality of that memory came back.

Those were bad times. Whether Father resented Jonathan's takeover or not I don't know. I do know that battles between them would suddenly erupt. Servants would scurry from the halls and the sounds of the two male voices—so alike in depth and resonance—would fill the house.

They frightened me, those voices. To get away from them I would run out of the house and proceed to break one (or several) of the rules (increasingly strict, as Father got older and crankier) that governed my life.

I climbed endless trees, ran under the great waterfall in the heights behind the house, slid my bare legs over the backs of horses in our stables and, before anyone could stop me, took them out. I played with the children of the cane cutters, I went to the witch's hut and (later) bought a statue of Jonathan I could stick pins into, and more than once spent the night in a cave up in the green hills back of the waterfall and woke up when the huge red sun lifted itself out of the eastern sea.

But always, sooner or later, Jonathan would find me. He ordered me to come down out of trees, forbade me to ride the big horses in the stable, threatened the cane cutters' families so they wouldn't let their children play with me and, when I defied him, turned me over his knee and lashed my thin bottom. When even that didn't work, he locked me in the nursery.

Only in dreams now does my mind go back to that night of the fire. I have tried since then to go over it moment by moment, to exorcise it, stare it down. But my conscious, waking mind refuses. It remains a blur of night and blackness, of the sound of fire crackling near me, my own screaming at a locked door, the smell of smoke and the memory of unspeakable fear.

I was not afraid of Jonathan now. But even so, if it were not for Nick, I wouldn't be going back to the island. Somehow, despite the caption in that magazine, I didn't think Nick would be marrying his Lovely immediately. I don't know why I didn't, but I didn't. As long as Nick was free I had hope. And as soon as I started teaching, I would have money.

The plane circled down. The ground came hurtling up. There was a rush of green past the window and then we were bumping along the Band-Aid-sized airstrip. Finally we stopped. The pilot opened the door, and the lush swampy smell of the island poured in. For a moment what I wanted to do was cry out of the sheer joy of being back. I had forgotten how much I loved it.

"Come on, Sedgewick," I said. "We're home!"

A tall, good-looking young black was waiting by the airstrip. Behind him was what looked like a taxi.

"Miss Kilgaren?"

I nodded. "Yes."

"Sir Jonathan sent me to get you. I'll get your bags."

I had forgotten how English the island English

was. When he came back he looked doubtfully at Sedgewick. "That your dog, Miss?"

"Yes," I said a little aggressively, so as not to sound apologetic. "That's my dog."

Sedgewick, sensitive to the slightest critical atmosphere, sat down, as near my legs as possible. To show he was not intimidated, he gave a short bark, then wagged his tail, then wiggled back a little.

The young man said softly, "Maybe your dog doesn't like blacks."

There was something in that gentle voice that made me decide to clear the matter up immediately. Sedgewick had led a harried enough life as it was. It was time he enjoyed some peace and quiet.

"My dog's name is Sedgewick, which is a sort of a joke, because he came off the streets of New York and his problem was people who kicked him around. I don't think he knows black from green or white from purple."

The young man gave Sedgewick a look of cool contempt, shrugged and opened the car door for me. "Maybe he should fight back."

I stood in front of the door. "Fight whom and for what?"

The black eyes stared arrogantly into mine. "For his freedom. For his right to his share."

It was an astonishing conversation to be having within three minutes of my arrival. I remembered Mother once saying, "People going to the island think it is very slow motion, very tropical, very mañana. But some things—strange things—happen amazingly fast." I wondered then what she meant. Now I was beginning to have an inkling. And I was quite sure that this hostile young man was simply using Sedgewick as a device for getting a message over to me. I pushed Sedgewick into the car and got in myself. Absently I stroked his back and felt the quivering of his skin.

"What's your name?" I asked the young man.

After a second's pause he said, "Seth." Then he added, "Miss."

"All right, Seth. I'm not your enemy and Sedgewick's not your enemy. So let's not have any silly misunderstanding."

"You're still part of the family, Miss."

We circled away from the airport and took the road that ran up the west coast of the island. Bamboo and eucalyptus trees lined the road. To my left, on the east side, I could see the tall green walls of sugar cane. On the right was the ocean, its color, at that moment in the early evening, an aquamarine. I drew in my breath. It had been—how long?—nearly eleven years. Yet it was as though it had been a year or two.

Absently I said to the young man in front whose bony shoulders seemed to exude anger and resentment, "Yes, I am. But that still doesn't make me the enemy."

"Your brother, Sir Jonathan, is. So you are."

My first feeling was to be annoyed to be included with my brother. My next was that I couldn't repudiate him, however much I might dislike him personally.

"What would happen if I told Sir Jonathan that you're talking to me like this?"

The black eyes, a little almond-shaped, looked at me in the rear-view mirror. "Nothing. You haven't been around for a time, have you Miss?"

"No."

"It's not like it used to be. Not so many young people now to do his work for him. They're going to Jamaica, which is now free. Independent. That's what we want to be. That's what we're going to be."

He spoke as though he were reading it out of some revolutionary's speech. Yet, although it was parroted, it carried conviction.

"Does—does Sir Jonathan know you feel this way?"

Then he laughed, looking suddenly much younger, his cheeks round, his skin almost as smooth as a child's. "He knows, Miss. He *should* know. We tell him every way we know how."

The car started to climb. The trees seemed to part and I saw the house, a long pile of graystone with a lot of chimneys, a European transplant, ugly and alien and yet, by now, as much a part of the landscape as the bamboo or the palm trees.

"That's Four Winds," I said aloud.

"Yes, Miss. That's Winds."

3

*E*verything was in a state of dilapidation: the drive, the thick bushes that had taken over what I dimly remembered as the front lawn, the front of the house, which had a strange, mournful look due, perhaps, to the fact that since the house faced northeast, it was now in evening shadow. Vaguely I noticed that the louvres seemed shut on most of the windows. To the left the sky was dark, to the right, orange.

As I got out of the car the front door opened and out stepped a tall man with broad shoulders, black hair, light eyes and a prominent, crooked nose. It was Jonathan.

"Hello, Barbara. Welcome."

Despite all my mental pep talks to myself about not being afraid, I felt my muscles tighten. He came down the front steps. I could hear Sedgewick behind me, flopping out of the car. Then Seth put my bags on the drive beside me, got back in the car, and started the engine.

Jonathan came up to me and before I knew what he was doing leaned down and kissed my cheek. "Did you have a good trip?"

I was so astonished I gave the automatic answer of the well-mannered schoolgirl. "Yes, thank you."

He picked up my bags. "What's that?"

I didn't even have to turn around. "That's Sedgewick. He's a dog. And he's mine. Where I go, he goes. Like Ruth and Naomi."

He put down the bags. I braced myself and wished that Seth weren't rolling down the drive with the car. If Jonathan was going to turn nasty about Sedgewick, then I was going back to New York, job or no job, money or no money, even Nick or no Nick.

"Come here, Sedgewick!" Jonathan said. Wriggling his wretched stump of a tail, Sedgewick went up to him and, to my unspeakable disgust, licked the hand that was held out to him.

"Sedgewick," I said coldly, "may not be the best of breed—"

"He isn't any breed at all, best or worst." Jonathan rubbed Sedgewick between the ears and ran his hand down his side. "What are you doing about those sores?"

"I have some ointment the vet gave me. And if you're going to object to his sleeping in my room or on my bed because of that—"

"I don't care where he sleeps." Jonathan picked up the bags and started up the steps to the front door.

I remembered the hall as huge, swallowing up an immense sofa, a table and two wing chairs. In the center a staircase went up, branching out on either side. Portraits lined the paneled walls and a chandelier hung suspended from two floors above. It had been splendid and baronial and inappropriate and very English. It was still very English, but the general dilapidation was visible here in a light coating of dust on the hall table, in the faded coverings of the furniture, and on brass ornaments dark with tarnish. There had been a row of them along the wall, the brass decorations that used to be worn by the huge shire horses in England and that some Kilgaren had collected and mounted. They were still there but they looked dirty.

"I remember those. But they were a lot brighter," I added tactlessly.

"There used to be a lot of servants," Jonathan said. And for the first time I realized that no servant had come out for my suitcases, and there had been none in the hall. According to an old joke, there used to be at least six for every member of the family. I tried to remember some of the names, but all I could recall were the black and brown faces above white coats that seemed to be everywhere.

"What happened to them all?"

"I'll take these up," Jonathan said, walking towards the stairs. I followed.

Following him up the dark wood stairs, I asked him again, "What happened to the servants?" I remembered what Seth had said, but I wanted to hear Jonathan's version.

"Nothing happened to the servants, Barbara.

What happened was to the family. We lost most of our money. The young blacks—those that aren't cane cutters or have other jobs—are going to Jamaica or Cuba. Even if they don't, they don't want to serve here."

"You mean you have nobody?"

"I have Hamish, a Scot, and some blacks who come in occasionally by the day."

By this time we were up on the second floor. Jonathan walked down the southeast wing. "I'm putting you here next to Evelyn."

"Who's Evelyn?"

Jonathan walked into a big square room with windows on two sides and a cool cross draft. Three lamps and a ceiling fan went on as he touched some wall switches. Putting my bags down on two suitcase stands he turned. "There's a bathroom through that door. Dinner will be in half an hour. I'll wait for you downstairs." He went out, closing the door.

I stood there for a minute, then I turned off the lights again and walked over to the French windows straight in front of me, opened one side, and stepped out on a small balcony. The house was high. The air was cooler up here. The sky was a deep blue. It was almost, but not quite, night. Immediately in front of me was a dark mass that I knew were the hills that reared themselves up at this end of the island. Although I couldn't see them, in those steep heights were the cave I spent the night in, the waterfall I slid behind, the thick tangled underbrush I used to hide in during the wild happy days of my early childhood.

I still couldn't believe I was back. I couldn't believe this was the house I had been born in and grew up in, at least to the age of eight. It felt so strange. And then, suddenly, borne by the breeze came the cool, damp smell, and everything became real.

The sound of running water a few feet away made me jump. I turned around and went back into the room and switched on the lights again. Behind the closed door leading to the bathroom a tap had been turned on. There was a light under the door and the noise of splashing.

Suddenly I remembered that Jonathan had said, "I'm putting you next to Evelyn." But he had never told me who Evelyn was. I knew perfectly well that to knock on a bathroom door—unless there were a very good reason—was not, in Mother's phrase, done. But I had spent my life doing, as a matter of principle, what was not done. So boldly I went to the door and tapped.

"Who is it?" said a peevish alto voice. The accent was English English, not island English. Obviously, this was Evelyn.

"Barbara. Barbara Kilgaren."

"Oh. You're the American."

Something in her tone removed any tentativeness I might be feeling. "Yes. I am. What are you?" (As if I didn't know!)

"English, of course. Couldn't you tell?"

"Not necessarily," I lied. "The islanders speak English English, too."

"They do *not*. You can't have any idea what real English is like if you think that."

I grinned to myself. I had struck a nerve. Up the Revolution (American-wise)! I decided I could now afford to be polite. "Whenever you're through I'd like to use the bathroom."

"Whenever I'm *finished*, I'll let you know, of course. But I shan't be for a while. I have to wash my hair."

"Wash your *hair*? Dinner's in less than fifteen minutes."

"I expect I shall be late, then."

"And what am I supposed to do for a bathroom? Jonathan, my brother, said I could use this." Maybe, I thought, that would provoke from Evelyn some information about herself. I should have known better.

"Did he now? There's another one in the other wing. I'm sure no one will be using it at the moment." These kind words were followed by the unmistakable noise of a shower bath being turned on.

If I had been my old bratty self, I might have kicked the door to relieve my feelings. But, I realized, that would simply be letting Evelyn, whoever she was, know that she had got under my skin. "Down, Rover," I said aloud. Sedgewick, sitting in the middle of the floor, thumped his tail and gave a short bark.

The shower next door suddenly went off. "What's that?" Evelyn asked.

"That's my Great Dane."

"It doesn't sound like a Great Dane."

"I thought you were washing your hair."

"You're not supposed to have dogs up here."

"On whose authority?"

There was a slight pause. "My father's."

"And who—?" I started, when there was a brusque rap on my own door.

"Come in," I called.

Jonathan came in. Sedgewick barked enthusiastically in a way I deplored. I saw no reason why he should look upon Jonathan with approval.

"That's not a Great Dane," Evelyn's voice came through the door. "I can jolly well tell—"

"She's washing her hair, whoever she is," I said. Jonathan gave me an odd look, then opened the bathroom door and marched in. "OUT!" I heard. "I told you you were to use the other bathroom while Barbara was here. Now get your clothes on and move!"

I was torn between approval of Jonathan's clearing the bathroom for me and disapproval of his authoritarian manners. I could hear Evelyn's voice, feeble and protesting. More running water. Then off, then what was obviously the other door being opened, then the sound of Jonathan moving around in the bathroom. Finally he opened the door and came into my room. "You can go in now. I'm sorry about that. Hamish will sound the gong in about five minutes." And he was out the door before I had a chance to ask him any questions.

The bathroom was large, had obviously been converted from another bedroom, and bore signs of having been hastily cleaned and picked up. I looked around for any telltale clues to show me with whom I would be dealing. But there were none. Fresh towels had been laid out. Very well then, but I would be putting questions to Jonathan the moment I got down. As I was splashing cold water on my face, the gong went.

"In here, Miss," said a gnarled-looking old man in a short white jacket as I came down the staircase. "You'll be eating in here." The Scots' Doric lingered in his voice.

"You're Hamish," I said.

"Ay." He held the dining room door open for me. Something vaguely crossed the back of my mind. "Were you here when I was here before?"

"Ay, Miss, I was. It's like your mother you are." He obviously didn't mean it as a compliment.

I looked him in the eye. "Thank you," I said, with a passing wonder that I would be sticking up for Mother.

Unexpectedly, the browned-apple face cracked into a grin.

"Go on in now, the master is waiting."

Master. It was not a term I liked, smacking of feudalism and servility. I was about to walk into the dining room when I stopped. "Hamish, who is Evelyn?"

"Did ye not hear me? The master is waiting."

With spikes sticking out all over me I went into the dining room. It was certainly not a banqueting hall in the large and Elizabethan sense of the word. After all, this particular house was built on the site of the previous one only about a century before. But as far as gloom and dimension were concerned, it had all the drawbacks. The ceiling was high, the paneling dark and the sideboard massive. On a Yorkshire moor of a hundred years earlier it would, if one's taste ran that way, have been appropriate. On an island in the heart of the tropics it was a crass idiocy, managing to be both bleak and stuffy at the same time. Jonathan was standing behind an enormous carved chair at the other end of the table.

"Come in," he said. "I've put you here." He indicated a place setting to his right. This was a room I had seldom entered when I was a child, and I had almost no memory of it. When I got to my place I saw I was opposite a huge portrait.

"Who is that?"

"Our father. Don't you recognize him?"

The moment he said it, I did. But I could see why at first I didn't. My father was past fifty when I was born. I remembered him as aged beyond his years by illness, bent and white-haired. I was staring at a man of about Jonathan's present age, that is, his late thirties. I put my head on one side. "You look like him, Jonathan, but he was fairer. I mean, his hair was black, but he wasn't as dark as you. His eyes were very blue and yours are—" I looked at him—"a sort of slate gray going into hazel."

"He didn't have my Spanish ancestor," Jonathan said lightly, pushing in my chair as I sat down.

"Spanish ancestor? Which one?"

"It was on the other side of my family."

"I didn't know Lady Margaret had any Spanish ancestor."

"How should you?"

Unless you realized how much islanders considered Father had stooped to marry his second wife, my mother, and how much, despite her Bolshie views, they looked up to Lady Margaret, his first, you wouldn't be able to understand how much the cool way Jonathan said, "How should you?" made me want to take him down a peg.

"Of course. That's the *good* side of the family, isn't it?"

"Don't be impertinent, Barbara. You should have grown beyond that."

"And don't be so superior. If you think I'm bratty, why did you ask me to come and teach your wretched children?"

"Because I couldn't afford anyone else."

To anyone used to Mother's euphemisms Jonathan's abrasive candor was like a brisk, fresh wind.

"Well," I said grudgingly. "That's honest, anyway. If unflattering."

Hamish wobbled in with the soup. I noticed the place-setting on Jonathan's left. "Who's Evelyn?" I asked.

"Your main pupil."

"I thought you wanted me to teach the island children. That's what I came for."

"There'll be those. You'll be assisting Mrs. Gutierrez, the principal."

The name stirred something in my memory. I paused a moment, trying to track it down, but decided, finally, that I must be wrong. "You haven't told me who Evelyn is."

The door opened. Jonathan looked up. "See for yourself. Come in, Evelyn, and try to behave yourself."

I turned quickly. And then stared like an idiot.

As I should have known, if I had not been misled by the light alto voice, Evelyn was a boy of about fourteen, and, barring a sulky expression, one of the handsomest I had ever seen in my life. Over his head tumbled a mop of slightly damp gold hair. Widely spaced blue eyes above a short nose and sullen mouth topped a graceful, slender body.

"My hair's still wet," the vision said crossly.

"It won't hurt you. Sit down."

Evelyn slid into his chair and picked up his soup spoon. "It'll probably be cold."

"Almost certainly. You should have been down on time. Barbara, let me introduce you to Evelyn Kilgaren. My son. Evelyn, as you know, this is your Aunt Barbara."

"Half-aunt," Evelyn said, as one would say only half-diseased.

I came out of shock. "You never said you had a son. Or that you were married. Did Mother know?"

He paused for a second. Then, "I spoke of it in the

letter I wrote asking if you would come down here."

The blood rushed to my face. "Mother can be pretty devious. But I don't believe that."

"Did she ever show you the letter?"

As a matter of fact, she hadn't. Jonathan was watching me, a satiric look on his face. "Next time, before you agree to something, ask to see the terms."

"Why didn't she tell me?"

"Would you have come if you had known about Evelyn?"

I knew immediately I wouldn't have. Teaching the children of exploited blacks was one thing. Aside from bringing me money to go to Rome, it made me feel useful and idealistic. Jonathan's son, if I had known he existed, was something else. "No."

"Well, that's your answer."

"If she's an American, she probably doesn't know enough to teach me anyway," the charmer across the way said. "Their education is notoriously bad."

Jonathan spoke evenly. "Like your manners. Either apologize or go upstairs. Now."

"But I haven't had dinner."

"You can do without."

Evelyn mumbled something that sounded like a grudging "Sorry."

"Don't deny him his dinner on my account, Jonathan," I said righteously. "His rudeness doesn't affect me. He probably doesn't know any better and can't help it."

"I'll have you know, *Aunt* Barbara—"

"QUIET! Both of you. Evelyn, you know what the

headmaster said, either you considerably improve your French and Latin and pass another test at the end of the summer, or you don't go back next term. It's up to you."

"I could easily have learned French with Mother—"

"It is your mother who sent you here. She says she cannot afford either to send you to France or pay for your tutoring in England. I'm told Barbara speaks French like a native. Also Italian, and she probably can keep one jump ahead of you in Latin." Jonathan turned to me. "Your mother says you want to go to Rome. If you can teach Evelyn well enough to pass his tests in September I'll pay your fare next summer to Rome plus enough to enable you to live—cheaply—for six months.

My heart leapt. "It's a deal," I said happily.

"Good. I thought so."

"Well it isn't with me," Evelyn said. "I don't see why you should hand me around as though I were some kind of a bargain." Despite my dislike of him I sympathized with that.

Hamish came in and took the soup plates, put down other plates and slowly, almost audibly creaking at every joint, handed around chicken and vegetables that managed to be both overcooked and lukewarm. While he was doing this we were silent. When the door to what was obviously a kitchen passage finally shut behind him, Jonathan said, "Well, Evelyn, your choice is this: You pass the exam and go back to school—which you tell me is what you

41

want to do—or you stay on the island here with me and learn the sugar business."

"I thought all Kilgarens went back to school in England."

"All *male* Kilgarens," I put in.

"Quite. The ones that count."

"Now look here—"

"Let him alone, Barbara, he's only baiting you. Yes, Evelyn, they did. When they had the money. I don't have the money. If you pass this exam your headmaster has agreed to a scholarship. But it's either/or. In the meantime, I suggest you take advantage of what I am told is Barbara's French. Why don't you say something in fluent French, Barbara, just to show him."

The look of condescension on Evelyn's face didn't irritate me as much as the irony in Jonathan's voice. So he thought Mother was exaggerating! I said something I had picked up from Mother's dresser one time when we were living in France with Mother's third husband. It was fluent, idiomatic and rude. Evelyn looked blank. Where, I found myself wondering, had I seen that short nose and sulky mouth before? Somewhere. Then I glanced at Jonathan. He had that frozen look around the mouth that I suddenly remembered meant he was trying not to laugh.

"Why don't you teach him yourself?" I asked, embarrassed that he had understood. I really was terribly rude!

"I thought you wanted money so you could go to Rome."

He had me there. *"D'accord,"* I said with as much loftiness as I could, and with an accent that would not have shamed the *Académie Française.*

"Entendu," Jonathan replied amiably.

I decided to ignore him.

The rest of the dinner was mostly silent. There were a lot of questions that I was going to put to Jonathan, but not at the table where I felt Evelyn's hostility coming over to me in a steady wave, and where Hamish would burst in from time to time, taking out finished dishes and putting down others.

After dessert, which was, to my horror, rice pudding, Jonathan pushed back his chair. "Coffee will be served in the living room."

I got up. "I want to talk to you, Jonathan. Alone."

"All right. Come into my study. Hamish, bring Miss Barbara's coffee and mine there."

Hamish, muttering to himself, went back to the kitchen.

"And what about me?" Evelyn asked indignantly. "I suppose I'm to have my coffee by myself."

Jonathan got up and stood a minute looking down at him. "We'll join you shortly," he said in a kind voice. "You are not being left out of anything that could possibly concern you. After all, my sister and I are entitled to a private chat."

"It's hard to think of her as your sister. After all, she's nearer my age."

"Nevertheless, she is my half-sister and your half-aunt, as you put it. Come along, Barbara." And he held the dining room door open for me.

I followed Jonathan down a longish hall in the northwest wing and into a square room at the end. As soon as I was inside the room I could feel the difference in atmosphere. The rest of the house was dying. This room had a used, active quality. The furniture was cheap and modern, the kind that could be bought in any office furniture store. There was a large calendar on the wall and some vivid watercolors of obviously local scenes. And there was one protrait, this time of a woman in the dress of the late twenties. One would know anywhere in the world that that handsome, rather horsy face belonged to an English aristocrat. But there was more there than just breeding, more even than the obvious and considerable intelligence. I stared at it for a moment, trying to define the other quality.

"Lady Margaret," I said, rather than asked.

Jonathan was pouring out the coffee. "Yes."

"She did a lot for the island, didn't she?" The truth was, I was envious. I wished she had been my mother, instead of the beautiful, pleasure-seeking woman with whom I had so little in common. The woman who, even now, could be talking to Nick, who could, despite what she said, have afforded to give me what Jonathan had just offered, money enough to be in Rome.

"Why are you getting so angry just looking at my mother's portrait?"

"How do you know I'm angry?" I asked suspiciously, taking a coffee cup.

Jonathan sat down on the edge of his desk. "When you were a little girl two red spots would appear in your cheeks whenever you were having one of your tantrums."

I looked straight at him. "I suppose that was why you locked me in the nursery the night of the fire."

I don't know what I expected him to do: Turn away? Look down? He did neither. He said coolly, "You were making a nuisance of yourself."

The coolness of it took my breath away. "And you're offering that as an excuse?"

"No. No excuse. A reason. I've never offered you, personally, any apology for that, have I, Barbara? Well, I do now. I am truly sorry."

"You're truly sorry. For ruining my face. And you think an apology can balance that out?"

"No. I don't. But, speaking of your face, do you know that your scars are barely visible? That if I hadn't known where to look, I might not even have noticed them, and if I had, could have thought they were the result of an unimportant accident?"

Curious. To be unscarred was a desire I had thought about every day of my life since I first stole a mirror after the fire and looked into it. I waited for the sense of release. But it didn't come, blocked, probably, by the arrogant way in which Jonathan tossed around his responsibility.

My ready anger flared. "I don't accept your apology. I never will. If you made it every day for the rest of my life and brought me a bag of gold in addition, it wouldn't make up for it." The mental image of Nick's handsomeness mocked me. "You don't know what it's lost me." I walked over to the empty fireplace and stared down at it.

There was a silence.

"I should think," Jonathan said, "that by now you'd be over having hysterics about it. As I told you, your scars are barely visible. But I suppose once a crybaby, always a crybaby. You really are very like your mother."

It occurred to me even then that his words, deliberately offensive, were chosen to snap me out of my threatening tears. If so, they certainly succeeded.

I gasped. Then I turned around, all desire to cry vanished. "That's what Hamish said, that I was like my mother. I thanked him, so I'll thank you."

"It wasn't a compliment."

"I'm not stupid. I don't know whether you're trying to make me hate you, Jonathan. But you're certainly succeeding."

"I thought you already did—hate me, that is."

"Oh there's always room for a little more. Did you know I went to see the witch doctor when I was young and bought a statue of you to stick pins in?"

"No, did you? You should get your money back."

"You mean because you're so successful? Like all the servants running around here? Your thriving business?"

"Don't be deceived by appearances."

I looked at him there, sitting on the edge of his

desk, swinging his leg, and decided not to satisfy him by enquiring further. His angular, rather austere face, deeply burned after a lifetime in the tropical sun, relaxed into a smile that struck me as sarcastic.

"But," he said, "you came to inquire about Evelyn, didn't you?"

"Yes. I did. How come no one ever knew about him before?"

"Perhaps because I didn't know myself."

"I don't believe that."

"Suit yourself."

I really should have walked out of the room, but curiosity won. "How could you not know about him?"

"It's not that difficult. Fathers, you know, are not like mothers, my dear Barbara, or hasn't anyone told you?"

I was about to give him the kind of answer he deserved when he went on. "I was in London on business. Evelyn's mother—who was married—and I had a—er—fling. I left. She discovered Evelyn was on the way. The obvious thing for her to have done was to palm Evelyn off as her husband's. But in view of the fact that they merely resided together—if you follow me—this proved unfeasible. So she induced a school friend and her husband to adopt him."

"But didn't her husband *see* that she was pregnant?"

"He didn't live in England."

"So the friend and her husband brought Evelyn up?"

"Well, the husband died when Evelyn was about three. So it was plain sailing after that. And Evelyn's mother footed all the bills. But then, it seems, the money ran out. So the friend, who by that time was feeling put upon, wrote to me. I got in touch with Evelyn's mother, who then told me what I have just told you."

"Why didn't *you* bring him up?"

"On this island? With my father still alive?"

That did give me pause. It was not the kind of thing Father, that great Puritan, would have appreciated, from the little I had remembered and from everything I had heard. "If you had loved her—"

"Who said anything about love?"

"Well, I may belong to the liberated generation, but I think your morals absolutely stink!"

"Your chaste outlook on such carnal matters is deeply gratifying—"

"And furthermore, the whole thing sounds fishy to me. I bet you welched out on your obligations and tried to pretend he isn't your heir. Won't he inherit all this?" I waved my arm around.

"No. He's illegitimate. According to the original charter, if there are no legitimate heirs, the island reverts to the Crown."

My heart leapt up. I had absorbed the overwhelming importance of the Kilgaren succession with my first porridge. "You must hate that," I said happily.

"You'd better hold your joy for a bit. I'm not yet that gone in years. There's nothing to prevent me marrying and having six bouncing boys all nicely in wedlock."

"Are you planning to?"

He stood up. "Yes, I think so. It's fully time the succession was settled."

"That's the most pompous thing I've ever heard. You sound like a feudal monarch."

"Yes, I thought you'd say that."

"And I suppose you have her all picked out, the lucky girl?"

"Of course."

I had to ask. "Who is she?"

"You don't suppose I'd put that piece of information into your destructive little hands?"

"What do you think I could do about it?"

"Knowing your ingenuity, I don't want to find out."

I tried another tack. "I hear tell there's a revolutionary movement that would like to throw you and the whole family off the island and declare its independence—a separate nation by itself."

"And you'd like to help?"

"Yes. I would. I think it's outrageous in this day and age that everything and everybody on this island belong to one person. That's peonage. The Kilgarens have been lords here since good Queen Bess. They've owned everything and everybody. When Father spoke, about thirty servants inside and out ran to do his bidding or help somebody else do it. He owned the input and the output and all the means of production. Without that kind of money and/or private army—"

"You sound like a freshman civics class in a third-rate Marxist college."

In a flash of memory I was six years old, determined not to come down out of a tree. Servants had tried, our local constable had tried, all of them pleading with me from half way down the tall trunk which was as high as an adult could go. And then, while I was preening myself on having foiled everyone, Jonathan came at me from the roof of the house and lifted me out of my fork as though I were a fly. I felt the same rage then that I felt now, and the same helplessness. I remember beating my small fists uselessly against him, while he laughed. He was smiling now. I clenched my fists to my sides to keep them from attacking him.

The laugh suddenly went from his face. "You look," he said wryly, "as though you wanted to kill me."

"I can't think of anything that would give me as much pleasure." And I started to walk out of the study.

"By the way," he said as I reached the door, "if you have any papers of any importance, I can put them in the safe here."

"Where? Behind Lady Margaret?"

He grinned. "Why not? She was the repository of many secrets."

Afterwards I remembered that sentence, so casually tossed off. At the time I was merely amused at the idea that I could have any important documents. "What papers do you think I would have?"

"Your passport. Your birth certificate. Your will."

"My *will!* You must be joking. First you have to have something before you can will it."

For several seconds Jonathan's eyes never wavered from my face. Then he said lightly, "There's always Sedgewick."

"So there is. I'll discuss it with him."

"Incidentally, school starts at eight tomorrow morning."

I paused. I had forgotten how early everything started on the island.

"Or would you prefer to wait a day or so?"

I didn't want his kindness. "Tomorrow will be fine."

I started to open the door, then stopped. "And when do I coach Evelyn? After lunch?"

"In the late afternoon. It'll be cooler then."

"You really intend for me to earn that money, don't you?"

"But I thought that, in view of your warm, loving, sisterly affection for me, you wouldn't want to receive anything from me unless it were for services rendered."

He was laughing as I slammed the door.

4

I had breakfast alone the next morning at seven-fifteen, Jonathan having eaten and gone (I assumed) and Evelyn not down yet. Laid next to my place was what looked like the island weekly newspaper. I had remembered it as the *Kilgaren Tatler*, copies of which were mailed to Mother for years after she left the island. In that earlier manifestation it had been a tiresome imitation court calendar, a gushy list of social notices concerning the forty-some white people on the island and their friends and relations in England. Anything that could possibly drag in the mention of a title was printed in as great a length as possible. When the Governor General of Barbados, the younger son of an earl, stopped overnight at Four Winds the entire paper was devoted to it.

Now it was called *The Carib Challenge* and read like one of the more violent of the American underground papers that could be picked up on any newsstand in New York's Greenwich Village. On the front page there was a huge picture of Fidel Castro plus a breathless report of the splendid progress of Cuba's sugar crop, its educational facilities, its medical plants and so on. On page three was a photograph of some happy-looking islanders all carrying machetes and all wearing placards announcing that they were on strike. On page two there was an editorial that described Jonathan and all other Kilgarens in terms usually reserved for the late Adolf Hitler. Carib Islanders would proudly starve, the editorial concluded, before one more pound of capitalist sugar was harvested.

I was finishing the last of the rhetoric when Jonathan came into the dining room. Yesterday he'd had on a pale gray twill suit and a light blue shirt and striped tie, which on the island passed for dress. This morning he was in a short-sleeved faded khaki shirt and blue jeans, the island work uniform.

"You know, Jonathan," I said, looking at his surprisingly muscular arms, "you're almost too brown for comfort. Or are you offended by my saying that? One forgets the island touchiness on the subject of color."

"But you don't, Skimp, do you? You must be descended from a long line of elephants, because I don't think you've ever forgotten anything." He went to the sideboard, got a clean cup, then came to the table and poured himself some coffee.

But he was wrong. It had been years since I had heard his old nickname for me, Skimp, and I had forgotten it. It was derived, of course, from skimpy, which will give you an idea of what I looked like.

I looked—hopefully—to see if he was offended by my comments on his brownness, but he had that smile on his face that I always thought of as sarcastic, but I now would probably describe as satiric.

"Your Spanish ancestor again, Jonnie?"

"Plus about half a dozen years of cane cutting."

"*You*, a Kilgaren, cutting cane? I don't believe it."

Jonathan drank some coffee. "You saw the local rag. The regular cutters have been on strike for months. I have had to bring in workers from Louisiana, Trinidad, Venezuela—anywhere I could get them."

"Strikebreakers!" I had the good liberal's scorn for any such dirty pool.

"Yes, that's what your paper there calls them. I must get you a personal subscription. Another way of putting it would be to keep good sugar from rotting, to fulfill our contracts and not lose what markets we still have, and to feed those—the old, the children, the young mothers—who don't work but who get regular stipends anyway."

"Benevolent despotism," I said coldly.

"You're going to be getting some of it, or would you rather turn it down?" He looked at me over his coffee cup.

I got up. "I'll be ready in five minutes."

We went in a jeep, descending rapidly by a narrow

road shaded by the huge trees. Within fifteen minutes the temperature and humidity had both gone up ten to fifteen degrees as we reached the coastal area. Suddenly I remembered Seth, the driver who had brought me from the airport, and his hostility. I had forgotten about him in discovering Evelyn.

"Who is Seth?" I asked Jonathan. "The one who drove me from the airport. He was hostile and rude and talked about me being part of the family and how the—er—revolutionary movement is always trying to let you know how it feels."

"He is Seth Williams and one of the militant leaders. He also did his best to get the strike stirred up." Jonathan glanced at me. "Did you tell him that you were ready and willing to join?"

"No. I even stuck up for you."

"Why?"

After a minute I said, "Atavism, I suppose."

Jonathan glanced at me. "It's hard to be in the middle."

I scowled into the windshield, trusting Jonathan least when he was being forbearing and understanding. "How would you know that?"

"You'd be surprised."

"Are you being devious?"

"Probably."

By now we were riding through dirt paths cut through the cane which rose tall and green on each side, looking a little like enormous stalks of corn.

Suddenly he asked me, "Do you remember Mrs. Gutierrez?"

"No. But the name is familiar."

He slowed down. "She's the teacher you'll be assisting. Her late husband was a Venezuelan who used to come here on sugar business. Before that, when she was a girl, she was Mother's personal maid. Her mother was our grandmother's maid, brought from England, although further back there was an island strain."

"You mean what is euphemistically called 'a touch of the tarbrush.'"

"Precisely. A black strain, African, plus, I believe, some Carib Indian."

"How did it get to England?"

"According to family history, one of our ancestors, the grandfather of our grandfather, took his personal servant, an island black, with him once to England. He himself returned, but the servant married in England and settled there. The feudal instinct which you so deplore made any Kilgaren from the island get in touch with the servant's family when in England. And when our grandfather's bride came over here, she brought one of the old servant's granddaughters back with her. She was Mrs. Gutierrez' mother."

"Where did Mrs. Gutierrez get her education to become a teacher?"

"Mother sent her to Jamaica, which had English schools then, and from there to a college in the States. She stayed there a while, teaching in schools in the South and then up North. But she wanted to come back here and did. She married shortly after she arrived, but taught anyway."

"What about her husband?"

"He died."

"How many pupils does she have?"

"About twenty-seven. She takes them only to the age of twelve. After that they go to the school in the village, which is run by the older brother of your revolutionary friend, Seth."

"If he's such a revolutionary why haven't you fired him—Seth's brother, I mean, from the school? After all you own that—along with everything else."

"What makes you think he is a revolutionary?"

"Well—Seth is. I can't see any brother of his being an Uncle Tom."

"Yet that's what they—the hardcore militants—call him. One of the things they want to do is replace Gervase with Seth."

"How come they're so far apart politically? Gervase and Seth?"

"There's nothing particularly unusual about that. Brothers frequently disagree—look at the American Civil War. But in this case it was aided by the chronological difference as well. Gervase is the oldest of a large family, Seth the youngest, and there's almost twenty years between them. But that doesn't mean Gervase is any Uncle Tom. He is a democratic socialist—one of Mother's true heirs."

I did some rapid arithmetic. "Well she must have taught him in the cradle then. Because Seth is around twenty, which would make his brother around forty. Didn't Lady Margaret die about thirty years ago."

"Perhaps you should teach Evelyn arithmetic. He

didn't do well in that either. But as to your question: Yes. She died when I was six, so it would be thirty-one years ago. Gervase does remember her and she did take an interest in his education. But I said he was her spiritual heir because *his* teacher was the man Mother brought from the London School of Economics."

"The one Colonel Fortescue called 'that Bolshie cad.' "

"The same. Did your mother tell you that?"

"Yes. Is he still the Chief Constable?"

"He is indeed. And he's convinced Seth and his cohorts are going to take over the island."

"Aren't you?"

Jonathan turned. Four hundred years of Kilgaren ownership and arrogance looked at me out of those light eyes. "No. I am not."

Despite myself I was shaken. "What makes you so sure?"

"Because I won't let them."

"You think you can stop them?"

"Oh yes. I can stop them."

"With the Third World rising up all over the place and giving one another aid and comfort everywhere you think you can keep them out of here? You're mad!"

"Ah! But I have an ace in the hole."

"What?"

"That, my dear little sister, like the identity of my intended, I shall keep to myself. For all I know you might rush to town and give it to Seth."

I was about to deny it vehemently (why, I don't know; theoretically I was on their side) when I saw the mocking look on his face in the rear view mirror.

"Yes. I might."

Jonathan laughed. At that moment the narrow walls of cane suddenly broadened and the jeep stopped. We were in a clearing near the village under the shade of huge oaks and eucalyptus and palm trees. A little to the back, nearer the trees, was what had once been a shed for the cane stalks. But the walls had been almost completely removed. Thin bamboo poles held up the leafy roof. Inside, a concrete floor was raised several inches above the ground, which could become a mire in the rainy season.

"That's new," I said. "At least, it was a barn."

"It's now the elementary school."

"What happened to the old school?"

"It got burned down."

"It wasn't much of a loss."

"No. I think that's why it was burned down."

"You mean it was deliberate?"

"I think so. Your friend Seth and his merry men. They were all set to make an issue out of it when I foiled them."

"How?"

Jonathan got out of the jeep. "I went to Mrs. Gutierrez and asked her what she wanted."

I looked at the cool but primitive schoolroom. "What happens in the rainy season?"

"That's when they have vacation. But there are

panels that lock into the sides to make it rainproof."

"Ingenious. What are those long roll things just under the roof?"

"They are rolls of specially treated canvas that can be let down to keep out light rain or too much sun. They fasten at the bottom. There are others zigzagged under the roof inside so that a portion of the room can be divided off to make two classrooms."

I thought about some of the schools at home. "She could have asked for a solid concrete school complete with labs and gyms, such as they have in the States."

"Yes. She could. But she designed this herself."

"I'm surprised she wasn't immediately dubbed an Auntie Tom."

"No one, and that includes Seth, would have the nerve to. She taught them all and somehow managed, permanently, to put the fear of God into them. They may defy king, country and all the Kilgarens, but not Mrs. Gutierrez. Are you getting out?"

As we walked toward the building I could see that the further end was enclosed. The schoolroom itself was filled with rows of old-fashioned desks. The teacher's desk was on a platform raised a few inches above the concrete floor. Back of her desk were blackboards. To one side of the platform was a door. Jonathan went up and knocked on it.

A woman's voice said, "Come in."

Jonathan opened the door and held it for me to pass. "Mrs. Gutierrez," he said, following me inside, "this is my sister, Barbara Kilgaren. She will be helping you."

I didn't see her at first, because facing me was a wall of picture windows, and she had been standing at the side, looking out. Then she moved away from the windows and I saw a tall, regal-looking woman in a black dress. I got an impression of high cheekbones, an arched nose and skin like dark ivory. Then she nodded her head and said, "How do you do, Miss Kilgaren."

I was impressed. She must have been in her middle fifties. There was more gray than black in the wavy hair pulled back into a knot. But her thin, ramrod-straight body was that of a younger woman.

The dark eyes looked coolly down at me. "I am glad you are here. It is a small school, but we have all ages up to twelve and it is hard to teach them at once. Perhaps you can take the younger ones off my hands so I can concentrate on those that are older."

"I'd like to do that," I heard myself saying in my nervous, well-brought-up voice. "I like teaching young children."

"Have you ever taught them?"

"Once or twice I took the kindergarten at school."

"And what school was that?"

Almost with shame I gave the name of my socially exalted boarding school. If I could have added, as a sort of apology, that it was academically poor, I would have felt better. But, of late years, it wasn't. As more of its graduates sat for their Regents instead of bowing at a cotillion, the school cut down on the hunting and riding and upped the academic standing.

"Yes," Mrs. Gutierrez said. "As you will see, things will not be exactly the same here."

Was that mockery on her face? I stiffened. "I imagine children, particularly young children, are pretty much the same everywhere."

"Do you? I'm not sure I agree with you. Some of these children have parents who are well educated—perhaps half a dozen. You will probably find them not too different from the ones you have taught. The others are the children of the cane cutters. Their parents are illiterate. You may have more trouble with them. When I say trouble, I mean trouble interesting them in academic learning. Even to the studious child, it's not easy to stay inside on an island like this."

"I know," I smiled, trying to feel at ease. "I had every inducement in the world, including a governess. But I wouldn't stay in." I glanced at Jonathan, who was leaning against the wall. "It was my brother here who was always coming after me and bringing me home."

She gave a faint answering smile but the iron quality of her face did not soften. By this time I had no difficulty at all in believing that Seth and a whole regiment of fiery revolutionaries held her in respect. If at that moment she had told me that I should stand on my head before the class every morning for half an hour I think I would have agreed.

Jonathan straightened. "I'll leave you here then, Barbara, and pick you up around noon. Good morning, Mrs. Gutierrez," he said, coldly, I thought, and with a nod toward me, opened the door into the schoolroom and left.

I glanced at the teacher, wondering how she was taking Jonathan being very much the Kilgaren of Kilgaren, but she was picking over some books.

"Now, Miss Kilgaren," she said. "Let us go over these."

It crossed my mind to ask her to call me Barbara. After all, the enormous difference in our ages—she was considerably older than Mother—seemed to warrant it. Yet there was something about her that stopped me. I wondered then if my hesitation was due to racial prejudice. Morbidly anxious not to be guilty of that I blurted out, "I wish you would call me Barbara."

She didn't even look up. "I think, Miss Kilgaren, that it would better if we kept to the formal address. There is nothing wrong with formality. It has its place, don't you think?"

I felt my cheeks go hot with the rebuke. "Of course." I was furious at myself for asking.

She smiled faintly. "And now let us decide which books you will use today."

I rapidly discovered that, just as Mrs. Gutierrez predicted, my previous experience counted for precisely nothing.

The dozen or so children I had dealt with in Maryland had been the well-bred, well-disciplined children of upper- and middle-class whites. They had all seen books and been read to. At least half, or so their mothers rather loftily told me, could already read. This usually meant that their extremely average offspring would look at a realistic picture of a cat sitting on an unmistakable mat and mouth loudly, "The cat sat on the mat. See, Barbara? I can read! That's what it says: The cat sat on the mat!"

But a few really could read. And they were all used to books and reading and talk about books and reading. When I told them to be quiet, they were (mostly) quiet. On that first day in Mrs. Gutierrez' open classroom, I found myself thinking of them with longing. Not that I didn't enjoy myself.

The children had started to arrive shortly after Jonathan left. They were all shades of light and dark brown and black, the girls dressed in brightly colored dresses and sleeveless shifts, the boys in shorts and shirts and T-shirts. They came up the paved road, walking and jumping, giggling, pushing, talking.

When they saw Mrs. Gutierrez they ran towards her. She stood there in her black cotton dress, her Nefertiti face exuding a kind of tender strictness, touching the children lightly, a soft, multi-braided head here, a shoulder blade there, as they crowded around.

"Now sit down, all of you. And be quiet. We have a new teacher."

The children ran and sat at their desks. We stood in front of the platform. Two rolls of canvas had been lowered on one side against the direct stream of the morning sun. A breeze stirred the cords that hung just over head height, attached to other rolls angled from the rafters.

"Children, this is Miss Kilgaren," Mrs. Gutierrez said.

The whispers, giggles, and murmurs that had been a soft noise stopped. There was a silence that was unnatural in a roomful of children. Then, rude and abrasive, erupted sounds known in America as the Bronx cheer, in England as the raspberry.

I felt my cheeks burn. Somehow I knew that under Mrs. Gutierrez' sovereignty this was as untypical here as it would have been in my eastern school classroom.

"Francis, William, Sarah, come here! At once!" The teacher's voice whipped out the command.

Stupidly I mumbled something about it not mattering.

"Of course it matters," Mrs. Gutierrez said in a tone that withered my bones and made me feel very much as Francis, William and Sarah, now slowly approaching up the aisles, must be feeling. "Bad manners are nothing but a display of lack of respect for the dignity of another person. And one of the lessons we teach here, perhaps the most important one, is that all people, *all* people, are to be respected unless they prove unworthy. Isn't that so, children?"

"Yes, Mrs. Gutierrez," came the choral answer.

The three dissenters from this were now standing directly in front of us.

"Apologize to Miss Kilgaren at once. All of you!" Mrs. Gutierrez said.

The three children, I reflected, must be at the

upper end of the age limit. The girl was thin, but developed, the boys almost as tall as I. The three brown faces looked at me with active hostility.

"Well?" The teacher said. "Are you going to try to pretend you didn't make that disgusting noise? It would be useless. I saw you."

"We made it," the taller of the two boys said. He was an extraordinarily handsome boy, his skin a rich chocolate, the eyes set at a slight angle above the high cheekbones.

"And we're not sorry," the girl said, "so why should we apologize?"

"Because I tell you to," Mrs. Gutierrez said calmly.

I marvelled at her. Whatever the right or wrong of such a stand, I doubted that nine teachers out of ten in the United States would even try it today, let alone get away with it. I would watch the outcome with interest.

"And if we don't?" the boy asked.

"You will then leave the school."

To children in the States who didn't want to be in school in the first place, this would hardly be a threat. But here, the three children didn't move.

Then the second boy spoke up. "Her name is Kilgaren," he said sullenly. "We don't apologize to no Kilgaren."

"Any," Mrs. Gutierrez corrected. She looked at them a moment and then said slowly, "I know that's why you made that noise. And that's why I am insisting that you apologize. Miss Kilgaren"—she seemed, almost, to lean on the name—"just arrived on the island yesterday. You're far too young to have remembered her when she was a child here. You know nothing about her. You were jeering at the name, not the person, the way some people jeer at the color of the skin, not the person, or the accent of speech, not the person, or the financial status, not the person. I won't have that. It makes a mockery of justice. And that's what we want, isn't it, justice?"

There was a silence. Then, almost as though on signal, the three looked at me and said,

"Sorry I did that. . . ."

"I did it because of your name. I'm sorry. . . ."

"Sorry. . . ."

Their faces were hostile, their voices as sullen. But they had got Mrs. Gutierrez' point. So had I. The teacher had very nicely let me know where she stood: She would not let an innocent person suffer because of a hated name. But that the name was deserving of hatred there was no doubt.

A section of the open classroom was curtained off by lowering two of the rolled-up canvases.

"That's pretty clever," I said, as Mrs. Gutierrez manipulated the cords above her tall head. "Jonathan said you designed the whole school."

"That's not true. It was as much his work. I am going to give you the ten youngest," she went on. "I want them to learn the alphabet thoroughly and in order. They sing it to a little rhyme every day."

This was not according to the latest educational methods as I had imbibed them. I started to tell her about the newest theory of phonics and visual recognition. She heard me out patiently. Then she said, "Yes, Miss Kilgaren, I remember the arguments about that when I was teaching in the States. In my personal opinion, the condition of the ghetto schools is at least partly the result of such theorizing. These children are going to be drilled in the three Rs, regularly, so they never forget them."

"But—"

"And on that," she went on implacably, "they can build anything."

The discussion, if there was one, was closed. A few minutes later I was standing in front of ten children ranging in age from five to about eight, listening to them sing and clap as they put the alphabet to an engaging calypso rhythm.

"That's good," Mrs. Gutierrez said, "except that I don't think two of you, Mary and Therese, sang the letters. Why don't you do it by yourselves?"

The two little girls seemed to be overcome. They giggled and scuffled and protested, but after that they raised piping voices and sang through the alphabet, turning their small bodies, clapping their hands, and stamping their feet. It was an appealing sight. I wanted to hug them.

"Now," Mrs. Gutierrez said to me. "Take them through again once or twice, then try them on simple combinations of letters. The older children, of course, on harder ones. After that you can go through the twice-times table, and the older ones can go through the three- and four-times tables. That should keep them busy for the rest of the morning." And she disappeared around the curtain and left me to it.

I like young children, and the time passed quickly. We sang the alphabet and did the multiplication tables, I read them a story, we sang some more and played games. There were four boys and six girls. They were, for the most part, sturdy and merry, and their attention span was so short that it kept me hopping to think up things for them to do. I could certainly see why Mrs. Gutierrez needed someone to occupy them while she dealt with the older children. There were two exceptions to this: two little girls, dark ivory, their hair curly rather than kinky. They sat a little apart, sang the alphabet and the twice-times table, and rather ostentatiously put letters together into simple words. Their names, I discovered, were Sylvia Martin and Marie Long.

Afterwards, while I was waiting for Jonathan, I asked Mrs. Gutierrez about them. "They seem a little different from the others," I said.

"They—or their parents—would be the first to agree with you," she said drily. "I suppose you were too young when you left to know the situation here, but the colored people are themselves divided into classes. George Martin, Sylvia's father, is an accountant and Bayard Long owns the dry-goods shop in the village. They and the other educated colored families hold themselves as aloof from the cane cutters as the white people do from them. If they—the middle-class blacks—could possibly avoid it, they would refuse to send their children to this school. But your brother will not permit another school. He says there isn't enough money even for one, let alone two at both the primary and the high-school level. And he's right. So the Martins and the Longs and the des Champs and the Chavezes and a few others have to send their children to class with the illiterate children of the illiterate cane cutters. It nearly kills them," she added, with what sounded suspiciously like pleasure.

"You don't approve?" I asked, rather obviously.

She looked at me with something close to contempt. "Of course not. The only hope the blacks have is to stick together."

I wanted to ask, hope for what? But I didn't, either because I didn't dare, or because I might find out that she was one of Seth's partisans, and I didn't want to think that.

I asked Jonathan about the matter when he was driving me back in his jeep.

"Yes, there's as big a barrier between the lighter, educated blacks and the cane cutters as between the whites and the blacks. That's the pity of it."

"Why pity?"

"Because, from their point of view, if they stuck together, they could take over this island in a week."

"You sound like Mrs. Gutierrez!"

"Even Colonel Fortescue would tell you that, although he would undoubtedly use it as a reason for the whites to build a concentration camp for the blacks and import mercenaries to keep them there."

"I thought you said you wouldn't let them take over."

"I won't."

"Then you're like Colonel Fortescue."

"No. I'm not like Colonel Fortescue."

"Well, you sound like him."

"And you sound like Seth when you say that. He is doing his best to persuade the island blacks that Colonel Fortescue and I are alike. That's his whole purpose."

I was silent. I didn't much like being compared to Seth. On the other hand, I, like Seth, thought that when push got to shove Jonathan would put up that concentration camp—any Kilgaren would. That reminded me of the incident this morning. I told Jonathan about it.

"They would be Sarah and William Jenkins and Francis Appleton. They belong to the Youth Party and have become regular little troublemakers. I have a strong suspicion that it was one of them who actually set fire to the old school—under Seth's orders, of course."

"Well, if you think that why don't you do something about it?"

"Now you sound like Colonel Fortescue."

We drove the rest of the way in silence.

5

*R*ight from the start, coaching Evelyn was trouble, but not because he wasn't bright—he was. And he had, when he chose to use it, an excellent memory for grammar and a good ear for accent. But, as the days followed one another, I learned two things: The first was that what did not serve Evelyn's interest at any given moment he didn't do. I would emerge at the end of the two hours of coaching far more worn down and irritable than after five hours' teaching at school. The difference was easily seen: The school children, for all their youth, fragile attention span, fits of giggles and, in the case of one or two, rebelliousness, were basically good natured and, on the whole, wanted to learn. Evelyn didn't. Or at least from me. The second thing that became obvious was that beneath almost everything Evelyn said to me ran an undercurrent of hostility. He had a wicked tongue and an instinct for my soft spots, and he used both.

"Look," I said one particularly galling afternoon,

"if you hate so much being coached by me, why don't you tell Jonathan? Maybe he can find someone else."

Evelyn sailed a paper dart past my ear. "But then you wouldn't get your money to go to Rome, would you? No money, no Nick." He looked at me from under his golden lashes and folded another dart. One of my childhood habits that I have never been able to subdue is my violent blush. I could feel it now, surging up my neck into my face. One reason I hate it is that when I blush my remaining scars go fiery red. Without thinking I put my fingers up to the scar that ran through my brow into my temple. It was hot. I didn't need a mirror to tell me it was crimson.

"Dear, dear," Evelyn murmured. "I did hit a nerve, didn't I?"

I fought silently with my desire to kill him on the spot. Or, failing that, to create a situation which would conclude with him at my feet, prone, begging for mercy. Or perhaps to have my slaves take him out and suffocate him slowly.

What I said was, "Who told you about Nick?"

"Oh, walls have ears."

I decided I shouldn't even feel guilty about ordering his torture. "And to which wall was your ear pressed?" I asked, and then suddenly remembered Mother's letter to Jonathan. "Oh, I see. You read your father's mail."

It was a shot drawn at random, but to my surprise and gratitude it landed. Some pink flew into Evelyn's tanned cheeks. "Don't judge others by yourself. In England—"

"—you were snooping before the Pilgrims landed. And if you're so patriotic, why did you flunk that exam? If you don't pass your re-exams at the end of the summer you won't go back at all. I should think you'd be working morning, noon, and night."

"Oh I can pass that bloody exam any time I want to."

"Then why didn't you?"

"You wouldn't understand."

"Like you couldn't?" More than just getting my own back was involved here. I was trying a little baiting of my own to see if it would produce some information. It worked.

"Of course I could. So could the other chaps who flunked, as you put it. We simply didn't want that particular master back. He was a thorough-going second-rater from a second-rate public school. We knew it was touch and go whether he'd be asked back. So we made sure he wouldn't be. We didn't want types like that around us."

It was almost unbelievable and, from a fourteen-year-old boy, ludicrous. But there was a very unyoung, fanatic look on Evelyn's face.

"That kind of snobbery is a bit passé, or haven't you heard?"

"There are certain kinds of discrimination that are never passé, but I expect you, being an American, wouldn't know about that."

"Oh yes, I would! Discrimination of taste, for example, which would rule you out to begin with." As I said it, it struck me that I had descended to his level and that we sounded like two children exchanging insults in the nursery. I wanted to laugh.

Unfortunately, Jonathan walked in on us at that moment, and it obviously struck him the same way, because he told me so in no uncertain terms.

"I brought you here to coach Evelyn, not to match childish witicisms with him. We have a deal, Barbara. If he doesn't pass his exam you don't get to go to Rome—at least not on any money that I give you!" He turned to his son. "And as for you—I thought you wanted to return to that school, certainly that's what you were always saying. And the only way you'll get back is to learn enough French and Latin to get through those tests."

"Yes, sir," Evelyn said, with a docility that I would have found surprising if I had not caught the complacent expression in his cerulean blue eyes a second before he lowered them. So he was playing games! A spasm of anger went through me.

I said nastily, "*Wanting* to pass seems to be Evelyn's problem, *not* not knowing enough."

Jonathan, who was turning over some books I had brought down, looked up at his son. "Oh? Well, Evelyn, you go back to England whether you pass that test or not. But if you don't pass you'll attend a state school."

"Like that poor master you were talking about," I couldn't resist saying. But I should have tried, because I encountered from Evelyn a look of astonishing malevolence.

"What master?" Jonathan asked.

"Just a school story Evelyn was telling me," I said, a little ashamed of my tattling and, if truth be known, a little frightened.

"All right. Get on with it." And Jonathan left the room.

Whether or not it was because of Jonathan's threat, Evelyn proved less trying for the next several days. We managed to get through the daily reading and translation without his usual sneers and put-downs. My memory of that evil look faded. It was probably, I decided, still a little ashamed of my role in the whole affair, my overheated imagination. He wasn't basically hostile, just adolescent, and was really not too bad if you took the trouble to know him. Thus lulled, I was off my guard and, of course, fell into a trap. It started off with a familiar brisk exchange.

I had elected to have the coaching sessions in a large, screened-in porch at the end of the southeastern wing. By that time of day the sun was over at the other end of the house, and the breeze that sprang up in early evening was moving the heated air out. Also, when things got too difficult or too boring, I could look at the mountains.

I was doing this one afternoon, thinking about the caves and waterfalls and green tunnels hidden on those slopes that had, when I was a child, been my playground and hiding place. I hadn't had a chance to go there since I had returned to the island and I decided now to remedy this soon. Evelyn (for once) had been so quiet translating that I had forgotten him, a very dangerous oversight. Staring at the mountains, I hummed something that after a bit I recognized as a measure or two of plainsong to which, at least once a week at school evensong, we sang my favorite psalm:

I will lift up my eyes unto the hills, from whence cometh my help. . . .

Without realizing it I sang the words and then jumped when Evelyn commented acidly,

"Well, if you're expecting any help from there you'll be disappointed."

It was funny, and I couldn't help grinning, even though I was embarrassed. But I noted the smug, slightly malicious expression.

"Tell me, Evelyn," I said, "What's in it for you? Being so generally repulsive? I mean, you look so pleased with yourself. Like a dog with two tails."

He lowered his eyes. "Speaking of dogs," he murmured, "where's Sedgewick?"

As he said it I realized with a guilty pang that I hadn't seen Sedgewick since early morning when I had left for school. I always left Sedgewick at home in the morning to roam at will, glad that for the first time in his driven life he could run and chase and tear around without the danger of gangs or police or cars or other urban pitfalls. Usually he was back, waiting for me, by the time I returned for lunch, sitting on the front steps, his tongue lolling, his backside wagging with joy at my return. Today he hadn't been. I decided he must have found a new, interesting smell to pursue and thought I would look for him after lunch. But when I got upstairs after coffee, I had made the great mistake of lying on my bed just, I told myself, for a minute, and woke up five minutes before the evening coaching.

Remorse and fear added themselves to my guilt but I made an effort to sound offhand. "Who knows? Out pursuing new and delicious scents. Why?"

"No particular reason." Evelyn was as offhand as I, which stepped up my suspicion without allying my rising panic. "It's just that—well, Jonathan said there was no use worrying you, but a favorite island sport is to capture stray dogs—you know, ordinary curs, starve them for a bit and then set two at a piece of meat or torment them until they fight to the death. It's a sort of change of pace from cockfighting."

Even while I noted the triumph he couldn't quite hide, I remembered rumors and stories of such a custom when I was a child.

Evelyn was watching my face. "You didn't know? Too bad. I thought you knew, or I would have mentioned it sooner. I hope Sedgewick is all right. I saw him headed in the general direction of the village this morning. Looking for you, I expect."

I tore out of the porch into the central hall. Raising my voice I called Sedgewick several times and whistled invitingly.

There was no answering bark or scrabble of paws. I went up the stairs two at a time. He could have come back and gone straight up to my room at the end of the southwest wing and now be asleep. At home in New York Sedgewick always waited for me in my room, having the good dog-sense to know himself unwelcome elsewhere, Mother and Renaldo not considering street mutts as dogs in the true sense of the word.

"Sedge!" I yelled now, bursting into my room.

But he wasn't there. I looked under the bed and in the big wardrobe and in the bathroom.

By this time I knew Evelyn had been up to something, but all I could think about was frightened, unheroic Sedgewick being trapped by some ghoulish cane cutter, starved, and then fed to a ravening hound twice his size. Sedgewick was no model of Dog Hero: He wasn't Rin-tin-tin or Lassie or Lufra or Gêlert. His street training had imbued him with one lesson: Whenever possible, run; a principle I thoroughly endorsed. I was convinced he owned his life thus far to abiding by it at all costs. But what if he couldn't run . . . ?

Like a lunatic I ran in and out of the countless rooms, snatching open wardrobes and closets, looking under beds, calling his name. Finally, something Evelyn had said floated to the surface of my mind: *Jonathan said there was no use worrying you . . . Jonathan—*

I flew down the stairs and through the other wing to his study and burst through the door.

"Jonathan—" I yelled, and then stopped cold.

Jonathan was sitting in a chair reading something. Beside him on the floor, a blissful look on his silly face while Jonathan scratched his back, was Sedgewick.

He gave a happy bark and leaped towards me. I bent down and hugged him and burst into tears.

"What on earth— What's the matter with you, Skimp?"

It had probably not been more than fifteen minutes since Evelyn had planted his poisonous suggestion, but it felt like a year. Sedgewick wiggled and licked my face and thumped his remnant of a tail on the floor, and I tried to get hold of myself and succeeded only in getting hiccoughs.

Jonathan got up. "Will you please tell me what this is all about?"

I took a deep breath and told him, and added, "And what's more, Evelyn said, or anyway implied, that you knew Sedgewick had taken off into the village area. He said, 'Jonathan said not to worry you.' Did you?"

Jonathan was staring at me, frowning, "You're sure he said that?"

"Positive."

"He did ask me if there was such a story, about setting dogs on one another, and I said yes, that I'd forbidden it of course. But that it still occurred. But I didn't mention it in connection with this hound here, nor did I know anything about his going towards the village. Maybe Evelyn just took a shot in the dark, hoping to worry you—not very nice, but maybe nothing worse."

"But then why would he say, 'Where's Sedgewick?' looking as though he'd swallowed a canary. How could he be sure that Sedgewick wasn't here? And he *was* sure." As I spoke it occurred to me that if I were a true heroine, the kind of noble and unselfish person I admired (in books), I would be the one to make light of this, to save Jonathan's paternal feelings. But, like Sedgewick, I was not of the stuff of heroes. Any contest between Sedgewick on one side and Evelyn and Jonathan on the other would be unequal. So it was up to me to watch out for Sedgewick. "Where did you find him?" I asked.

"In the kitchen, being fed by Hamish," Jonathan said slowly.

"When?"

"Half an hour ago, when I came in. I think I'll investigate this further." He went over to the chimney piece and pulled the old-fashioned bell beside it.

Neither of us said anything until Hamish came in.

"Hamish," Jonathan asked, "When did Sedgewick, this dog here, come into the kitchen? Miss Barbara and I are trying to find out where he's been all day."

"He'd been locked in the potting shed away to the back. I heard him yelping his head off. If I hadna gone there for a trowel I'd never have heard him. It's more'n two hundred yards back of the stables. So I brought him back and gave him a wee bite."

I said indignantly, "Why didn't you tell me?"

"Och ay—I thought you and the master'd learn soon enough. And he'd be the one to take care of it. Why go after trouble?"

I opened my mouth, but Jonathan spoke first. "All right, Hamish, but tell me if anything like this happens again."

"The sins of the fathers—"

"Yes, all right, Hamish."

Muttering, the old man left.

"He's having one of his attacks of Calvinism," Jonathan said.

"I know Evelyn's your son, Jonnie," I said, unconsciously using my childhood nickname for him, "but he's a vicious little beast. That was a horrible thing to do. And I shall take pleasure in telling him so." Not having a handkerchief, I started using my fingers to wipe the tears off my cheeks.

Jonathan pulled a clean handkerchief out of his pocket. "Here." Then he looked down at Sedgewick and absently bent and rubbed him between the ears. A look of idiot rapture came over the dog's face.

"Dogs are lucky in a way," Jonathan said. "They remember fear and pain, of course, and who's been good to them and who's abused them. But other than that they start every minute fresh, with a clean slate. No self-image problems. No worrying about how they appear."

"I suppose you're trying to drum up sympathy for Evelyn. Why should he have self-image problems? He's very good-looking."

"You have an obsession about looks. Being good-looking isn't the panacea to every problem."

"No? It's like being rich. Money's not supposed to buy happiness. But it can make you very comfortable while you're being unhappy."

Jonathan pulled Sedgewick's ear gently through his hand, while Sedgewick looked ecstatic. "And to think," Jonathan addressed him, "that I would hear such materialistic, capitalistic words from your power-to-the-people mistress. It saddens me."

Unfortunately, and because I was feeling sorry for myself, I said, "Oh it does! Well, if your face had been burned—"

Jonathan got up. "You remind me of that tired old story of the man, rescued after solitary years on a desert island, whose one reply when asked his impression of the new politics, the new economy, the new war, the new peace and the landing on the moon, was that they all reminded him of sex. Well, everything comes back to your face which for some reason you insist on still thinking of as disfigured. Look at it!" And with that he took me by the shoulders and pushed me towards an oval mirror to the right of the fireplace. "Now!" he said, dragging a lamp over and turning it up to full strength, "let's really see what we have. I can detect three scars, none of them actually on the front of the face, that are usually white to pale pink and are now much brighter because you're having a tantrum. Here and here and here." He held me in a steel grip with one hand while with the other he indicated the scars going through my brow to my temple, another coming down from above an ear to the back of the jaw and the third following my hairline."

I wrenched myself free. "And I suppose the rest of my skin looks as smooth as a baby's bottom!"

"I am not personally acquainted with many babies' bottoms, although you remind me of how much you're asking me to smack yours. No. It doesn't. Not yet. But give it time!"

"Time! I've had this all my life since I was six. Every hour of every day."

"Well then, instead of wallowing in self-pity maybe you can spare a thought for Evelyn, who every hour of every day has lived with a rather indifferent woman he thought to be his mother, and no father. So he made up for these deficiencies by adopting a snobbery that was the entrée to acceptance at his school, only to discover that he was really an unwanted bastard, the woman he thought to be his mother a paid surrogate, and his father a "—Jonathan paused and then went on—"his father seemingly oblivious of his existence. And instead of being, as he planned, with his friends during his summer holidays, he was forced to come to an island filled with people he had taught himself to think of as inferior and a father who—" He paused again. "You're very alike, you know, the two of you. You both feel sorry for yourselves and you're both self-obsessed. But there's more excuse for Evelyn; he's only fourteen. You ought to have grown by now."

By dinner time, two hours later, I had calmed down to where I remembered that I was here on this island for reasons of purest self-interest, and that if I went on packing my suitcases there'd be no Rome and no Nick. So I stopped packing and started slowly unpacking.

"But just remember this," I said to Sedgewick, who

was sitting on the floor watching the proceedings with a puzzled expression. "There's going to be no more fraternization with Jonathan. Your taste in people, present company excepted, is deplorable!"

Seeing the suitcases going back into the wardrobe Sedgewick started wagging his rear end. He didn't much care for traveling. I closed the wardrobe. The rage that had shaken me at Jonathan's words and the icy bite in his voice as he spoke them had faded. But all I had to do to start the fury again, quivering along my nerves like electric currents, was to recall a few choice excerpts. How dare he! How *dare* he talk to me like that! I suppose, I thought to myself, that his brutality was some form of self-exculpation for his share in damaging my face. Nevertheless, and even through my rage, I couldn't quite forget his statement that my scars were barely visible. I realized he had said it before, just after I arrived. I had put it down then to the wish being father to the thought because of his guilt. But this time, when he forced me to look in the mirror, something I did as seldom as possible. . . .

I went over to the mirror at my dressing table placed carefully across the corner where the light from two windows could fall on anyone in front of it. I would take a clear, unemotional look at my scars.

I couldn't see them.

I stood there not believing my eyes. For years people kept mirrors away from me. But there were always panes of glass, plate glass windows, other people's mirrors. And I could not remember when looking into my own reflection had not been agony.

There should, I thought now wonderingly, be bells or trumpets or cymbals. I was staring at a quite pretty girl with honey-colored hair, dark gray eyes and smooth, lightly tanned skin. . . . I was looking at someone called Barbara Kilgaren who was I and whom I did not recognize and hardly knew.

I stood there in a daze until Sedgewick, misinterpreting my tears, jumped up and pawed at my dress. "It's all right, Sedgewick," I said, patting his head. "I'm happy. Not sad. And I'm pretty. Pretty, pretty, pretty, pretty, pretty, pretty . . . ," I sang, taking Sedgewick's front paws and waltzing him around the room.

But in some strange way I did not fully understand, this did not prevent me from continuing to be furious at Jonathan.

I went downstairs to dinner coldly, not smiling and with great dignity.

Jonathan and Evelyn were waiting for me in the dining room. Jonathan's expression was grim and Evelyn was looking sullen. He said sulkily, "I'm sorry, Barbara. I didn't mean to frighten—at least, well, anyway, I apologize." He added, "It was only a joke."

"Not very amusing for Sedgewick, locked all day in a hot shed."

"I said I was sorry." In his surly state he was more like any cantankerous adolescent and less like his usual and nauseating rendition of something out of a Wildean play.

"Anyway," I said. "I'm glad for the warning about

the local sport. I shall keep Sedgewick within my sight at all times."

"Poor beast!" Evelyn said.

"I'll have you—"

"QUIET! Both of you!" Jonathan, in the big chair at the head of the table, was not at all amused. "My God! You're behaving like tiresome children. If this continues, Barbara, I shall send you back. Nothing you might do here or at the school is worth it to me to put up with this stupid, brainless bickering. Especially not at a time like this, when I need all the help— As for you—" He turned towards Evelyn.

But at that minute Hamish pushed open the swing door with his shoulder and came in with the soup. Perforce, conversation, such as it was, had to stick to innocuous subjects, such as a cricket match that was going to take place the following Saturday afternoon and, a week or so later, a dinner-dance to be held, I was astonished to learn, in my honor.

"But why?" I asked, not wanting to show how gratified I felt.

"You're a Kilgaren," Jonathan said briefly. "No excuse is needed to hold a dinner-dance and that is better than most."

Evelyn, who had recovered some of his languor, opened his mouth. Encountering a tight-lipped, unsmiling look from his father, he closed it again.

Eventually dinner was over. "You can serve the coffee in here, Hamish. One of us will bring out the cups when we've finished."

Hamish, who was piling the dessert plates onto a tray, muttered something under his breath.

"What was that?" Jonathan asked.

"I said, 'Tis a pity ye no can quarrel in the sittin' lounge so a body can clean the dinin' quarters in peace."

"All right. Put the coffee in the sitting room." He got up. "I have something to say to you both. So come along."

When we got into the sitting room and Hamish had brought the silver coffeepot and left, Jonathan said, "I haven't discussed too much our current situation here, Barbara, and I don't intend to now. Suffice it to say that it's serious. There are two separate and opposing factions, each of whom is quite ready to take over the island and kill the opposition. I don't intend to let either one do that—"

I interrupted, "I suppose you mean Seth and his militants on one hand, but who is the other? Colonel Fortescue?"

"I said I wouldn't discuss it."

"Why on earth not? If there's going to be trouble that could involve us I don't see why we shouldn't know."

Jonathan drained his cup and put it down. "Don't you? You can't stay in the room with Evelyn here for more than half an hour without falling into some childish quarrel with him. He can manipulate you as though you were a puppet. For him it's like stepping on one end of a seesaw. He says something calculatedly offensive to you and you predictably flare up. That's hardly the kind of person I need around if there's going to be pressure—and there is—or in whose discretion I could have any confidence."

The fact that he was right and I knew it didn't help. Strange, I thought, staring down at the muddy liquid in my Crown Derby demi-tasse: Upstairs, less than an hour ago, I had been wildly happy to discover that—at long last—I was pretty. Now—did it make me any happier to realize that in Jonathan's eyes I was a tiresome child—a pretty child, perhaps, but a child? For the first time I dimly understood what he meant by my over-preoccupation with looks. Did I like Evelyn any better for being so handsome? "I'm sorry," I said stiffly.

"It's all right, Skimp. I'm sorry to have had to scold. Now Evelyn, it's your turn." I looked over at his son and once again was struck by his resemblance to—whom? Where had I seen that perpendicular forehead, straight nose and short upper lip? Then it was gone.

"—I've tried everything I know," Jonathan was saying. "I know you've had a difficult time, and it certainly wasn't easy to discover the circumstances of your birth and your father to be what they were. I'm sorry about that. I have tried, and I will continue to try, to make it up to you. But as far as your stay here is now concerned, I'm giving you an order: Either you behave with civility and, if possible, courtesy to Barbara or you go back to England on the first plane from Jamaica. If that happens, you will attend a state school in the autumn. I'm not at all sure that wouldn't be better for you anyway."

Evelyn's face had gone completely white. "I can't stop you sending me back to England. But I will not now or in the future go to any state school. And you can't make me."

"No. I realize I can't. And I won't try. If you want to go back to your old school you'll have to pass that exam. That's up to you. But if you don't cooperate with Barbara now and treat her politely, then I can and will force you back to England. I am your legal guardian—you didn't know that, did you?—and I can have the law put you on the plane at this end and meet you at the other. Now—are you going to do what I ask?"

There was nothing languorous or effeminate or effete about Evelyn's face now. In fact, it was frightening. Because if looks could have killed, Jonathan would be dead in his chair at that moment. "All right," Evelyn finally said between his teeth. "I'll be polite to dear Aunt Barbara." And he got up and walked out of the room.

"If it's any consolation to you," Jonathan said in a tired voice, "it's not you he hates. He's just getting at me."

"Are you sure? That he's only getting at you through me? I think there's something else, something to do with me."

"Like what?"

"I don't know."

"Then I think you're being paranoid."

"Thanks a lot. Is he laboring under the delusion that you like me?"

"It's not a delusion. I do like you. When you let me."

We sat there in silence. Hamish, disregarding Jonathan's orders, came slamming through the door with his tray, picked up the cups, saucers, coffeepot, cream jug, sugar bowl and small spoons, all separately and with a good deal of noise, and departed.

Jonathan got up. "I have work to do. By the way, I got hold of a collar and leash from the old stable and put them on the table over there." He went over and brought them back to my chair. "They're a little large but they'll do. I'd strongly suggest that except when you take him for a walk, you keep Sedgewick with you and leashed."

"I don't suppose," I said doubtfully, "that it would be any use broadcasting the information that Sedgewick is of a new, rare and terribly valuable breed? Evelyn said they only pick up mongrels?"

"No use at all. No one would believe it. Sedgewick is pure cur. That's a large part of his charm. I'd put my name on his collar, Skimp, but I'm not sure if, under the present conditions, that wouldn't be his death warrant."

I shivered. "Your last dog must have been a Great Dane," I said idly, turning the huge collar around in my hands and noting where new holes had been made to accommodate Sedgewick's more modest dimensions.

"Yes, he was. When he stood on his hind legs his shoulders were on a level with mine. He weighed nearly two hundred pounds."

"I bet the island people didn't try kidnapping him."

"No. They poisoned him instead."

"How could they do anything like that? He wasn't responsible for their grievances."

"I don't suppose they thought he was. He died as a symbol, a warning."

"Couldn't they, the police, find out who actually did it, and punish him?"

"By 'they' I suppose you mean Colonel Fortescue. He's pretty much the police around here. He tried. But how was he going to find out? Who's going to talk? Anybody could have got the poison. Anybody could have put it down in a piece of meat. There were no witnesses."

"He was probably too busy downing gin and tonics at the club to put himself out."

"That sounds like something your mother might have said."

"Well—it was." I gave him a reluctant grin. "Was it unjust?"

"Yes and no. He certainly absorbs an astonishing amount of gin at the club. On the other hand, it's not true in the sense that he's there when he should be elsewhere doing his job. He does as good a job as anyone could with his handicaps."

"Such as?"

"He's white, an ex-army officer, and a friend of the

establishment, i.e., our family. He and our father were very thick."

"He sounds just like the kind of person Mother usually likes, but I think he made her feel inferior."

"He does have a talent that way," Jonathan paused. "But there was a time when he and your mother seemed to get on very well."

"Oh? She never told me. She always referred to him as that pukka bloody sahib."

Jonathan threw back his head and laughed. "I can just hear her."

It hadn't struck me before but Jonathan, being so much older than I, must have known Mother from another adult's point of view. Curiously, she had never said too much about him. Since Mother almost never failed to talk (unflatteringly) about everyone, this was more food for thought. I glanced at Jonathan and found him looking at me speculatively. "Now what's going on in that young mind of yours?" he asked.

What I wanted to say was, How did Mother seem to you? But of course I couldn't. So I said instead, "Your Colonel Fortescue sounds just the kind of person Evelyn would like."

"You're on target there. Evelyn has conceived a great admiration for him, and it appears to be mutual."

"He would." There was a grin on Jonathan's face so I said rather testily, "Well I just hope your intended will inspire him with the same respect, if she exists, which I doubt."

I don't know why I said that or what was going on in my head, because I hadn't, for more than a moment when he first told me, believed in Jonathan's intended. The whole thing, I was quite sure, was invented just to tease me and sound mysterious.

"Then it will be just in time," Jonathan said agreeably.

"What's just in time?"

"Your meeting at the dinner-dance with, as you call her, my intended."

"Come on, now. Tell me another!"

"You wound me, Skimp. Why do you find it so difficult to believe that some fair lady would place herself—to say nothing of her considerable fortune—in my hands?"

"You're joking!"

"But I'm not." Jonathan was staring down at my face. "You really didn't believe me, did you? You look absolutely stunned. How very unflattering of you!"

For a minute I was really shaken, until I remembered what a deadpan artist Jonathan always had been. "Fiddle!" I said.

I still thought he was pulling my leg.

Evelyn tried no more pranks. Jonathan's threat about a state school must have borne fruit, I decided. Still, his anachronistic attitude puzzled me.

"I thought England had undergone a social revolution since the war." I said to Jonathan.

"It has. What are you getting at?"

I thought of all the English movies I had seen lately. "Evelyn and his prejudices seem like something out of the past."

"Nothing happens all at once. There are rebels against the rebellion. Besides, I told you: Evelyn found himself a misfit everywhere until he fell in with this lot at school."

"Why don't you send him to another?"

"Partly because he's happy there for the first time in his life, and the school is a good one. Also, it's only the particular crowd he's with. I could send him to another school, but he'd find a few of the same, even in a state school. Besides, I told you: Finding out about me was a shock to him."

But I wondered. Following Mother's crowd around, observing them from the sidelines, I had had a chance to see every shade of snobbery from the ultra to the inverse.

"What did Evelyn's foster father do?"

"Nothing much. Hung on the fringes. Aspired to social status, mainly. Why?"

"Well, I bet that being illegitimate matters far less to Evelyn than discovering he's really the son of a three-hundred-year-old title."

"You're not exactly a fair judge, are you?"

No, I wasn't. But my opinion remained unchanged and I really saw more of Evelyn than Jonathan did. In fact, except in the rides to and from school and at dinner, Jonathan was never around. Frequently he'd drop me home for lunch and then immediately go out again.

"What does Jonathan do all the time?" I once asked Evelyn, as he and I were lunching alone.

He said loftily, "Administers the estate." His tone produced an immediate picture in my mind of acres of waving wheat, with dozens of tenant farmers in smocks all pulling their forelocks as the baronet rode past on his horse.

"He worrrks," Hamish growled, rolling his r's and slamming down our plates. "It wouldna harrm ye if ye did the same."

Evelyn raised his brows and tried to ignore the servant, putting him in his place, a singularly profitless endeavor, I thought with some amusement, since Hamish's place at any time was wherever he wanted it to be.

"Cutting cane?" I asked.

"Ay, and stacking and helping get it down to the pier and the boats and helping to repair the cottages. He's no bailiff now, ye know. He's his own bailiff and carpenter and farmer and anything else." He glared at Evelyn. "When I was a lad I could shear a sheep, thatch a croft, shoe a horse as well as a man."

Evelyn, bent on maintaining the proper distance between son of the house and servant, pretended he hadn't heard, but the effort sent his eyebrows almost up into his hair.

There were evenings too when Jonathan wasn't there and Evelyn and I were left to our own devices.

"He can't be cutting cane all night," I said one evening when Jonathan had left us immediately after dinner. Evelyn and I had taken to playing chess. It kept our minds occupied and off dangerous subjects. The only trouble was that Evelyn went up to his bedroom before nine, leaving me to roam through the downstairs rooms, dust-sheeted and silent, or take refuge in the library, or go out to the kitchen to talk to Hamish. It finally came to me that Hamish, in his surly way, was keeping an eye on me. On the rare occasions when Jonathan did not go out after dinner but holed up in his study, Hamish retired to his own quarters immediately after dinner.

"Where does Jonathan go?" I asked the old servant one night.

"To meetin's."

"What meetings? Whose meetings?"

The old man looked across at me. I could almost see him weighing the desirability of keeping me informed with the costly output in words. Finally he settled for, "Ask him."

So I did.

"Hamish should keep his mouth shut," was all I got in reply.

So I asked Evelyn.

"Haven't a clue," he said, but added, "Probably the counter-insurgency militia or whatever they call themselves."

"Against the militants?"

"Of course."

Refusing to be snubbed I said the next morning to Jonathan, "Evelyn says your meetings are to counter the revolution. Is that right?"

"Yes," he said, repressively.

"But—"

"That's all I'm answering."

One other odd thing happened. One evening when Jonathan was out there was, surprisingly, a telephone call for Evelyn. The slightly muffled male voice at the other end was English, but that didn't tell me much; most of the male voices on the island sounded English. I put down the receiver and went upstairs to Evelyn's bedroom, kicking myself for not asking in the best secretary's manner 'who is calling?' But I hadn't, and it was too late to go back down and do it.

I knocked on Evelyn's door, which must have been unlatched because it swung open even as Evelyn said, "Who is it?" Opposite the door was a long mirror. In it I saw Evelyn, lolling on the big bed, reading a book with what looked like a leather cover. As he saw me in the mirror watching him, he pushed the book under the bedclothes.

"What do you want?" he asked sharply.

I had never been in his room before and I was impressed, as much with the heavy, ornate furniture and the huge bed with its massive headpiece filled with knobs and carvings as with the size of the room.

"What grandeur!" I said. "Who used to live in this room?" Father's old bedroom, was, I knew, at the other end of the house.

Evelyn sat up in bed, his hand over the place where he had hidden the book. "I asked you what you wanted?" He sounded edgy.

"Telephone for you."

"Oh. All right. I'm coming." He glanced at me again. "After you've shut the door and left."

I turned to go out the door. "What are you reading? A dirty book?"

He gave me a strange look. "In a way."

He wouldn't move until I had left and started down the stairs. When he did come down he talked with his hand cupped around the mouthpiece. But there was such a provocative look on his face I was fairly sure that his conversation was about as inflammatory as the Saturday cricket match. Naturally, I wondered whom he was talking to, but I was not about to ask and invite a snub.

On the way to school I told Jonathan about the telephone call. "Who do you suppose it was?"

"I haven't the faintest idea."

"Are there any boys his age on the island now?"

"Plenty. But not among the white families. The boys they have are either older or younger and they're mostly away now anyway."

"I can't see him with the children of the blacks, even the middle-class ones."

"No. Neither can I." He sounded depressed.

"You sound as though that saddens you."

"It does."

"Why? I still don't see you as the great democrat."

"I can't hold myself responsible for your limited imagination."

"Thanks a bunch."

Jonathan glanced down at me and I saw his nice,

rather lopsided smile. Unexpectedly, he took his brown hand off the wheel and covered mine. Without any volition of mine, my own hand turned and held his.

"I still think," I said, "that he's up to something." And I told him about the book under the bedclothes.

Jonathan put his hand back on the wheel. "Why? Because he keeps a secret diary? What nonsense! You have an overheated imagination."

"I thought you said it was limited."

"It's probably both. Which just shows how talented you are."

I ignored that. "By the way, who used to sleep in Evelyn's room? It looks like the royal bedchamber."

"Mother." And as I looked blank for a moment, he added, "Lady Margaret."

6

I will never forget the night of the dinner-dance. For an occasion that started out so well, it ended, for me, in disaster.

Jonathan, Evelyn, and I got into Jonathan's rather battered car around six thirty to drive to the club, which was about two miles north of the house and on a plateau overlooking the northwest coast and the Gulf. Jonathan was in black tie and white jacket, Evelyn in a lightweight suit and I in a dress that Mother had bought me just before I left New York. For once, I was entirely happy with the way I looked. Mother and I had gone to the expensive floor of a famous New York specialty store, and Mother stood over the sales clerk till she produced this dusky pink chiffon that clung to my small breasts and narrow ribs and then flowed down into a swirl of sweet pea colors. There was absolutely no question about it, I thought as I examined myself in my dressing-table mirror, the colors, the shape and the style did things for me.

When I came down the stairs to where Jonathan and Evelyn were standing waiting for me, Jonathan glanced up.

He looked for so long without saying anything that I got nervous. "Do I look all right?"

"Ravishing," Evelyn said in a bored voice.

I stuck out my tongue at him and looked questioningly at Jonathan.

One side of his mouth lifted in that disconcerting smile of his. "As Evelyn correctly said, ravishing!"

"Truly?"

"Truly, Skimp. I'm just sorry the island doesn't sport more impressionable young men who could perk up your vanity."

"What do you mean, 'more'? Are there any?"

Evelyn, examining his tie in the hall mirror said, "If you like them hairy and political."

"Who's hairy and political?"

Jonathan explained. "Gilbert Palmer, our distinguished local journalist. Come along, we'll be late."

I pursued the matter in the car. "What do you mean by local journalist?"

Jonathan put the car in first as we started to descend. "He's editor of what used to be the *Kilgaren Tatler* and is now the *Carib Challenge*."

"The one that refers to Jonathan"—Evelyn never referred to his father except by his Christian name—

"as the Running Dog Despotic Owner of the People's Island."

"Jonathan, don't you support the paper? Father always did."

"In the sense that I own the printing press and used to pay the salaries, yes."

"Used to?"

We were now much lower and hotter. The road ran at coastal level for a while before climbing again. An intersection lay about a hundred yards in front of us, the main road continuing north to the village, another, smaller one, climbing up to the club.

"Somebody seems to have dropped a bag or a hat or—" I started, and then was flung against Jonathan as he veered the car violently to the left into what looked like a swamp. The front wheels were already beginning to sink as Jonathan threw the gear into reverse and pulled them out and stopped the car.

"Christ!" he said quietly.

I couldn't think what had happened. "What on earth—"

"It's a mine," Jonathan said.

"A mine!" I stared at the harmless-looking object in the rapidly darkening dusk. "Are you sure?"

Jonathan got out. Bending down he picked up a rock from the side of the road. With the accuracy of a man who had bowled for his school and university, he threw it. There was a flash of red and an explosion. "Yes," he said calmly, "I'm sure."

"One more pothole," Evelyn observed sourly.

"Better than three legless bodies." Jonathan started walking towards the jagged hole in the asphalt. I scrambled out. "Jonnie!"

He turned. "Get back into the car. At once!"

"Jonnie, it might go off again. Come back!"

"It's shot its bolt, quite literally. It won't go off again. Get back in the car!"

"Well, if it's safe why do I have to get back in the car?"

"Because I say so and because I don't know who's about."

Grumbling, I got back in the car. "You seem to take it very calmly," I said to Evelyn.

"Well, there's nothing I can do."

In a moment Jonathan was back. "That's all there seems to be for the moment."

"Don't you have any mine extinguishers—those things that look like vacuum cleaners? You always see them on TV news whenever there have been any terrorists around."

"No, I don't."

"It seems to me you could use them."

"I could. But for one thing they're too expensive and for another I'd need technicians who knew how to work with them without blowing themselves up." Jonathan started up the car. In the past few seconds it had grown suddenly dark, as it does in the tropics, so he put on his lights. We started moving slowly.

"Are you afraid there's another one down the road?" I asked after a few minutes of crawling.

"No. There won't be another one tonight. I'm

looking for the message that usually comes right after."

"What do you mean?"

"If whoever had put the mine there had meant to make it invisible, they would have made it invisible, or relatively so. I don't think he or they meant to blow us up. What was intended was a demonstration—you see, we can blow you up whenever we want! And after the demonstration, in case we missed the point, comes the moral. Ah yes, there it is!"

"I don't see—Good heavens!" The banner was held between stilts stuck into the soft ground to the left of the road. In crude letters was spelled out, *The island belongs to us, the People. All former owners and exploiters should leave while they can. This is a warning. Power to the People!* And underneath, the now familiar insigne of a clenched fist.

"They're serious," I said, stupidly.

Jonathan accelerated the car and we started back up the mountain. "Did you think they weren't?"

I realized I really hadn't taken it too seriously—children playing war games. But there was nothing childish or childlike about that burst of flame and powder and asphalt.

Jonathan said, "I've seen a man's legs blown off by one of those."

"Where?"

"Cyprus."

"What were you doing in Cyprus?"

"My military service. It was once a British colony. I was there during some of the upheavals."

I remembered a course at school in contemporary history. "Yes. Sorry. I forgot."

"It's typically American—" Evelyn started.

"It's not typically anything," Jonathan said.

I ignored Evelyn. "I suppose it was Seth and his revolutionaries who put that mine and that banner there."

"Possibly. It's also possible that the right-wing extremists put it there wanting you to think just that."

"I feel as if I'm in Rhodesia."

"Rhodesia," Evelyn said pontifically, "is slightly larger. In your American schools—"

Jonathan cut it. "If you say anything like that just once more, Evelyn, you can get out and walk home. And I meant what I said about sending you back to England."

At that point we turned yet again, up a still steeper incline, and there, ablaze with lights, was the club.

Jonathan parked the car and we walked across the springy, carefully nurtured grass. The building itself was white frame, with rather stubby wings on either side and a front porch, now outlined with lights and full of women in brightly colored, full-length dresses and men in the standard evening dress for the tropics, black tie and white short jacket.

"You know it's funny," I commented as we walked, "Mother used to talk a lot about the social hooha here, but she never said much about dances at the club. They all seemed to be at the house."

And as I said that I was suddenly six years old, in my white cotton nightgown, my face pressed to the gallery railings as I looked down at the guests in the great ballroom at Winds. My nurse, Nemi, was behind me, her arm around my shoulder, whispering to me, pointing out the notables. . . .

There's Sir Arthur and Lady Waring. He's Governor General of Jamaica. There's Mr. Maitland, from Nassau, Lord John Dexter from Barbados. There's Mrs. Huett and Mr. Formby. There's Colonel Fortescue, dancing with your mother. . . .

Strange, that that should suddenly surface in my memory: *Colonel Fortescue, dancing with your mother.* Nothing that Mother had ever said about Colonel Fortescue, and it wasn't, admittedly, much, had led me to believe that dancing together would be something they would ever do. . . .

". . . which is where this whole thing ought to be," Evelyn was saying. "To welcome back a member of the family there should be a ball, not a dinner-dance, and it goes without saying it should not be here but at the house."

"If you can arrange for me to have about fifty servants, cheap, I'll be happy to have one. Until then, Skimp will have to make do with this bourgeois version."

"Why do you call her Skimp?" Evelyn asked, for once deterred from his ruling passion of correct social observance.

I could almost feel Jonathan choosing his words so

that my ever touchy feelings would not be hurt. I decided to be generous. "Because I was so skimpy," I said. "My other nickname was Mosquito."

"You will have to grant," Jonathan said, as we approached the steps of the porch, "that I have not used that once since you came back."

I was looking up at the porch, which was lined now with strangers waiting to greet us, and, despite what my mirror had told me a bare hour before, I felt the chilling touch of my old neurotic fear of social gatherings where I was quite sure people would be staring at, or trying not to stare at, my face.

"I now understand Pavlov," I said idiotically, and thought that Jonathan would think I had gone mad. But he didn't. I felt his hand come under my elbow. "Just remember how pretty you are," he said. And then, more loudly, "Hello, Derek. As you can see, I've brought the guest of honor."

Several things came sharply to memory from that evening:

I had remembered the club from Saturday afternoon matches and occasional Sunday teas to which I, along with other children, had been invited, as imposingly large and glamorous. Now it seemed to me small and a little dingy. There were specks on the lights where the insects had flown through the open doors and stuck on the yellow globes. The floor was polished, not with the old shine of constant rubbing, but the metallic sheen of too much varnish. I had remembered the people as rich and beautiful and redolent with that quality that the French call *race*. Now, as I stood with Jonathan and Evelyn greeting people and waiting to go through the double doors into the lounge where the cocktails would be served, I realized that either my child's mind had romanticized them out of all reality, or they, too, like Four Winds, had suffered from time, loss of money and social unrest. Because the men and women clucking around me, shaking my hand, were very ordinary, the kind that could be seen by the hundreds and thousands in the tennis clubs of provincial English towns, with this difference, that at home in England they could not be anything other than themselves. Here, at this last outpost of a vanished empire, they exuded a quality that Mother always called Extract of Poona Substation.

"My dear, how marvelous to see you again!"

"Jolly to have you with us once more!"

"You look so much like your mother!"

"I wouldn't have recognized you," followed by the hastily tacked on, "You look so *different*."

"My dear child, you've grown up to be quite lovely."

I smiled. The words were sweet. I was on top of the world. And then I saw coming towards me a face I remembered only too well. Jonathan, beside me, said, "You remember Dr. Templeton, don't you Barbara?"

How could I not? After the fire he came up to Winds two or three times a day, changing dressings, his perpetually cold, bony fingers probing painfully, so that Nemi and even Jonathan were summoned to hold my head.

I fought down a wave of antipathy. "Yes indeed." Beside the doctor and looking uncannily like him was his bleak and bony wife. "Poor little girl. You were such a pretty child. So like your mother."

Were, were, were. . . . The antipathy in me swelled into active hostility as I felt my happy bubble diminished like a leaking balloon.

"And isn't it nice that she's even prettier now?" Jonathan said pleasantly. His fingers were almost meeting each other through my arm.

"Clumsy butcher," I muttered as they passed on into the lounge ahead. "He made bad worse, according to the doctor in New York."

"I'm inclined to agree with him."

I remember my surprise when he said that. And I remember the moment when Gilbert Palmer walked up. Jonathan said, "I'd like you to meet Gilbert Palmer, Barbara. He's editor of our newspaper."

Evelyn's description, 'hairy and political,' fitted exactly. A scowling young face looked out at me through a thicket of auburn beard below and a dark red thatch of hair on top. Unlike all the other men, who were in tropical evening dress, he had on a crumpled seersucker jacket over a striped shirt, bright blue slacks and a surprisingly sober striped tie that looked slightly familiar.

"Hello," he said, extending a rather dirty hand. "I'd like to interview you later on."

That made me nervous. "What for? I haven't done anything."

"Palmer is not so much interested in facts as in attitude. The two of you should get on," Jonathan explained. "I think your political hearts should beat as one."

The trouble with Jonathan was that the moment I started feeling fond of him or grateful to him, as when he put Mrs. Templeton in her place, he'd turn around and infuriate me. I opened my mouth to suggest that he leave my political leanings alone when he said, with an amused look on his face that made me want to hit him, "Will you forgive me if I drag myself away for a minute? I'll be right back."

I watched him go towards the porch and walk towards someone—a woman I thought, but I couldn't be sure because he was effectively blocking her. Something that wasn't quite fear settled itself in me.

"I want to do a piece on the return of the local princess," young Palmer said to me, rummaging in his bulging, out-of-shape pockets. He produced the chewed remnants of a pencil and some grubby-looking paper.

"And why should I help you with an article that's going to make me sound like the last of the Bourbons?"

"The Bourbons aren't finished, worst luck. There's that chappie in Spain."

"Don't be so literal. Anyway, I'm on your side, as

you heard Jonathan say. I'm against all this feudalism stuff."

"If you were really on our side you wouldn't be living up there in that palace with your anachronistic brother. You'd be agitating with the rest of us, giving us your support and name. As a matter of fact"—he paused and started scrawling something on the dirty paper—"that would be a better story than the one I planned. "Tyrant's sister joins the people. Something along that line."

"Oh no you don't!"

"What do you mean, Oh no I don't? I shall write anything I like."

"The printing press belongs to Jonathan."

"Trying to muzzle the press, are you? I was right the first time. You're bad as your brother."

"Ninety percent of what you publish in that sheet that you dignify with the name of press is sheer garbage. The Kilgarens don't have any money any more. You surely know there isn't a servant up at Winds except old Hamish, who's white."

"I thought you were supposed to be for us. You can't say your brother's not a tyrant and be on our side." His sherry-colored eyes looked at me scornfully. "I can see you're nothing but a Laodicean."

"A what?" Somehow, despite (or perhaps because of) his outrageous words, it was very hard to take him seriously.

Unexpectedly he said, "So then because thou art lukewarm and neither cold nor hot, I will spue thee out of my mouth."

"And what is a good radical like you doing quoting the Bible?"

He had the delicate skin that goes with red hair and it flooded crimson. He started to turn away.

"Don't be cross," I said. "I didn't mean to offend you."

He hesitated and half turned back. "My father was a vicar," he mumbled. "I had to learn yards and yards of the Bible. Besides, I can make a very good case for socialism from there. If you had heard Bishop—"

"I have. And I told you. I'm on your side. By the way"—I glanced again at his tie—"where did you go to school?"

As though admitting to a jail sentence he mumbled the name of a famous English school.

I grinned. "I thought I recognized it."

He blushed again and looked abashed.

"Anyway, as I said, I'm on your side. But Jonathan's not a tyrant."

"Perhaps not. But as a symbol he must be represented as such."

I thought of Jonathan's Great Dane who had died as a symbol. "I don't like people and . . . other things used as symbols. You can die—being a symbol, I mean." I suddenly remembered the mine in the road. Perhaps whoever had put it there—leftist? rightist?—had meant it to be seen only as the conveyor of a message. But what about an animal who didn't know that, whose legs could be blown off? "Why don't you write a real story," I said without thinking about the possible effect of my words.

"Such as?"

I told him about the mine.

"And of course your brother put it down to the militants? Yes, I can write a very good story about that. Kilgaren accuses leftists," Palmer said, scribbling rapidly.

"No—"

"Thanks for the story." And Palmer started to push past me. I was beginning to understand a little of Jonathan's problems with our local press. "Look here, Mr. Palmer. Be fair. You could *help*."

"Help whom? What? There's no such thing as fair, didn't you know that? What's fair about these blacks being here, brought here, or their ancestors were, as slaves? What's fair about the condition they're in now? What's fair about their starting everything from behind the eight ball?"

"But some of the blacks, the middle-class ones, own stores here, are in the professions—"

He all but spat. "Those bourgeois sellouts. All they want is to be admitted to the ranks of the whites. Then they'll be happy."

"That's not true. What about Mrs. Gutierrez? I don't see anyone—you or Seth Williams or anyone—calling her a sellout."

"Why not? She started off as the sainted Lady Margaret's maid, up at the big house, among the white folks, absorbing their viewpoint. She was also your revered father's little plaything, when he got tired of climbing into bed with the aristocratic old warhorse. *Droit du seigneur* and all that. Then she gratefully took her education from the family that had dishonored her."

I let out a peal of laughter. I didn't know where he had picked up that tidbit or from whom, but it was obvious that he was too young and inexperienced to know when he was being had. "You sound as old-fashioned as a story about Guinevere and Lancelot. Talk about dishonored women doesn't sound a bit like a good leftist."

I shouldn't have laughed at him. The red tide rushed into his face. His brown eyes were blazing. "And there's your brother that you're so busily sticking up for. There are a lot of people who'd like to find out who Evelyn's mother really is. If my ideas and investigations bear out, and I think they will, that might shake the old family tree quite a lot. I know a man in London who—"

He stopped, staring past my shoulder. Then he said in a calmer voice. "Speaking of symbols, here comes one on your brother's arm that is the walking, living symbol, if anyone is, of every filthy exploitation in South and Central America. Those diamonds at her ears and neck were paid for out of the hides of Indians, blacks and God knows who else. It's highly fitting that, according to rumor, she's shortly to be your sister-in-law."

I whirled around.

I will remember as long as I live that first glimpse of Yolande walking beside Jonathan. Her dress was white. Diamonds as big as hunks of quartz flashed from her ears and from a pendant just above her neckline. Everything about her was simple, with that crushing simplicity of the immensely rich. Perhaps she wasn't, precisely speaking, beautiful, but the overwhelming impression was that she was not only beautiful but desired. It's a look any woman recognizes in another woman. And if it needed confirmation, the expression on Jonathan's face as he looked down at her confirmed the matter beyond doubt. That feeling in me that I had not been able to define now identified itself as pain. I heard myself asking young Palmer in a dull voice, "Is she as rich as she looks?"

"More so. Her father could buy her fifty Kilgarens, both man and island, as a wedding present."

It was like struggling against a powerful current to speak up but I said, "I don't think Jonathan would marry just for money."

"Come now, Miss Kilgaren. You don't know your family history very well. If he had to, any Kilgaren would do anything to hang onto this squalid little hell hole of an island."

Hadn't I said the same thing to myself? Why should everything in me rise to protest it?

In a sort of a haze I saw Jonathan remove his adoring gaze from the lovely girl beside him. "Yolande, this is my sister, Barbara. Skimp, I want you to meet Yolande del Arribe."

She held out her hand. "At last! Jonathan has spoken so much of his little sister. I am so happy to meet you." Her English was flawless—like the rest of her.

I don't think I ate dinner. I remember dishes being placed in front of me and then removed. As the guest of honor I sat at the center of the T-shaped table with Mr. Formby, president of the club, to my left, Jonathan two places to my left, Yolande across from him and a space on my right. On the other side of the space I saw Mrs. Templeton's angular, lantern-jawed profile. There were place cards, of course, and so my eyes searched for the card for the place to my right. But either it had never been there or, more likely, had been accidentally brushed off, because I couldn't find it.

"And how do you like being back on the island?" Mr. Formby, beside me, said, in a totally predictable opening gambit. For a second, just for a second, I debated telling him the truth: that at the moment I wouldn't give old Peter Stuyvesant's twenty-four dollars for this lousy little speck of land, smaller even than the Manhattan Island that the old sharp-dealing governor was supposed to have diddled the Indians out of. But again, atavism or custom proved stronger. And I heard my nice, phony, finishing-school voice answering all his questions politely, saying the things that he wanted and expected to hear: It was lovely to be back; no Kilgaren felt quite real away from the island; yes, it was a pity so many of the former servants had fled to Jamaica and Cuba; no, it didn't seem the same at Winds without the dinners and the balls; yes, my mother was quite well; yes, it would indeed be like old times to have a beautiful sister-in-law to reactivate some of the old customs of the island. And the pompous old bore might just as well have said wouldn't it be lovely to have all that Arribe money to pay for a new army of servants and open up the old rooms and halls and entertain on a grand scale again?

So that's what Jonathan meant when he spoke of his intended and her handsome fortune! Even I knew of Arribe money as I knew of Rockefeller or Getty money. I glanced down the table and across where Yolande was managing to keep the two men beside her and several across amused and entertained. It would have given me much pleasure to reflect that it was all her money. But it wasn't. She had a dark, fine-boned beauty that seemed infinitely feminine among the larger English and one or two American women. She was as Spanish and as feminine as the exquisite black lace shawl she wore negligently over her tanned bare arms. By comparison the other women looked drab or horsy or both.

She didn't make me hate her. She made me hate myself. I looked down at the dress I had been so proud of. Compared to the white satin moulded to her elegant little body it spelled bargain-basement. My tan looked like sunburn, my body skinny and unfinished. A depression that I knew to be a neurotic combination of resentment and self-pity and that I had not felt since I had been on the island descended like a nasty fog. On the other side of it I could hear Mr. Formby's voice going on and on. I knew, from past experience, that I must break out of it, or I would become totally isolated. The quickest way to do that was to say something. I opened my mouth—

"Good evening, Miss Kilgaren. I'm so sorry to be late. But it's so delightful to see you here again."

Someone on my right had done it for me. I turned.

A tall, thin man in his fifties had sat down in the empty place. Turned towards me was a narrow, intelligent, oddly attractive face with blue eyes and gray hair.

"Colonel Fortescue," I said, and was astonished at myself. I had no conscious memory of ever seeing him. His name had summoned no mental picture. Yet I knew instantly that this was he.

The blue eyes took on a surprising warmth. "I'm extremely flattered that you remember me! You were so young when you left—what was it? Seven or eight?"

"Just eight."

"Thank you," he said to the servant who put his first course down. "Forgive me while I catch up. There was a nasty little business at the end of the island that kept me late."

I thought about the mine, about Palmer and Seth and what Jonathan had said—right or left? And what had happened to Palmer? I glanced quickly down the table.

"Looking for someone?"

I hadn't expected to like the colonel, probably because, thanks to Mother's references to gin and tonics on the club porch, I had anticipated Colonel Blimp, red, bloated, full of the waffles and wattles of the cartoon stereotype, what-whatting his way through any conversation more demanding than a discussion of a cricket score. The wiry, intelligent man beside me bore no relationship to the portrait.

"As a matter of fact," I said, "I was wondering what had happened to Mr. Palmer, the editor of the paper. He was here earlier and threatening to interview me."

"You should be grateful then that he hasn't. You probably wouldn't recognize yourself in the result."

"I'm not sure that he won't write the story anyhow. He seemed to be debating between revealing me as the rich, spoiled princess or the unrich radical member of the exploiting family siding with the repressed islanders."

He smiled. "Which would you say comes nearer to the truth?"

I decided to do some gentle probing of my own. "Why don't you make a guess?"

"Then I should say probably a little of both."

No fool, Colonel Fortescue. "But you don't like radicals, Colonel, do you?"

"Is that an inspired guess or information received?"

"To quote you, I should say a little of both."

He signaled to the waiter, who removed his soup plate and brought the fish course that we were all working on. "No, I don't like radicals."

I could feel disapproving glances being bent in my direction from across the table and from the other side of the colonel. The English, I remembered from my encounters with them abroad, consider talking shop—and radicals, as far as Colonel Fortescue was concerned, were definitely shop—bad form. Well, I thought, tough! I'd had nearly half an hour of polite idiocies from Mr. Formby and another hour of them before that at cocktails with the other club members. Besides, the more I looked at Yolande spreading charm like rich pâté in every direction the more independent and boorish I felt. A little political tussle would divert me. "Don't you think that sometimes radicals, or being radical, is the only way of bringing about reform?"

"What specific reform do you have in mind?" The look in his eyes and his smile said he was indulging me, the daughter of the island ruling family, playing with causes. I should have been irritated, as I usually was when somebody patronized me in this fashion. Instead, perhaps because of Yolande and one thing and another, I was hungry for interest and attention, and Colonel Fortescue was giving me both. Either he was genuinely interested, or he was a very skilled actor.

"I don't think it is right for one family to own the island and everything in it, which means that it has total power over everyone living here."

"Anyone who wants to leave is perfectly free to go."

"Yes, but why should they be forced to go? It's their home as much as it is ours." The "ours" slipped out.

"You don't believe in private property then?"

"Not when it includes the entire island and the . . . the means of production."

"But any farm anywhere does that."

"Not if there are other farms to compete with it both for labor and for prices."

"You will probably think it unkind of me to point out that that is a purely capitalistic argument."

Back to square one. I was silent for a minute, gathering my thoughts. It came as no shock to me that I had been argued to a standstill. Anyone could do it, including Sedgewick. But that was one of the delightful things about Sedgewick. He didn't argue. He just rolled over on his back and looked loving.

"I wasn't trying to belittle you, Barbara! May I call you that, by the way?"

"Of course," I said mechanically, wrenching my mind away from whether Sedgewick would indeed be safe with Hamish. I decided he would. Hamish was disagreeable and taciturn and probably an ardent misogynist, but he would be reliable. "You know, Colonel," I said, "I'm not an economist or a politician and it's really stupid of me to try to argue political philosophy, but I tell you what I do think: I think that any place, whether it's the size of Kilgaren or . . . or . . . the United States . . . or all the Russias, should be governed with the consent of the governed. All of them. Regardless of race and so forth. And I think that's what should be done on the island here."

"And do you find that your brother agrees with you?"

There was something odd behind that question. "What do you mean, Colonel?"

His brows went up. "Exactly what I asked. Does your brother agree with you?"

The words were the same but in some way I could not define, let alone point out, the question was different. I decided, for the moment, to take it on its face value. "I don't know. I haven't asked him in just those terms."

"Well, you might ask him, Barbara. We'd all like to know the answer to that question."

"Why don't *you* ask him?"

"If I thought he'd give me a straight answer, I certainly would."

I decided to take offense. "Are you suggesting he would lie?"

"My dear, many a good man has lied himself black and blue for a cause he thought right."

"And what cause do you think Jonathan would do that for?"

"I don't know. I thought that's what you might ask him?"

"And you, Colonel? Would you lie for a cause you believed in?"

He smiled. "And when did I stop beating my wife?"

I changed tack. "I've told you what I believe in? Why don't you tell me what you believe in?"

By this time we had worked our way through the fish and meat courses and were in the middle of dessert. The colonel pushed his spoon around the remains of a rather liquid ice and then put it down.

"I could ask in relation to what? But that would be fencing and I fancy you don't want me to fence, do you?"

"Isn't that what you've been doing so far?"

"To a degree. Will you forgive me? I wanted to see what kind of girl you had grown up to be."

"What was I like before?"

He thought for a minute. "Wild, lonely, spoiled, secretive." The words rolled out like stones. "And you weren't to blame for being any of those. If blame is the right word to use at all."

Suddenly the words . . . *Colonel Fortescue, dancing with your mother* . . . sprang into my mind as clear as when Nemi spoke them. As with Jonathan, I wanted to ask, And what was Mother like in those days? What was she like then? What am I like now? Where do the two come together?"

"And now," he went on, "you've grown into an intelligent and interesting young woman."

"I'd rather be pretty," I said, throwing a glance at Yolande before I could stop myself.

He broke into a laugh, and for the first time something wasn't right. The laugh, which was the ho-ho-ho variety, didn't go with the rest of him.

Quickly, while he was laughing, I said, "But you haven't told me what you really believe in, Colonel?"

"Why, my dear, doing the job I was hired to do. If

I were of an older generation—or perhaps if you were—I would call it doing my duty." Colonel Blimp had surfaced as the curtain had descended; he was being the grizzled officer to the sweet young thing in her first season.

The endless evening finally dragged to a close. I danced with Mr. Formby, the colonel, Dr. Templeton and several other men whose names I did not remember. It was the old-fashioned kind of dancing, waltzes and fox trots, where people danced hanging onto each other rather than the kind I had grown used to in New York. Across the shoulder of whomever I was dancing with I watched Jonathan and Yolande. Every single one of the women with whom I chatted between those dances said, looking at them, "They make a charming couple, don't they?" I agreed each time.

To my vast surprise Gilbert Palmer walked back into the clubhouse towards the end of the evening. He promptly came across the floor and asked me for a dance. Since he was about twenty years younger than any other male I was, despite everything I disliked about him, glad to see him.

"Well," I asked, as he hauled me away, a little, I couldn't help thinking, as though I were a load of coal, "did I come out as the spoiled tyrannical sister of the local despot or the idealistic rebellious sister of same?"

"Neither," he said rather truculently. "I decided not to do it."

"Why not?"

He trod on my foot. "Sorry," he mumbled. "This isn't my style of dancing at all."

"You chickened out," I said.

"Well if you must know, yes." The very young cheeks above the beard were bright red again.

"Thank you," I said, quite sincerely. "That was really nice of you."

"Well it just shows what a bad revolutionary I am. I should have put the cause above the feelings, if you follow me."

"I had an interesting discussion about causes at dinner. With Colonel Fortescue."

"I bet. What did he natter on about? The Flag, the Empire and the Ruling Classes?"

"No. He asked me what I believe in."

"Did you tell him?"

"Yes."

"And that is?"

By this time I was beginning to feel like a one-girl course in freshman civics. "To govern with the consent of the governed."

Palmer made a rude noise. Then he said, "There used to be something called dancing cheek to cheek. Let's try it."

So we did. It made a nice balm for the rancor inspired in me by the sight of Jonathan and Yolande.

It hadn't been a good evening. But the final calamity was to come. The orchestra had played "Goodnight Ladies" and "God Save the Queen." I went out to the hall to wait for Jonathan and Evelyn, whom I hadn't seen all evening.

The first to turn up was Evelyn, who came out of the so-called smoking room with Colonel Fortescue. They were talking. Evelyn's usual sneer was missing. In fact, he looked like any attractive adolescent when in the presence of someone on whom he had a hero-worshipping crush. Awed, respectful, even affectionate, in a properly distant way. And the colonel? He looked kindly and well disposed. They laughed at something, then the colonel patted Evelyn briefly on the shoulder and went off in another direction. Evelyn turned and saw me. His whole expression changed. And the change, infusing his face with hatred, was shocking. Why did he hate me so much? The reasons Jonathan gave were simply not enough. A sense of danger, like a warning, went through me. At that moment Jonathan and Yolande came into the hall from the porch. Her slender hand was tucked around his arm.

"There you are," Jonathan said. "I have some good news for us."

Somehow, I knew I would not consider it good. "Oh? What?"

"Yolande is coming to stay with us beginning tomorrow. Isn't that nice?"

I could feel his words trying to pull something out of me. There was something he wanted me to say. The silence stretched.

"Barbara!" Jonathan said sharply.

"Yes, it will be lovely," I said in a flat voice.

Yolande came toward me. The exquisitely tanned arm went around my waist. I moved away. I couldn't help it.

The proud, beautiful face tightened. "Perhaps your sister doesn't share your feeling about it, Jonathan."

"Then I must apologize for her." On Jonathan's face there was a white, frozen look. I realized suddenly how angry he was.

I pulled myself out of my trance. "I'm sorry, Miss del Arribe, I didn't mean to appear rude." Then I had an inspiration. "I—I was worrying about the fact that it might not seem right for you to be staying at Winds, you know, without a hostess."

Her face melted into a smile. "But you are the hostess, Barbara. And please, since we are to be sisters, call me Yolande."

Thus their engagement was announced.

The words fell into a silence. Then there was something like a sigh from the surrounding people followed by bright voices uttering banal but overwhelmingly sincere congratulations.

As someone thrust a champagne glass into my hand I looked at Jonathan. Under his dark tan the blood had receded and his anger was still there in the deeply etched lines and set mouth. I thought: I've really let him down.

Somebody, Mr. Formby of course, was proposing a toast. Yolande stood there reminding me in some way of a delicate prow of a ship. The congratulatory noise rose. I glanced around. Abstaining from the happy, almost hysterical hilarity were Colonel Fortescue and Evelyn, who stood a little apart, as though they were surprised, even, I thought, dismayed.

"Well," Gilbert Palmer's voice said behind me, "That saves everybody's bacon."

"What do you mean?"

"Don't be naive, Barbara! The Arribe millions have lifted the siege. The Marines have landed. Mafeking has been relieved."

As I continued to look blank he explained. "No more worry about whether the crops will be harvested; with enough money for police and mercenaries you can always put down a revolution; with enough money, in other words, white supremacy is secure. Catch?"

I caught.

7

*T*he next morning I came down with Sedgewick on his leash. Jonathan was waiting for me in the jeep. I threw my wide-brimmed straw hat—no one on the island moved without one—on top of Jonathan's on the seat between us and put Sedgewick on my lap.

I had not slept well, and Jonathan, I noted, looked as though he hadn't either. There were deep shadows under his eyes and the lines in his face and the hollows under his cheeks were more pronounced than usual.

We rode in silence for a while. Then Jonathan said, "I want to talk to you."

"Well, here I am, a captive audience."

"And being smart-alecky isn't going to help, either."

There was a new, biting note in his voice.

I didn't say anything. Quite apart from Jonathan's stricture, I couldn't dredge up many funnies this morning. "All right."

"I shouldn't even have to ask you this. But it seems it's necessary—just as it was necessary to order Evelyn to be polite to you. I must insist that you treat Yolande courteously. At all times. Is that understood?"

"Yes, Jonathan."

He glanced at me as the jeep bumped down onto the eastern side of the level plateau at the base of the hills. "I can't think why you should be so rude to her. After all, she's a nice girl. Most people like her."

"I'm not most people. And anyway, men look at things differently."

"A more obvious statement I can't imagine."

"And besides, I wasn't rude. I was just surprised."

"That isn't what your face conveyed."

"I'm sorry about my face and the way it looks. I always have been. But you must share the glory for that."

With an exasperated gesture he stopped the jeep. "You know perfectly well I'm not talking about that. But, of course, the moment that you receive the slightest criticism you move the conversation back to your favorite subject—Barbara, girl-martyr, innocent victim."

He was right. But knowing that didn't help the way I felt. I stared through the trees to the green ocean beyond. There was the usual scattering of boats, sails, fishermen and, in the center, like a jewel, a small white yacht.

"Yolande's?" I asked nodding at it.

"Yes."

"And she's living on that until she comes to Winds?"

"Yes."

"Why is she coming? Surely nothing Winds can produce in the way of comfort can touch that little toy?"

"Maybe not. But there's something you seem to have forgotten. However dilapidated and run down it is, Winds stands for something. And Yolande wants what that is."

I turned to face Jonathan. "Something else it stands for is slavery, white supremacy, colonial rule and exploitation. That's the deal isn't it? She gets the title and the prestige. You get the money to keep the status quo."

"You know, you sound just like the editorial in today's *Challenge*. Was Palmer trying it out on you last night?"

Right again. "If it's such a *quid pro quo* with you and Yolande, then why are you pretending to be in love with her?"

"Am I?"

"Well, you certainly looked adoringly at her."

"What makes you think it's pretense? Can you deny she's a beautiful and desirable woman?"

No, I couldn't deny that. At that moment I discovered I was 1) miserable and 2) in a trap of my own making. "Let's go, Jonathan. I'll be late."

"In a minute. I haven't received your assurance that you will behave."

I looked at him. "Do you have to be so pompous? I'm not a child."

"Then don't act like one. I brought you here to be a help, not an additional headache." That was the old Jonathan, the arrogant disciplinarian with the whiplash voice.

My hand started to shake. I knew what that meant—tears, a culmination of all the strains of last night and the quarrel this morning. It was an entirely involuntary reaction that has bedeviled and embarrassed me all my life. Hastily I stroked Sedgewick to see if I could divert what was about to happen. But it was no use. The tears overflowed my eyes and started to roll down my cheeks.

In the same contemptuous voice he said, "And stop feeling sorry for yourself."

In another minute I would begin to cry, and I was humiliated enough as it was. "Come along, Sedge," I whispered, and jumped out of the jeep. Keeping a firm hold on the leash I started to run.

"Barbara! Come back!"

But I ran on, not down the road towards the school, but through the cane. I wanted to find a hole and hide until the storm had passed and I could get hold of myself again.

"Barbara! Don't go through the cane!" I could hear his voice behind me.

Determination took hold of me. "Come here, Sedgewick," I whispered. Quietly, I veered from the narrow path I had been following and plunged into the thickest of the seven-foot-high green stalks. Then

I burrowed down, my arms around Sedgewick, one hand around his muzzle so he wouldn't bark. I could hear Jonathan thrashing through the cane, calling me.

"Barbara don't be an idiot. The fields are full of snakes! Where are you?"

I hadn't thought about the snakes, although I remembered now that the island sported its native vipers, swift, venomous, and deadly. They abounded in the forest that rimmed the island and would periodically appear in the cane. That was the reason cane cutters were always supplied with boots and were specially trained to keep on the alert for them.

Sedgewick, hearing Jonathan's voice, wiggled in my grasp and tried to bark. I tightened my grip. I knew I was being foolish. I knew that both Sedgewick and I could be bitten and killed; that I should behave like a mature adult, get up and walk out and, in a rational manner, discuss the whole matter of Yolande and the arrogant way he had used my presence to invite her. I had a perfectly legitimate grievance. I was, I assured myself, in the right. But I stayed where I was.

"Just a minute more," I whispered to Sedgewick.

I heard Jonathan walking through the cane and calling both me and Sedgewick, and I could tell by the sound of his voice that he was getting angrier and angrier. For a few minutes I was certain he would all but fall over us, because his voice came steadily nearer. But then I heard him stop, swear to himself, and start off in another direction. The footsteps receded and finally I couldn't hear them.

After about twenty minutes of complete quiet I eased to my feet and took my hand off Sedgewick's muzzle. "Come on," I whispered to him.

Sedgewick, of course, promptly barked.

"Be quiet, can't you?" I said in a voice just as loud as his bark. Then I bent down and hugged him in case his feelings were hurt. I have always felt with Sedgewick that it was absolutely essential to keep his self-image and self-esteem braced up, because he is not some pure-bred born with an over-developed and boring sense of his own superiority.

"It's not you," I went on, whispering this time, and stroking him while he wagged his behind. "It's just that we want to escape Jonathan."

He looked disapproving.

"Yes. I know you think you have a crush on him just because he knows how to scratch that special place on your back you can't reach. But that doesn't mean he's been nice to me. And I don't wish to discuss it any further. Now," I went on briskly, "we're going in the opposite direction."

If Sedgewick could have talked he would have said opposite to what? And I would have replied, opposite to where I think Jonathan is waiting to pounce on us. But since I wasn't sure where that was, it wouldn't have been very enlightening.

I looked up at the sun. It seemed at about a forty-five degree angle in what I took to be the east. I had been running, I decided, from the southeast. If we had continued in the jeep we would have been going northeast. Therefore I would go northwest. I jiggled the leash and we set off.

You cannot make progress through cane quietly, especially not if you're watching for snakes, so as soon as we struck a path that seemed to head, more or less, in our direction, I got onto it.

As I look back on it now, knowing what was bothering me, I can see the rationale to my irrational behavior. Because it *was* irrational—and dangerous. I was attempting to cross the cane fields at their widest part as the sun was mounting to its morning peak. There was no shade. I had left my hat in the jeep. Furthermore, I was heading directly away from the school where I was already overdue. But all I could think of was getting away from Jonathan.

Sedgewick and I walked and walked, getting hotter and hotter. By this time the nuttiness of my behavior had presented itself even to me. In a pique and a pout, I was cutting off my nose to spite my face, but, I assured myself, there was one thing to be said about an island: If I just went on long enough I'd hit the edge of the cane fields and the rim of forest bounding the ocean. Therefore it made sense to go on.

The sun climbed. Sedgewick's tongue started to loll out.

"Yes, I know, Sedgewick. We'll find some water soon."

By the time the edges of the trees reared themselves above the cane stalks I was doggedly putting one foot in front of another and I had no idea what time it might be. Finally the rows of cane came to an end. We staggered off the path into the shade of the trees and sat down. I had just enough sense not to let Sedgewick's leash slip from my fingers. "In a minute we'll go and look for some water," I said, and lay back. Sedgewick, following my example, stretched himself out.

It was absolutely still. The relative cool of the shade was pure bliss. There was no sound of cars or voices or people. There was nothing to see over our heads but a patch of sky showing through thick branches. I knew it wasn't safe to lie there too long. Not there in the lowland where the smell of the swamp mingled with the moist hot odor I always associated with our tropical rain forest. I knew that, but was too tired and hot to move and so, of course, I did what was inevitable: I dozed off.

I awoke some time later, and for a few seconds had absolutely no idea where I was. Then I sat up suddenly. "Sedgewick!" I called. The handle of the leash was still around my wrist. But the leash itself had been neatly cut about a foot beyond that. The strap dangled from my arm. There was no sign of Sedgewick.

I had been walking and calling for more than an hour. The sun was like a huge furnace directly over me. Nobody ever went hatless on the island, not unless they were in deep shade and intended to stay there. In early photographs of my father he and some of his guests wore pith helmets, but as these symbols of the British Raj grew less welcome around the world, the generally used headgear became the big, wide-brimmed straws worn by most of the cane cutters. There was a row of them on pegs near the front door. My own hat was, of course, in the jeep. I knew now that if I didn't put something on my head I would have sunstroke. I could, of course, take to the edge of the forest and keep in the shade, but I didn't think that I would find Sedgewick that way, and finding him was more important than anything else.

My mind had been alternating between pictures of what might be happening to Sedgewick and, when I pushed those away, to the faceless person who might simply have come across us as I lay sleeping, but who also might have been watching us since we emerged from the cane, who might very well be watching me now. My fear about Sedgewick, my sense of being watched, and my remorse at having allowed myself to sleep, or even further back, of having given free rein to my childish tendency to run away, went round and round in my mind. Surely, if he were alive or conscious, Sedgewick would have barked when someone tried to take him away. That thought did nothing for my peace of mind. But, watched or not, I was going to have to do something to cover my head, and the only thing I could do was to fashion some kind of turban or burnoose from my half slip. Still walking, I stepped out of the white cotton petticoat. I tore the hem off, then, folding the slip several times, tied it on top of my head, bringing the hemstrip under my hair at the back. If I were a cane cutter, I thought, I could weave some of those broad leaves in a few minutes. But I wasn't. My slip would have to do. Miserable and anxious as I was, I grinned at the appearance I must present. Lawrence of Arabia in drag, I decided.

I was walking now almost due north, shouting every few seconds, "Sedgewick! Sedgewick!" Then I would whistle. Sometimes I would say, "Come on, Sedgewick, I'm right here. Make a noise! Anything!" I realized, as I went, that I could have chosen just as well to return the way we had come. There was nothing to indicate that Sedgewick's captor had taken him in this direction. I could be walking away from him.

The sun climbed higher. I knew my arms and throat and face were getting royally burned. School would be over soon. What would Mrs. Gutierrez think of my absense? Would Jonathan tell her? At the thought of Jonathan my anger picked up. He'd certainly given up easily. And then I knew I was being the spoiled brat again. I had run away. I had hidden. He had tried to find me. I couldn't unload this on anyone else. Why had I hidden? Jonathan and I had been getting on very well—until he decided to use me to invite Yolande to stay. Well, why shouldn't he? He was in love with her.

But, curiously, my mind turned away from that as from a wall. For whatever reason, I didn't trust or like Yolande. All of which had brought me to where I was now, walking along the edge of the cane fields in the broiling sun, my mouth dry with shouting, looking for a small dog who might now be dead. At that point I stumbled over a root and fell, and for a minute just lay where I was. All I could think of were cascades of water, cool, blue water, flowing down my throat, glasses of it, buckets of it. My mouth felt as though it were filled with pitch. I sat up. Lights jumped and danced in front of me. I said out loud to myself, "You're just dehydrated. There's nothing wrong with you beyond that. Get up. Now."

I struggled to my feet and stood still, as there were more spots and stripes and lights. I had to go on looking. Staggering slightly, I started off. Ahead about a hundred yards the path bent. Beyond that it was hidden by tall grass and shrubs. The forest came nearer. But, I reminded myself, the island would be getting narrower around here. The main road, cutting towards the other side, couldn't be that far away. If I could just get to the road I'd flag down a car and get myself taken to Colonel Fortescue's office as fast as I could. He could rout out some of his part-time constables to help me find Sedgewick. If Sedgewick were still alive.

I fixed my eyes on the bend in the path and the picture of the main road. I felt if I could just keep my mind on those I'd make it. My legs felt like pieces of spaghetti. I was beginning to shake and vaguely, at the back of my mind, admit to myself that dehydration could be dangerous. Moist as everything was down here, I had sweated out the fluids from my body. What I should have had were salt tablets. But I didn't. Keep going, I told myself. Eventually I came to where the path veered, and found myself in a clearing. To the left, hidden until now, was a huge tree, throwing shade for thirty yards. Tied to the tree was a small brown and white dog with something wrapped around his mouth and head. My wavering legs started to run. "Sedgewick," I called, telling myself he must be alive because he was sitting up. As I got nearer I could hear his whimpers. Finally I reached him. A strip of white cotton cloth, not too unlike the slip now on my head, was holding his muzzle together so he couldn't bark. The moment I came near he strained at the rope and jumped all over me. With quivering fingers I unknotted the cloth. Joyous barks greeted me. I sat down in the shade, hugging him while he licked my face. It was all very emotional.

I don't know how long we'd been there when I heard what, after Sedgewick's bark, must have been the most welcome sound in the world: falling water.

"Let's go," I said to him. He was still wearing the collar and the leash. I made a small loop at the cut-off end and twisted it around a couple of fingers. Then I gripped the rest with my hand and we started off towards that blessed gurgle. It was inside the forest, which had grown thicker here. No matter. We plunged in. There was no path. Within a few minutes all sight of the sun had vanished. What light there was was a dark green. It was as though the whole forest was inside a huge emerald.

I had never been in this forest before, not even as a child. My hiding and escape places had always been up towards the green mountains at the back of the house. Truth to tell, I had always been afraid of the swampy lowlands and the small forest that bunched at the upper end. There were strange tales about it: That it had been used in the past by the cane cutters for some of the weirder practices brought from Africa; that from time to time drum beats could be heard coming from there; that animal—some even said human—sacrifices had taken place there. None of this was believed up at Four Winds, certainly not by my father or mother or Jonathan. But Nemi talked about it sometimes, when she had been drinking, and I did know that a lot of the servants wouldn't go anywhere near it.

I took a tight grip on the leash and kept it short as Sedgewick and I picked our way, climbing over roots and creepers. You couldn't even see the floor of the forest. And there were a hundred small noises indicating that though nothing visibly moved, we were invading a living world. But the sound of the water kept me going. Finally we came to it, a tiny waterfall, the clear white water falling from a couple of rocks into a small pool. I had never had the slightest hesitation about drinking the water up in the hills. Whether it was still pure down here or not I didn't know. But I was going to try it. I put the end of the leash between my teeth and held out both hands, cupped, under the fall of water. I didn't want Sedgewick lapping it from the pool. Who knew what was in it or how stagnant that still water might be. I was taking as few chances as possible.

I held my cupped hands, full of water, down at Sedgewick's level and he drank and drank. After he had had his fill I wrapped the leash around my wrist and drank myself. Nothing in my life ever tasted as good. I splashed the water over my face and head. Then I drank some more. Then I splashed some over Sedgewick. Then he had some more to drink. I thought about taking off what few garments I now had on and going in under the tiny fall with Sedgewick. But in this tropic forest we could mildew before we got back to the sun, and there was always that watcher. I had not forgotten him for one minute. He could be hiding in the cane, waiting to see me discover Sedgewick. He could have seen us enter the forest. It didn't seem likely he could have followed us without my knowing, but then it hadn't seemed likely that he had followed us before, either. Nothing that had actually happened seemed likely.

It was after Sedgewick and I had finally had our fill and I turned to go back that I realized that "back" had no meaning. I knew, in general, the way from which I had come. But would that be enough? I had simply followed the sound of the water. Could I find our way back by choosing a direction where the sound steadily, and perceptibly, decreased? Fear, which had stopped the moment I found Sedgewick, came back. We could very easily be lost.

"The thing for us to remember—" I said aloud, and then stopped, appalled, as there was a great flutter of wings and scuttering of leaves. My human voice had disturbed the citizens of the forest.

"The thing for us to remember," I said, in a much quieter voice, "is that the forest is just not that wide." The trouble was—and I couldn't help thinking about it—that though it was true that if we kept to a line going across the forest we would reach either the inner or outer rim in a reasonable time, we could just as easily choose one going through, that is, parallel to the outer edges, and that would take us, picking our way at a quarter of a mile an hour, a very long time indeed, because the forest on this side ran from the tip of the island to where the heights began.

It was a very depressing and rather frightening thought.

"Never mind, Sedgewick," I said. "We have each other."

At that point it was very obvious that what Sedgewick wanted was 1) dinner and 2) a long nap. He was dancing around in that peculiar manner that at home meant, Let's make for the kitchen. Since he was on a short leash, his movements were restricted, but his meaning was unmistakable.

I closed my eyes. "Dear Lord," I said aloud, "Please send us in the right direction."

Then I opened my eyes and turned very slowly around in an arc, keeping the waterfall at my back. I was trying to see if there was any slight difference in the light. If there was any direction in which the green seemed more translucent, I would head that way.

It seemed a good idea at the time. An hour or so later, I knew that it hadn't been. I didn't know where

I was going. I couldn't hear the waterfall, but I didn't know but what I had circled it and was making towards the outer rim. In which case, I should soon reach the water's edge. On the other hand, I could be plunging northeast towards the tip of the island. That was several miles away and I was very tired. I was also hungry. And Sedgewick, trotting very close to my feet, his tail down, was plainly tired and hungry, too. I thought about my prayer. For some reason best known to Him, the Good Lord had appeared not to answer it. Or at least not to answer it the way I had planned for Him to.

And at that moment I struck a very faint path. In almost no other context would it be called that. But here, where every foot was covered, it was an unmistakable parting in the undergrowth. A path went somewhere, and I was beyond arguing where it might be going. We would follow it. I peered at my watch, which said eleven thirty. I brought it up to my ear and listened for the tiny tick. There was none. I tried the winder. It was completely loose. As I wound it I reflected that I had no idea how long ago eleven thirty might have been.

We followed the path and, with only one interruption, it proved much easier going. But the one interruption gave me enough of a scare to last me for some time. I was moving along fairly rapidly, trying to ignore the soreness of my feet and the growing blisters that were not improved by the damp, when Sedgewick suddenly stopped and made a whining noise. I stopped too. "What is it?" I asked him.

He sat down and whined again, his muzzle facing forward and a little to the left. I looked there. For a moment it just looked like a mound of whitish sand or earth. Then I saw it moving.

"Dear God!" I whispered. I knew what they were. Soldier ants. I bent down and picked Sedgewick up in my arms. Then, giving the mound a wide berth, I left the path, keeping it in sight, and struggled on over the roots and stumps and undergrowth for some time before I returned to it. Then, quite suddenly, there was a small clearing. And in the clearing was a broken-down abandoned hut, made of sticks and palm leaves and dirt.

It was an eerie ruin, its few planks sagging, the roof looking as though at any moment it might slide off. Nemi's stories of witchcraft and voodoo revelry drifted unpleasantly through my mind. As I looked at it I became aware of the stillness. There were no forest sounds here, no birds, only Sedgewick's whine as he strained at the leash. Again I wondered about a watcher, the same silent figure that had walked up and cut Sedgewick's leash while I was sleeping. Sedgewick whined again and gave another tug.

"All right, all right! We'll go over and have a look," I whispered. "But I don't like the look of it."

But it seemed to change character when I got up close. Somehow it was bigger than I expected. I had thought one or two gaping, squarish holes were windows, almost, by now, grown over. But close to I saw that beneath the green leaves was earth and board. Odd. We walked around it. Along with being larger, it was less of a wreck than I had thought, too. In fact, it had a surprisingly solid quality. And those sagging planks seemed to have nothing to do with the structure. They appeared to be tacked on here and there with no relation to each other or anything else. The door was almost entirely overgrown, the creepers and vines meeting and in some cases crisscrossing. Curious, I parted them. I don't know what I expected to find—slats, I suppose, loosely held together by nails. But the wood underneath my fingers was amazingly solid. Still keeping Sedgewick's leash tightly gripped in one hand, with the other I felt the door all the way up and down, and then all the way across, not just in one place but at various levels and heights. It was as sturdy as the front door of any valuable mansion, and the wood was thick, too. I could tell that by the dull, solid sound it gave off when I rapped it.

Sedgewick, in the meanwhile, had not been idle. I don't know how much, if any, terrier there was in his ancestry, but he was pawing and digging the earth just under the wall beside the door. I suppose my mind was on a possible snake, because I said to him, sharply, "What have you got there?"

At that moment, several things happened. The fingers of my right hand, still absently feeling the door, encountered a round, raised, smooth surface. I peered at it, unable to believe my tactile sense. Underneath packed mud and paint was an extremely modern lock. Whoever had painted it had done a sloppy job. Where my fingernail had cleared some daubed mud showed bright, new gilt. I hadn't really absorbed the meaning of this when a shot rang out and something went whizzing past my ear.

If I had given one second's thought I would have dropped to the ground. Fortunately, my native panic took over. I picked up Sedgewick and flew over the few feet of clearing behind the house. Another shot rang out just as I reached the trees.

For the first time I blessed the almost shoulder-high bushes, shrubs, plants, creepers and general undergrowth that had made my journey of the last several hours such a snail's-pace affair. At least I would be hard to find. But as I said that, I heard the unmistakable sounds of someone behind me. No one could walk quietly in that forest, although whoever wanted to kill me was making a lot less noise than I had. If I went on he would catch me.

For the second time that day I put my hand around Sedgewick's muzzle and crouched behind a huge bush, praying that no snakes or scorpions or ants were near, that Sedgewick would stay still so that we would make no sound, that we would be invisible, that whoever it was would go past us.

My prayers were answered. The footsteps came nearer, paused, went on, paused. I wanted to see who it was but the bush that hid me was too thick and wide to see through or around. I crouched there, my heart pounding, one hand around Sedgewick's muzzle, the other around his rib cage feeling the rapid beat of his heart. I held my breath. Then the feet moved on and away. I strained my ears, hearing the steps continue regularly until they went out of hearing range.

I don't know how long we were there. Fear had driven out all thoughts of hunger and exhaustion, but after what seemed a year, when we still hadn't heard the sound of anyone returning, they came back. Slowly, stiffly, I stood up. This time I didn't make the mistake of taking my hand from Sedgewick's muzzle. I had done that this morning. Who could tell? Perhaps that was when the silent watcher, the one who wanted to kill me, who had stolen Sedgewick, had heard us.

I had no choice as to which direction to take. Ahead lay our pursuer. Back of us lay the hut. I struck out, away from the path, across the forest. I wondered if it were still daylight. It didn't matter. All I could do was go on. Hating the cruelty of it, I tied poor Sedgewick's muzzle together with the white cotton bandeau that I had pulled off him before and stuffed in the pocket of my dress.

"I'm sorry about this, but I have to do it," I whispered in his ear. My fingers encountered what felt like some embroidery. In the dim light I couldn't possibly see what it was, nor did I have time to look. Later, I thought. Then I heaved Sedgewick over my shoulder and picked my way.

I was so dazed and exhausted that I had been staring ahead at something for quite a few minutes before I realized what it was—daylight. I almost cried out and ran. But I forced myself to walk as slowly and carefully as before, sticking to the thickest part of the trees. Walking into the light, I would make an excellent target. At any moment I expected to hear a shot and feel a bullet between my shoulder blades, although, if it hit me, would I hear anything? I was still puzzling this highly technical point when I reached the trees' edge and heard, in the near distance, the most beautiful sound in the world next to running water—a car. I had come out near the tip of the island. The main road up the southeast side of the island was less than a quarter of a mile away.

Ten minutes later Sedgewick and I were standing by the main road waving at a car coming towards us.

8

*I*t turned out to be no accident that the car that picked us up was carrying one of Colonel Fortescue's part-time constables, a soldierly young man who cut cane, drove a truck, and did various other jobs while he was working his way through a Jamaican college.

"Your brother has been very worried, Miss Kilgaren," he told me in his polite, soft English. "Everybody is out looking for you."

"Then I should think if they shouted I would have heard them and shouted back and they would have found me."

"But they were looking mostly on the other side of the island."

"I was in the forest."

"But none of us—not even your brother—thought you would go there. Nobody goes to the forest. It's not safe."

"I learned that," I said bitterly.

"And besides," he went on doggedly. "If you were

lost in the forest, why do you have that—covering—on your head, and why are you sunburned?"

I put my fingers up to my face. "Does it show that much?"

He smiled, that smile of pure good humor that so many of the islanders have, and adjusted the rear-view mirror so that I could see myself. I looked up and winced. My face and throat were pure lobster. I glanced down. So were my arms, although they were more bronze than pink.

"You're going to have some beautiful blisters," he said, "You must have had a long walk through the cane before you got into the forest."

I nodded tiredly and then sneezed, a habit of mine when, after being out of the sun, I am suddenly exposed to it again.

"Your dog sure looks worn out, too. What kind is he?"

Everything about Sedgewick drooped—his tail, his ears, his head. He was half on my lap and half between the driver and me and more than half asleep. I opened my mouth to say he was a fine new experimental breed being cultivated at great expense in the United States, when something in the young driver's intelligent face told me that that would be a lost cause. I was too exhausted to put any conviction in it. Like Sedgewick, everything about me drooped.

"All sorts," I said, and sneezed again. Without thinking, I put my hand in my pocket and took out the handkerchief there. "Why was my brother so convinced I would be on the other side of the island?"

"He said, When you were a little girl, that was always where you went, up where the land rises and goes into the mountains."

It was true. The island rose more steeply on the southeast coast and reached a higher altitude. And Jonathan was always looking for me up there when I was a child.

"But I was headed towards the other side when I—" I didn't quite want to say "ran away from him." It didn't sound right. To give myself time I untied the hem of my slip from around my head and took off my homemade burnoose.

"That sure looked funny, but I guess it was a good idea," my escort said.

"Better than sunstroke," I agreed, and sneezed again. I was smoothing the handkerchief and felt again the embroidery. My memory was jolted. This was the strip that I had taken from around Sedgewick's head. I looked at it more closely. It was obviously part of a handkerchief. The embroidery, torn across, had formed half of a monogram which looked vaguely familiar. My tired mind chased the matter around for a bit but failed to come up with anything.

In the following fifteen minutes until we arrived up at Four Winds I learned from my companion his name—John Richardson—and the various jobs he did while taking courses at the Jamaica college. His mother, it seemed, had once worked up at the house and he had been there with her as a small boy.

"I think the thing I remember best was how cool it was, even on the hottest day, compared to our house down in the village. 'Course you had those big fans."

I wondered then, How did he feel about the Kilgarens up at the cool, big house with their large, efficient fans, their money, their servants? Did it make him a secret follower of Seth Williams? Did he have his job with Colonel Fortescue as a revolutionary placed in the middle of the police force—such as it was—waiting for his moment to attack from inside? Did he ally himself with the small middle class of shopkeepers, accountants, and professional blacks? Or was he a loner, interested only in bettering himself?

As we drove along the road I thought that if my mind were less fogged I might be able to ask clever questions that would elicit the answer to all these imponderables. Subtlety was never my strong point, even under the best of conditions, and these were not the best of conditions. I debated a bald question: Are you an admirer of Seth Williams? Would he answer? And if he did, would I believe him? I met his eyes in the mirror.

"You're giving me a very speculative look, Miss Kilgaren," he said, smiling.

I don't know what made me say it, but I said, "I was wondering if you were a revolutionary."

"No. I'm not a revolutionary. But I am for self determination, by everybody, everywhere."

"You want to kick out the Kilgarens?"

"No. I think they should have their say, like everybody else. No more. No less."

"Have you ever talked to my brother about this?"

His smile broadened. "Often, Miss Kilgaren."

"What does he say?"

"Well, Miss Kilgaren, I think if you don't know you should ask him, don't you?" And with that he swept up through the gates of the house, and brought the car around to stop in front of the steps mounting to the front door. He leaned across me and opened the door. "I hope you feel better, soon. And Miss Kilgaren: Stay out of the forest. It's not a good place."

I looked back as Sedgewick and I got out. "I thought all that was old superstition."

"Sometimes superstitions are very useful for covering up things people don't want generally known. I'll let your brother know you're safe." And with that he half saluted, turned the car, and drove off.

To my great relief Jonathan was not home. I didn't feel up to encountering him at that moment. Or anyone else. I went back towards the kitchen. Sedgewick needed something to eat, and so did I.

As I passed I looked at the big clock in the hall. It was ten after three in the afternoon. My body felt as though it was much later. I walked up to the clock to see if it had stopped. But the stolid tick, tick, tick was going steadily.

The kitchens were back of the dining room connected by a small, dark corridor tucked away behind the wing of the house. I hoped very much that it was empty, and it was. Hamish had undoubtedly retired to his room, I thought with relief. I went straight to the big refrigerator, poured myself some orange juice, and, while I was drinking it, got out a whole cold chicken. After taking out the bones of one half I gave it to Sedgewick and was gnawing the other half when there was a clackety-thump and in walked Hamish.

"Wha ye doin' with yon chicken?"

"Eating it, Hamish, of course."

"It was for dinner, when the young lassie will be here."

I lowered the chicken leg. "What young lassie?"

"Señorita del Arribe." Somehow that very Spanish name sounded quite Celtic as it emerged from Hamish's mouth. "She and her crew will be coming before dinner. More work. More cooking, and not a hand to help me."

Incredibly, I had forgotten, temporarily, that Yolande was coming today. I had been standing, but I sat down. I put the half-chewed drumstick on a plate, uninterested in it.

Hamish was looking at me out of his shrewd little eyes.

"Ye didna know?"

"I had forgotten."

He peered again. "What hae ye been doin? Ye look burnt."

"I am burnt. I was lost."

"Ye're a naughty lass. Makin' trouble for Master Jonathan. Ye'd no right. No right at all."

"No right to do what?" I asked, indignant.

But he had pottered out of the big, cool, dark kitchen and I could hear his uneven steps going out the stone corridor that led, I supposed, to his room.

Sedgewick was now drinking noisily from his big water dish. "Come, Sedgewick," I said loftily. "Time for our nap."

I was asleep before I knew I'd found the pillow. Sedgewick jumped up on the bed and curled up at my feet. That was the last I remembered.

I woke up several hours later, feeling as though every bone in my body were broken and I had sustained a beating. My face and neck and arms were hot.

It took all the control I had not to stay where I was. But I knew I had to go downstairs. To stay sulking up in the bedroom, which I dearly wanted to do, was to announce to Jonathan that I was afraid to meet him. And I didn't want that.

But when I had opened the louvres, turned on the lights, and looked at myself in the mirror I almost got back on the bed. I was burned and scratched and bitten. I closed my eyes. I could look at the whole thing negatively and dwell on the fact that after my brief, happy appearance as a pretty girl, I had gone back to being plain old ugly me.

I opened my eyes. On the other hand, the positive

side was there, too. My current beat-up façade was so total that old scars didn't show, not even the ones around my hairline. "You win some, you lose some," I said to Sedgewick.

I took a long shower: hot, medium, and finally cold. I washed my hair. When I got out the lobster was already beginning to turn to bronze. If I could just not peel, I might have a good tan. My humor started to improve.

Then, just as I was leaving to go down, I glanced at the top of my bureau where the maid had placed the washed and ironed laundry I had put into the hamper. I knew that Hamish, though the only live-in servant, had outside help of various kinds from the village and the cane cutters' huts. And in this climate, laundry was done on an almost daily basis. Sitting on top of the heap of underwear was a large, folded white handkerchief. It was the one Jonathan had lent me that day in his study, and I had put it in the wash basket to be laundered before I returned it to him. I stared at it. There was a monogram in one corner, small, beautifully embroidered, nothing like the large vulgar splashes one sees even in the best stores. These had been done on the island by the same fine seamstress who had done so much for Mother. Tiny stitches, perfectly even, silk-smooth. I couldn't mistake it. I went over to the dress I had taken off and put in the hamper, and looked in the pocket. There was the strip that had held Sedgewick's muzzle together. I ran my hand along it and found the embroidery. It was only half of the monogram, but easily recognizable.

As I approached the sitting room I could hear the sound of voices from the big back porch opening out from the lounge and looking into the mountains. I went slowly out there.

Yolande was standing by the railing, her elegant back to me. Jonathan was beside her. Up this high the mosquitos were only moderately bad. Still, screens had been installed. It spoiled the view a little, but was better than being eaten alive.

Yolande turned. "Barbara! I am so glad to see you. Jonathan tells me you had an adventure this afternoon. Ach! You were out in our sun. Silly child! You should never expose yourself like that. Never mind, it will tan. You'll see. I have some miracle cream or other which will help. I'll bring it to you this evening."

By this time she was beside me, her cool arm around me, and she had kissed my cheek. I wanted to tell her to keep her cream. But aside from the fact that she was a guest in the house, I didn't have the heart for a fight. I didn't look at Jonathan.

He said, "Well, Skimp? Was that trip necessary?"

Yolande's merry trill of a laugh rang out. I looked then at Jonathan. He was not smiling.

"I thought so," I said steadily.

"Did you? We must discuss the matter more fully later."

"There is nothing to discuss," I said. Above all things I wanted to avoid a tête-à-tête with Jonathan.

"We shall see."

"Come now, Skimp—is that the nickname?—you mustn't make things difficult for Jonathan."

Yolande, I thought, was being the lady of the house with a vengeance. She might have called me the hostess, but she had already, in everything but formal name, pre-empted that. I turned to her. "Skimp is an old nickname, Yolande. I'd just as soon everybody forgot it. My name is Barbara."

There was a silence. Her nostrils arched a little. The corners of her mouth tightened. Behind the sweet features loomed the shadow of Father, the tycoon.

"Of course, Barbara." She threw a saucy smile at Jonathan, who was staring down at his drink. "We must be careful, mustn't we, not to call her that?"

"Where's Evelyn?" I asked, for something to say.

"I'm here," his voice said behind me. I glanced around. He looked pointedly at the others. "Sorry to be late. The bathroom was occupied for *hours*."

"You could have used mine," Jonathan said.

Yolande showed her pretty, three-cornered smile. "I expect Barbara was having a long soak. We females love that."

Evelyn examined me. "More like boil."

Jonathan got up. "I think Hamish must be about ready." And as though this was a signal, the gong started its evening clatter.

We started towards the dining room. Sedgewick,

who had come into the porch with me and had sat unobtrusively at the back of my feet, a little nervous with a stranger in the room, accompanied me now into the dining room. Normally, he would have been jumping all over Jonathan, but he was as zonked out by the day's adventure as I, and he always kept a very low profile when any unknown quantities were around. And Yolande was an unknown quantity. Then she noticed him walking beside me.

"Good heavens! What is that little mongrel doing here? Dogs should never be in a dining room. He must be taken out at once. Hamish—"

"Yolande—" Jonathan and I said at once, I with murder in my heart.

But it was Hamish who settled things. "The dog rests here, with Barbara. And there's no argument." I gave the grumpy old Scotsman my best smile.

"Careful," Evelyn said, sitting down. "Barbara's neurotically attached to her mangy little beast and I strongly advise you—"

"Shut up, Evelyn," Jonathan said. "Yolande, Sedgewick, Barbara's dog, is part of an interesting experiment in selective breeding and is extremely valuable."

"Valuable! Do you think I'm a fool, Jonathan? You can see dozens of curs like him all over the streets of any city." It was plain that Yolande, whatever her other considerable assets, had no sense of humor. She was staring at poor Sedgewick with growing distaste. "And he has had mange. One can see the patches. This must be some kind of bad joke.

I do not like dogs of his kind. I will give Barbara a poodle, for her own. She will forget this—this *perro*."

"If anyone lays a finger on Sedgewick—"

"Be quiet. No one will touch him. Yolande, I have explained the matter to you. There it stays."

Yolande lifted perfectly arched brows. "But of course, Jonathan. If you wish it. You have only to say." And she gave him her really beautiful smile.

His face softened. He smiled back, and, leaning over, picked up her hand and gave it a quick kiss. "*Muchas gracias!*"

She glanced down at her plate. I found myself reflecting that, according to Gilbert Palmer, her family had cornered the market on most of the valuable minerals in a large hunk of South America. The children of pirates, I found myself reflecting, are frequently pirates, and I could not believe in the docility of her present expression. I put a tentative foot under the table. Yes, there Sedgewick was. And there he would stay. Right where I could keep my foot on him.

She glanced up, her expression serene. "It will be so much pleasure for me to do over this room. To paint the walls a light color, to hang new curtains. It will be a show place again."

I didn't say anything. Neither did Evelyn. After a while Yolande said to me, "Has Jonathan told you of our plans for the island?"

"No. What plans?"

She looked at him and smiled. "You tell her, Jonnie."

I swallowed my resentment of her use of my childhood name for him.

Jonathan put his knife and fork on his plate. "Yolande thinks, and I agree, that we could stir up quite a brisk tourist trade to the island. We could build a hotel on the cove, charter a fishing boat or two, fence off that part of the beach, and make a new, expensive watering place in the Caribbean. With Yolande's friends' patronage, it could become the new status place."

"You mean that cove on the southeast side?"

"Yes. Below the heights there."

So they would take my green hidden slopes and make a resort out of them. My face must have shown my dismay.

"You do not seem to like that idea, either," Yolande said drily.

"But that's the best beach the island has. If you fence that off, then the people who live here wouldn't be able to use it."

"They don't use it much anyway. And besides, they have the whole rest of the shoreline," Jonathan said.

"And a resort would provide money and jobs for the islanders," Evelyn put in. "Unless, of course, you prefer it to become some kind of annex to Cuba."

I stared at Evelyn's face below the tousled blond hair, at the straight blunt nose and short upper lip. Again there was a flash of déjà vu. Then it vanished.

"Why are you staring at me?" Evelyn asked.

"Sorry. You remind me of someone. But I can never remember who."

"But," Yolande said helpfully, "Of yourself. Naturally. Aren't you related? You look so much alike!"

"Yolande, I thought—" Jonathan said. Then he stopped. "I thought I explained."

"But explained what, *querido*? He is your son. She is your sister. Why should there not be a resemblance? I myself look more like my aunt than I do my mother."

"Barbara—" Jonathan started.

"I really am *not* flattered," Evelyn said on a strong note of grievance. "I am told I look like my mother. I—"

"Telegram for you, master." Hamish wobbled in with a rather crumpled envelope on a silver tray.

"Don't they telephone them?" Yolande asked.

"Not if the messenger boy lives near here anyway." Jonathan reached out for the telegram and tore it open. "Excuse me," he said, and proceeded to read it. There was a silence.

"But what is it?" Yolande said. "You look so—so unpleasantly surprised."

Jonathan glanced at Hamish. "Thanks. No answer." And he put the telegram in his pocket. "I think we'll have dessert and then coffee in the lounge for Miss del Arribe and Evelyn. Miss Barbara and I will have ours in the study."

Before dinner I would have refused to go back there with him. I still didn't want to. But Sedgewick's body next to my leg was a reminder of a debt. Or was it a real debt? Had I handed my strange brother a hold on me through this idiotic dog of mine? Through it he could keep me on more or less civil terms with him, even grateful, when I now had evidence that he was behind the cut leash and (incredibly) the shot of the afternoon.

Of course, I thought gloomily, there was always Othello.

But then, in that case, or rather in this particularly snarled plot, who was Iago? I would dearly love to cast Evelyn for any villain going around. But despite everything, I couldn't. In a sense, his total self-absorbtion militated in his favor. I couldn't believe that he ever took his mind off himself long enough to plot against anybody. Nor could I imagine him leaping through miles of cane under the noon sun, even if he knew I was there and available for being frightened out of my wits. That reminded me of what Yolande had said about the resemblance. The sheer ridiculousness of her allegation kept me from being too upset. For one thing, much as I loathed him I had to admit that Evelyn was a remarkably handsome boy. Whereas I—But that was just that old self-hatred again.

Jonathan got up. "Now if you and Evelyn will excuse us? Come along, Barbara."

As we left I heard Yolande say, "Evelyn, would you like to try a game of chess with me?"

"Is she any good at chess?" I asked Jonathan as we crossed the hall and went down into the other wing.

"Very."

I sighed. "It doesn't seem fair."

He glanced down at me as we walked. "That she should have all that and brains, too?"

"Yes."

"Don't underestimate Yolande."

"I won't. I don't underestimate her at all. I'm terrified I'll come home one day and find she's persuaded you to have Sedgewick dispatched to the cane cutters' happy games or dog heaven so that I can have a well-bred poodle."

We had reached his study. He opened the door and held it as Sedgewick and I went in ahead. Then he shut it.

He touched a wall switch and the big fan overhead started turning. "Don't worry about Sedgewick, Barbara. Yolande won't hurt him, however much he outrages her sense of the fitness of things."

"Can you really be sure of that, Jonathan? I'd rather leave the island tomorrow than risk her doing anything to poor old Sedge."

Jonathan had been picking up some papers from his desk and glancing at them, but he looked up at that. "You mean you'd sacrifice that money with which you were going to Rome and capture Nick? My, my! Is it that you love Nick less or Sedgewick more?"

He was watching me. I opened my mouth and closed it again, appalled to find that I had forgotten about Nick.

Jonathan started to laugh. "Where are the snows and the loves of yesteryear? Routed by a brown and white mongrel. That should take care of Nick's vanity once and for all."

I was furious, but before I could say anything Hamish banged on the door, pushed it open with his foot, slapped down the coffee tray and went out, muttering to himself the whole time.

Jonathan nodded towards the tray. "Why don't you do the honors?"

I poured the coffee.

"Now," Jonathan said, taking his, "What happened to you today?"

His cool authority, to say nothing of his pretense of ignorance, was too much. I said sharply, "You should know!"

"What do you mean by that? I ask you to treat Yolande with some degree of courtesy and you run off into the cane in a tantrum, don't answer when I call you, worry everybody half to death, and force me to rout out half the island looking for you."

"And of course you didn't know where I was and what I was doing. And you didn't cut Sedgewick's leash or fire a shot at me." The moment I said that, put it into words, I was hit by the sheer, total unlikelihood of it.

Jonathan had been leaning against the desk, looking irritated. But he straightened. *"Fired a shot at you?"*

"Well, somebody did, and it was part of your handkerchief that was around Sedgewick's jaw."

He stared at me, his face expressionless. "Start from the beginning and explain."

I did, leaving out nothing. When I was through he said, "And you're sure it was part of my handkerchief?"

"Yes. It's just like the one you lent me in the study here that day."

"Go get it."

"Don't you believe me?"

"I'd still like to see it."

"I suppose you think I'm lying."

"Compared to being accused of tying up a dog's mouth so that he could easily suffocate and be unable to defend himself, to say nothing of taking a potshot at you, lying strikes me as a peccadillo. Please get the handkerchief."

I went up the stairs two at a time and raced down the south wing to my room. I had left the torn, stained, dirty dress in the hamper, but I was pretty sure I had put the handkerchief strip on the bureau along with the laundered handkerchief. I burst into my room and turned to the bureau. The clean, washed, and ironed square was there. But there was no torn strip. I went to the hamper and took out the dress. The pockets were empty. I emptied everything else out on the floor. The strip wasn't there. Then I looked in the bureau drawers, on the floor, under the bed, in the bathroom. It wasn't in or on any of those places. But nothing else in my room had been removed. All the clothes that I had left to be washed were still there, waiting to be picked up by the maid tomorrow. I closed the door and went downstairs. The answer to who could have taken the strip was obvious: Evelyn. He had been in the bathroom and had come downstairs after me. I paused, my foot on the bottom step. Should I go and question him? Standing there I heard his and Yolande's voices, laughing over something. For that matter, Yolande could have gone upstairs after Jonathan and I had retreated to his study. And Jonathan? Had he left the room at any time? No, but Hamish, who adored him, could easily have gone up during dinner.

Slowly I went back to the study.

Jonathan was sitting at his desk, going over what looked like an account book. "Find it?" he asked.

I shook my head. "No. It's not there." I walked over to the empty fireplace (who but a Kilgaren with baronial ambitions would have built a fireplace in a climate like this?) and stood looking down into it.

"So you believe that I not only followed you, took Sedgewick away, tied up his mouth, followed you again into the forest and took a shot at you, but now I have caused your evidence to be removed. By whom, by the way? Evelyn? Yolande? Hamish?"

I didn't say anything for a minute. Then, "I told you the truth," I said stubbornly.

"But if I told you such a tale and then failed to produce any evidence whatsoever, would you believe me?"

"No, but—" The illogic of it struck me.

"No, but that's not the same, you're about to say. Turn around. I'm tired of talking to your back."

I turned.

Jonathan, sitting in that chair, in his white jacket

and black tie worn in honor of Yolande, looked so much like my father that it was a shock. Same stern mouth with the deep furrows on either side, same cold eyes. "Well," he said. "which of my accomplices do you suspect?"

"I don't know."

He got up and walked around the room. Then he seemed to make a decision. "All right. I've tried to overcome your mistrust and dislike. But I'm going to accept now the fact that I can't. If A wants to believe the worst of B, then anything will do as an excuse. If he doesn't, then nothing will do. The feeling comes first, any evidence one way or the other second." He came and put his hands on the chimney piece and looked down for a minute. "I always felt that you got the wrong end of every deal. Father had no use for daughters. Your mother considered you an albatross and let you know it, and there's been nobody to take either place. And you hold me responsible for the burns on your face which no longer exist but seem still to be a permanent part of your mental equipment. I've tried to make up for my share in that. I still owe you one. But at this point, I don't care what you believe. I'm tired of the whole thing."

He went back to the desk and picked up a piece of paper. "The telegram I got tonight came from your mother. She'll be here around eleven o'clock. Colonel Fortescue is picking her up at the airport."

That bit of news stunned me and halted, for a moment, the wave of unhappiness that was threatening to engulf me.

"Mother? Here? Why? Where's Renaldo? Why is she coming?"

"I have no idea where Renaldo is, although I suspect he's still in Rome. The reason your mother is here is to protect . . . to protect her child's interests."

"To protect my interests? What interests? What are you talking about?"

He got up and walked restlessly around the room again, coming, finally, to stand near me, looking down at me. The cold, angry look softened a little. "Not your interests, Skimp. Evelyn's. You see, she's Evelyn's mother, as well as yours."

9

I stared at Jonathan stupidly. "Evelyn—Evelyn is Mother's son?"

He nodded.

For a minute all I could think of was—of course. That's why his face kept reminding me of someone's. It was Mother's: that soft, curved mouth with its indented corners and short upper lip, the wide-apart eyes, the springy, curly blonde hair. And that was the explanation for Yolande's statement. Because I, too, resembled Mother. "Then he's my half brother," I said slowly.

Jonathan was pouring something out of a cut-glass decanter into two delicate glasses. "Here. Have this. Under all that red you look almost green."

Numbly I took the glass but held it in my hand. "Then you and Mother—?" Curiously, that was the part that hurt.

Jonathan looked at me quickly. "It was a brief time more than fifteen years ago, Skimp. I'm not proud of it."

My mind was moving slowly. "Mother was still living with Father."

"Yes. Hence the need to have someone adopt him."

"But wouldn't Father have known? He must have known she was pregnant?"

"Your mother was away a great deal of the time, more and more as the years went on. For the crucial period, she managed to be as far away from here and Father as possible."

I looked at him. "And you—"

"I said I'm not proud of it!"

"Father was a lot older than Mother, wasn't he?"

"Yes. And before you condemn her too much, he had had his little flings, too."

"*Father!* The Great Puritan?"

"They make the most flagrant sinners. Didn't you know that?"

There was another pause while I tried to put the pieces in some kind of order. But there was no order in my head, only a vast confusion. I knew there were a dozen questions jostling together at the back of my mind, but none of them surfaced enough for me to ask it.

"You'd better sit down," Jonathan said. He went back to his desk. He sat there, playing with his pen, looking down at the ledger, saying nothing.

Finally I asked, "Does Yolande know?"

"No, not yet. I'll have to tell her before your mother comes. She has a quick eye and the resemblance she pinned down between you and Evelyn she'll certainly see in your mother. That, by the way, is why I am telling you. You might have seen it, you might not. But I couldn't take the risk of having it blurted out in front of you without your being forewarned."

I sat in the armchair looking down at the glass in my hand. Mother, of course, had known who Evelyn was from the beginning. Then why was she coming now? After sending me here? What had happened between our last conversation before she left for Rome with Renaldo and her decision to come here?

"Why is Mother coming now?" I asked.

"That's what I'm not entirely sure of."

"But you said, To look after Evelyn's interests."

Jonathan toyed with the pen, picked it up, put it down and pushed it away. "If anything should happen to me, who would inherit Kilgaren?"

"Well I wouldn't, of course, not given the male chauvinism of the Kilgarens."

"To say nothing of the law of primogeniture."

"What's that?"

"The law that says the eldest son inherits."

"Yes," I said after a minute to digest that. "But that's always been true. I mean, Mother's always known that and she's always known about Evelyn's being her son—obviously. So—what's happened to make her all of a sudden come and look after his interests? That looks as if there's a possibility—at least she thinks there is a possibility—that something might happen to you." A little shiver went through me.

"Nobody's going to bump me off, Skimp."

"What makes you so sure they won't try?"

"I'm very hard to kill." He smiled a little. "I have a vested interest in keeping me alive."

"Well," I said, striving to match his tone, "since you put it that way. . . . But anyway," I added, as a thought struck me, "Evelyn's illegitimate."

"Not legally. He was born to her while she was legally Lady Kilgaren, living—legally—with her husband. Who's to say he was not her husband's son?"

"Well, then, why did she have him adopted by a foster mother? I should think that *anyone* would think there was something pretty fishy there."

"Yes. But suppose someone who knew the family very well—Colonel Fortescue, for instance—should swear that her husband had been maliciously misinformed about her and Evelyn, thus banishing him to a foster home. But that there were papers to prove that, just before he died, he had discovered Evelyn indeed to be his son and was making arrangements to have him brought here, when death intervened."

"Then why wouldn't that have been discovered by his executors or whatever they call them, when Father died and his papers were examined.

"Perhaps the wicked older son"—he jabbed his thumb in his chest—"I, who was one of the executors, had stolen those papers and hidden them away."

"But why should you?"

"Yes, why should I? That remains to be uncovered, doesn't it?" Jonathan looked across at me. "You don't seem to be unduly stricken by this sidelight on your revered mother."

I made a gesture. "You see, I was never really that much with her. And I don't think she ever really loved me. You said I was an albatross—"

"I shouldn't have said that."

"Why not? It's true. I was. She didn't make any secret of that. And besides, I didn't love her."

"Whom have you loved, ever?"

"Nemi," I said finally. "And a cat I had once named Floyd. And Sedgewick. And Nick, of course." And, I wanted to add, you, long before the fire. But my memory of that was all mixed up with resentment and anger.

"Not a long list," Jonathan said.

"Well, what about you? How many have you loved?"

"Like you, not many. But let's postpone the remembrance of things past."

"But you love Yolande?"

"How could I not? She's beautiful, intelligent, and rich."

And devious and sly and I don't trust her an inch, I thought. Jonathan was looking at me. A great ache filled me; I tried to pull my mind back to the problem.

"But why Colonel Fortescue? Why is he meeting her? I didn't know they were such friends. Why is she getting in touch with him?"

"They were old friends and the colonel was very devoted to Father, you know."

I thought it over. "That doesn't answer my question. She was always very snotty about him."

It seemed to me that Jonathan was picking his words carefully. "Well, they had their differences. And you know your mother is not one to co-exist with somebody who disagrees with her. But they were also friends and allies."

"Allies?"

He sighed. "Don't pin down my words so, Skimp."

"But something has happened between the time she went to Rome and now to make her come here, and Colonel Fortescue has something to do with it."

"Yes."

"And you're not telling me what it is."

"Skimp—"

"And even if she can get away with saying Evelyn is legitimate what difference does it make? He'd still be younger than you." I stood up. "Does that mean something is going to happen to you?"

"Now Skimp—"

Jonathan got up and came and put his hands on my shoulders. "I don't know the answers to any of these questions. Truly."

"But you know things I don't."

He hesitated. "About what?"

"I don't know. Maybe about what's going to happen, or why Mother is here. Jonathan, please tell me. And you can't say it doesn't have anything to do with me because it does."

Jonathan didn't say anything for a while. He seemed to be staring over my shoulder at the portrait of Lady Margaret over the chimney piece. I turned and looked also at that square, well-bred, and—strangely, in view of her strong socialistic views—arrogant face. "Why are you looking at her picture?"

"Because in her way she was just as manipulative and despotic about shaping events according to what she thought was right as her husband. More so. And what is happening now is because of what she did. She had a funny saying, 'relationships are everything.' I never realized how right she was."

"What do you mean?"

"You were right. There is an element in here you don't know." He dropped his hands and put them in his pocket. "I thought only one other person besides myself knew this. Now I don't know."

But he wouldn't tell me what that other element was. When I asked him he just shook his head.

"We'd better go back to the living room with the others," he said, putting our coffee cups back on the tray.

A curious thing then happened. He came over to where I was standing and looked down at me.

"Are you very unhappy, Skimp?" he asked gently.

I looked up at him. "Yes. No. Yes—I don't know." And I didn't. At that moment, standing there, I wasn't unhappy, which was strange, considering the presence of Yolande and what Jonathan had just revealed. But I said, "I wish she wouldn't call you Jonnie."

There was a silence.

"Why, Skimp," Jonathan said lightly, "are you jealous?" That odd, characteristic smile was on his face, one corner of his mouth lifted.

I heard myself say to my astonishment, "I'm sorry I ran away from you this morning, Jonnie."

"Are you? And what about that monogrammed handkerchief? Am I still the villain? Do you still suspect me?"

I shook my head. Here, with him, I couldn't suspect him of anything. Not only that, all my old resentments seemed to be vanishing. How illogical could one be, I wondered?

Jonathan was looking down at me. "Now what's going through that funny mind of yours?"

"I suddenly realized I'm not mad at you about anything, not even the fire, but I don't know when I stopped." I thought that over. "But I wish I had felt that way before you got engaged to Yolande."

"Why? What has one to do with the other?" He was watching me carefully.

There was an answer there, but I couldn't quite find it. And then I remembered his question and I knew he was right. I was jealous. It was a shattering and humiliating thought.

"Now what?"

His hands rested lightly on my shoulders again. Then one came up and touched my cheek. "Don't, Skimp! Don't look like that, whatever it is!"

I don't know what took hold of me then. But the

next thing I knew was that my head was against his shoulder and his arms went around me.

"Jonnie—" I said. I could feel his cheek against my head.

He said in a very strange voice, "Skimp—Everything will be all right. I promise you. Trust me."

"I do. I do. Oh Jonnie—I love you!"

I could feel his face turning against mine. Some warning in me cried out. But it was too late. And anyway, I was beyond heeding it.

His mouth found mine, or mine his. My arms went around his neck. For one blissful brief moment everything resolved and came together.

Then he pulled his mouth away. For another second his bleak, unhappy face stared into mine. Then he strode out of the room.

After Jonathan had stalked out of his study, Sedgewick and I went up to my room. I lay on the bed and tried to sort things out.

At the end of a period that could have been an hour or fifteen minutes, in which names and faces and pictures and feelings tumbled around and chased one another, I decided firmly that what had happened was the result of too much sun and too many events creating a kind of emotional indigestion. Incest is an ugly word. I pushed it and all it meant away from me and from Jonathan. What I was suffering from, I told myself, was the entirely commonplace jealousy of a younger sister when a beloved older brother marries or becomes engaged.

Beloved? That still, deep voice in my mind objected: *I thought you hated him!*

Of course I didn't really hate him, I said crushingly to the voice.

Then you were conducting a very good imitation of it, the voice said back to me.

My hands went up to my face in the old familiar gesture. But the old familiar scars were no longer there. Had they been a refuge? Had I hidden behind them? Was my face, as designed by nature, now out in the open—like everything else?

Along with what else? *You should be miserable,* I told myself. But I wasn't. I was filled with an odd, detached euphoria. *It won't last,* I told myself again, and drifted off to sleep.

I awoke later and lay there with the feeling that something was happening. And then I heard, remote and distant, voices. One of them I would know anywhere: Mother's.

I got up, washed my face and combed my hair.

Everything Jonathan had told me about Mother and himself and Evelyn came back. Pushed to the background by what had happened later, it had been forgotten.

I tried to discover whether I cared, and was not too surprised to discover I didn't. Certainly not much. If I cared about anything it was the thought of Evelyn's being my brother.

"Yuch!" I said to Sedgewick.

He thumped his tail.

We went downstairs. Mother, Colonel Fortescue, Jonathan, Yolande and Evelyn were standing in the hall. Jonathan glanced up. "Here's Barbara."

"Darling!" Mother said, staring up at me. A look of dismay crossed her face. "Couldn't you have acquired a tan more scientifically? You're lobster-colored! I have some cream—"

"So has Yolande," I said. It hadn't occurred to me before, but Mother and Yolande should be an interesting combination to observe.

"You and I will take her in hand," Yolande said matily. "We will make her beautiful."

But Mother's attention had strayed. Her eyes were on Evelyn. I saw now why Jonathan had felt compelled to tell me about the relationship. Evelyn was far more like Mother than I. They all stood there for a moment, staring at one another.

I heard myself say, "Have you eaten, Mother, or would you like for me to fix you something?" I had said it, I realized, to forestall Yolande's saying it. After all, and until the knot was tied—I hastened away from that thought—I was still hostess at Four Winds.

But Yolande was not easily second-guessed. The dark eyes regarded me calmly. Then she said, "Barbara, why do you not go to tell that man—Hamish (plainly her Spanish mouth did not find that barbarous Celtic name congenial)—that your mother is here and would like something, no doubt, to eat and drink?"

It was so ludicrous I grinned and caught Jonathan's

eye. The corners of his mouth quivered. He glanced at Mother. "Well, Sylvia, what about it?"

"What about what?" Mother said, her eyes still on Evelyn, as though, I found myself thinking, he were a piece of sugarcake.

Jonathan laughed. Yolande frowned. Colonel Fortescue picked up the bags again.

"Which room?" he asked, coming towards the stairs.

Jonathan's eyes brushed mine. I held my breath.

"Northeast wing," he said. "Large bedroom at end."

I relaxed. I didn't want Mother near me. As though he read my mind Jonathan went on, "The one opposite Yolande's."

Now for whose benefit was that, I wondered? How would the colonel know which bedroom Yolande occupied? But he came ploughing upstairs as though everything was laid out clearly in his head.

"Well, Barbara," he said. "I hear you've been having an adventure. You should stay out of the forest, though. It's not safe."

"Yes, I know. The whole thing was very silly of me."

"Oh, I don't know. Your brother can be frightening sometimes."

"Not to me," I said firmly.

He reached the head of the stairs. "Then why did you run away?"

"I told you," I said, walking with him down the long hall, "I was being silly."

"Tut! You should have grown beyond that by now."

It was a sign of something that I felt no resentment of this at all. "Yes. I should," I replied meekly.

He gave me a sharp look. "Well, take care of yourself, won't you?"

It was obvious he was warning me against Jonathan. But it wasn't obvious why. Strangely, my faith, so easily undermined before, was firm now. I opened the door into the huge bedroom that used to be Father's and switched on the light. "Why? What do you think could happen to me?"

He followed me in and put down the bags. "What an odd question, my dear Barbara. My constable, Richardson, tells me you were in a state of both exhaustion and fright and near sunstroke when he picked you up and that, along with your other misadventures, someone had taken a potshot at you. Surely it's hardly to be wondered at then if someone suggests that you take care of yourself."

I suddenly remembered the hut in the forest, with its faked look of decrepitude and its neat, modern lock. I also recalled that I had not mentioned the hut or the shot to anyone—except Jonathan. I said, taking his cue, "Did Richardson tell you where the shot came from?"

Colonel Fortescue was watching me carefully. "No. Did you tell him?"

I decided I wasn't going to mention the hut, not till I could talk to Jonathan. "No. I thought maybe he could have heard it."

There was a second's silence. The big fan, that went on automatically with the light although it also had a separate switch, whirred above. I remembered what the young constable had said, how cool the house had been compared to the roasting shacks most of the islanders lived in. How rich and all-powerful the Kilgarens must have seemed, I thought now. The silence stretched and became increasingly uncomfortable. It was as though, I thought, my skin beginning to prickle, the colonel was waiting for something. Or making his mind up about something. To break the stillness I said, "Do you think we're going to have a revolution here? Peasants advancing on the house? Executions galore? Heads on pikes?"

The stern, tight mouth smiled a little. "You have rather old-fashioned ideas about revolutions. If it comes, it won't be like that."

"If?"

"Perhaps I should have said 'when.' "

I had never really, until that moment, accepted the fact that there would be a revolt, an uprising. A hasty muddle of my oft-stated political views, Gilbert Palmer's surly face, Lady Margaret's in the portrait, all tumbled through my mind. It had never been quite real. It had all been a joke. Now it wasn't.

"When is 'when'?" I asked.

He started pacing slowly around the room. "Who knows? It could be tonight, it could be a week from tonight or a year." He had arrived at the enormous, imposing bed. It had been years since I had seen it, and I was more than a little surprised that Jonathan had allotted it to Mother.

The colonel, looking at the bed, the high ceilings, the heavy, now rather faded, hangings, the paneling, said, "This was your father's bedroom. He died in here."

And in here he had begotten Jonathan by Lady Margaret and me by Mother. I tried to imagine the face of the horsy-looking Englishwoman lying there on one of the pillows. It was not easy. One didn't think of that face in connection with bed and pillows. It was easier with Mother. After all, with her, there had been so many beds, so many lovers, so many husbands.

I came to realize Colonel Fortescue was watching me. He said, "I still think you should go home."

"Why?"

"Isn't it enough that someone should not only shoot at you but cut your dog's leash? I hear you're very fond of him."

Was it my imagination, or was there the faintest hint of threat in his voice?

I had the feeling I had had before, when I was with Jonathan. I could imagine the colonel embroiled up to his eye sockets in any intrigue going around. He was of the sort, not that created empires, but that kept them going, which meant that he was a manipulator of events. But, as with Jonathan, there was something else, an unknown quantity that was almost palpably present.

"What are you trying to tell me?" I asked abruptly.

"Just what I've been saying: that you should probably return to America."

"Did you tell Mother that? Have you said that to Yolande?"

"Your mother and Yolande, my dear, are grown women. You're not. Besides, Yolande's safety is very much your brother's concern."

"And mine isn't?"

It was then I became certain that the colonel knew all about Evelyn's relationship to Mother. I don't know how I knew, but I knew. Jonathan had, of course, hypothesized that the colonel might know, and that he might manipulate that knowledge for his own and Mother's and Evelyn's sakes. I remembered how chummy he and Evelyn looked at the club. But if that were the case, what did it mean for Jonathan? I tried to remember the exact words of his speculations: *Supposing there were papers to prove that before he died Father discovered that Evelyn was truly his son, but that the wicked older brother, I, had hidden them?*

Why then all that would be needed for Evelyn to inherit would be the disposal of Jonathan. I felt that shiver again.

"I'm staying," I said abruptly. "Nothing is going to drive me away. After all, this is my home. Jonathan is my brother."

I don't know what I expected to see on the colonel's face—anger, withdrawl, glacial reserve—any or all of those would have been entirely in keeping with everything I knew about him. After all, I had seen them before. But the look that flashed into the usually cold blue eyes was something else.

I turned on my heel and went out of the door, still thinking about it. I was halfway downstairs when it occurred to me that the word I was searching for was regret, even sadness. I was so surprised I stopped, one foot on one stair, one on the one below. But I barely had time to absorb the possibilities that discovery opened up before something else hit me like a bomb: How on earth did Colonel Fortescue know that someone had cut Sedgewick's leash? I hadn't told him, nor had I told Richardson. Besides myself and Jonathan, whom had I told, who could know? Only the person who did it . . . or who ordered it done . . . or, at the very least, had been informed by one of those and therefore, presumably, was in cahoots with them.

Interesting, to put it mildly.

10

*I*t was a very strange few weeks that followed.

The two women, Mother and Yolande, settled in and showed no sign of leaving.

I waited for Mother to say something to me about Evelyn, indicating, perhaps, a trace of concern about my reaction to discovering an illegitimate half brother sired by my own half brother. As Lady Margaret had said, Relationships are everything. Mother may not have agreed with Lady Margaret's dictum, but a gesture on Mother's part that this was a trifle unconventional for a supposedly gently reared daughter like me to swallow would have been, I thought, in order.

I should have known Mother better. Early on she had learned the virtue of the old adage, Never apologize, never explain. As the days passed with no explanation, I, in my turn, got stubborn. I would not bring up the subject.

"You'd think," I said to Jonathan one day when he

was driving Sedgewick and me to school, "that she'd say *something*."

"Such as?"

"Well, how's this?*Darling–In case you're thinking it's a trifle odd that your brother Jonathan and I. . . .* or, *By the way, it slipped my mind all these years, but. . . .*"

Jonathan gave a snort. "Have you lived with Sylvia all this time and not discovered that she explains nothing?"

Jonathan was his old brusque self. That moment of tenderness between us in the study seemed incredible. It was hard now to believe it had happened. For a minute I felt a sense of loss and almost put my hand out. But I remembered in time not to. There was no place in our lives for that gesture.

My second wonder was that Mother and Yolande seemed to deal so well together. Aside from Mother's role in Jonathan's past, they were the kind of women that, I would have sworn, were born to be natural enemies. But some sort of unspoken (so far as I knew) truce reigned. Yolande went around the house staring at walls and hangings and paintings and making copious notes. Books of colors, patterns and designs arrived with every mail. I found this depressing. The place was hideous and an anachronism, but in a strange way it had a kind of dignity, and it was filled with stuff, frequently ugly, that nevertheless had been chosen and loved or used by some Kilgaren. I dreaded waking up one day to find a battalion of decorators busy converting this lumbering old galleon of a dwelling into a luxury yacht. In the meantime Yolande would pass me with a vague look and a sweet smile, both of which I found phony. Whether Jonathan had spoken to her or not I don't know, but she didn't again launch on a campaign to improve me, nor did she patronize me. Insofar as she could, she ignored both Sedgewick and me. It all seemed very bland and harmless.

But after a while, I began to understand what Jonathan had meant when he told me not to underestimate her. I had never said a word to her about my qualms over her decorating plans. But at the dinner table, which was about the only time we were all together, she would discuss her plans in detail: this wall knocked down, that room divided, a door put here, a picture window there. "You'll hardly know the place, Sylvia"—she nearly always addressed my mother, more so than she did Jonathan—"when I get through."

Was I paranoic, or was most of that meant for me? I had no hard evidence that it was except an occasional swift sidelong look and a small, set smile that made me want to kick her.

And Mother would smile and say, "How nice," or something equally noncommittal.

Frequently, now, we were asked out. The white families were all vying with one another to entertain us: There were sherry parties, Sunday luncheons, buffet dinners, evening picnics. I couldn't help remembering what Gilbert Palmer had said: With the Arribe millions everybody's bacon would be saved. At the very least the revolution could be postponed; most optimistically, forever. This probably accounted for the slightly hysterical note that seemed to me to lie just below the general conviviality of all conversations. Something else I noted: At almost every function, some of the men would be missing altogether, or they would arrive late or leave early.

"Isn't Dr. Renfrew going to be with us tonight?" I heard Mrs. Formby, that evening's hostess, ask the dentist's wife.

"My dear—would you believe it? He had to be flown to Jamaica for somebody's abcessed tooth."

"Good heavens, aren't there any dentists in Jamaica?"

"Precisely my words. But apparently they're on vacation or leave. Such a bore!"

Jonathan, too, was missing for the first half of that affair. It was something, he said when he finally arrived, to do with one of the cutters' houses. I could tell from the pronounced arch of Yolande's nostrils that she was not pleased with his absence. "But how dutiful of you, *querido!*" she said, a slightly brittle note to her voice. "It could not, of course, wait until tomorrow morning."

"Afraid not," Jonathan drew her arm through his. "Such are the joys of a farmer's wife."

Mrs. Formby rushed in to forestall a lover's quarrel, envisioning, perhaps, the Arribe millions withdrawing to the yacht (still anchored off the island) and sailing away. "My dear, *all* the Kilgaren wives have had to put up with this. Lady Margaret—" She stopped, appalled at the *gaffe* that in her eagerness she had started to commit. One did not, in that circle, mention Lady Margaret, whose name, synonymous with every kind of reform, had become anathema.

"Yes?" One of Jonathan's brows was slightly up and there was a sardonic glint in his eye.

Poor Mrs. Formby, caught between her *gaffe* and the impropriety of criticizing Lady Margaret to her son, bustled off to find Jonathan a drink.

Sometimes Jonathan refused invitations altogether, pleading business that must be completed before the rainy season set in. If Yolande didn't like it, she made no further fuss. Whenever I could, I too stayed home, pleading a headache, early school, too much homework, anything. I've never been much of a party-goer, and it was at functions given by this small, ingrown group of people that I felt most alien. It was even a group within a group. There were whites, such as the Renfrews and the Masons (he was one of the teachers in the high school) and, of course, Gilbert Palmer, who were as much outside the inner circle as I. But if I was out, Evelyn and—most strangely—Mother were in.

Once I said to Jonathan, "Weren't people here shocked when you brought Evelyn here?"

"If they were they overcame it. Kilgarens have always been like petty kings—they can do no wrong."

"Do they know that Mother is Evelyn's mother?"

"Not officially. They may suspect. In fact, with the resemblance, they probably do."

"Then why do they accept her?"

"Because they don't have any choice. If this weren't an island, if it were attached to some other community—even a distant one—it might be different. But it's totally isolated and, right now, so scared stiff that everything else is minor. That's why they're falling over themselves to welcome Yolande. They think her wealth can build some kind of a holding wall, make them all safe [Wasn't that what Palmer had said?]. Hence all the social fuss. And they can hardly invite Yolande and me without inviting the other guests."

"Do they think you think the way they do?"

"Not really. But they take one look at Yolande and feel reassured."

For that matter, did I know how Jonathan thought?

One other question intrigued me. I posed it to Jonathan. "Did Yolande mind when you told her who Evelyn was, I mean that he was Mother's son?"

"Not overwhelmingly. Or if she did, she hid it very well. Spanish women are well-trained to turn a blind eye to male peccadilloes."

"How nice for you!"

"Yes, isn't it!"

I seethed quietly.

I don't know what passed between Mother and Evelyn. My determination not to query Mother extended to him. He most certainly would have snubbed me. Our coaching sessions dealt strictly with the business at hand.

In fact, if it were not for Jonathan, who insisted that I sit at the foot of the table as hostess, I sometimes would have caught myself thinking I was not there at all.

I couldn't get over the feeling that we were all waiting for—something. Sometimes I would look up from my plate and see all of us, as though caught in a tableau, listening for—what? The conversation revolved mostly around Mother, Yolande and Evelyn. I'm not adept at small talk and Jonathan has always been taciturn. So we would sit there, two silent poles, while the other three chatted away as though they were sipping drinks or dining in Cannes or St. Tropez or Puerto Vallarta. The marvel was Evelyn. Brought up in a middle-class English suburb, he bandied back the gossipy exchanges as though born to it—perhaps, I found myself thinking, they taught a course in it at school. More likely, he had chosen as friends those boys whose parents thus amused themselves. It appeared, not too long after Mother's arrival, that she and Yolande had met beside a casino table or a swimming pool or on somebody's yacht. So they kept the amusing, spicy, slightly spiteful, empty little phrases running easily as Hamish creaked in and out with the plates and Sedgewick scratched behind his ear just under the table at my feet.

Sedgewick stayed by grace of Jonathan's edict and only by that. I couldn't be entirely sure that Jonathan didn't do this as much to irritate Mother and Yolande as to please Sedgewick and me. In fact, except at odd moments, he appeared as oblivious of Yolande's presence as she was of mine.

Once I commented on it to him. "I thought you were supposed to be in love with her. The two of you certainly don't waste time in billing and cooing."

"I prefer to do my billing and cooing in private," he snapped.

"Well, no need to get in a state about it. It was just an idle observation."

"I don't suppose anyone of your generation would understand that," he said acidly.

"That's right. We like to let everything hang out."

"We don't."

Three nights later I could believe it. I was out walking Sedgewick before going to bed when I came across Jonathan, his arms around Yolande, kissing her with an intensity that shook me and made me turn around and go in the opposite direction, but not before they had heard me. I heard Yolande's laugh. Jonathan, his voice harsh, said, "What are you doing, Barbara. Following us? I told you, we prefer privacy."

The incident made one thing abundantly clear; Jonathan's brotherly embrace of me that night in the study was just that—brotherly, the tempered regard of a sibling, nothing else.

I decided the next morning that I would walk to the school. After all, the road was clearly marked. It was the coolest part of the day. There was no reason on earth why I shouldn't.

Getting up an hour and a half early, I made myself coffee in the big kitchen before Hamish was even stirring. Then, putting Sedgewick's leash and collar on, I started out. I was about a quarter of a mile from the school feeling, despite the hour, very hot and sticky, when I heard the jeep behind me.

It drew up beside me. "Get in," Jonathan said.

"It's only a short bit more," I said.

"Get in, Barbara."

So I got in, putting Sedgewick, who seemed, in my opinion, to be unnecessarily glad to see Jonathan, on my lap.

"Now," Jonathan said, "I'm not interested in your girlish feelings or wounded sensibilities. But don't try to make this walk alone again. Or you go back to New York."

Knowing perfectly well what he meant, I nevertheless said indignantly, "What do you mean by 'wounded sensibilities?' Why should I be wounded by—"

I stopped, horrified at what I said.

"By what?"

"Well, by everything," I ended weakly.

"You mean, don't you, by what you saw last night?"

"How ridiculous! Why should I be upset by that?"

"Yes. Why should you?"

We stared at one another. He started up the jeep. "Just don't go on any more solitary walks."

"Are you just being your old bossy self, or are you afraid something might happen to me?"

"You took a solitary walk and you know what happened to you—and to your wretched hound."

I ignored the rude reference to Sedgewick. "But that was when I went through the fields and into the forest. Besides, I was fooling around that hut that somebody is obviously using for something. But here, I'm sticking to the road and going to school the way I've been doing right from arriving here. Why should anyone want to do something to me for that?"

By this time we were at the school. Jonathan pulled the jeep up in the shade. "I told you once that there was a lot going on that you didn't know. You didn't believe me. But it would be better if you did."

"Instead of these threats, why don't you tell me what it is."

"Because—" he was looking down at me. Then he stopped and looked away, pulling some of the blistered paint off the metalwork around the dashboard. "I have a good reason. I'm afraid that will have to satisfy you for the moment."

"Well it doesn't. Not hardly. And since you seem to think I'm in danger I think the least you can do is tell me why."

He said indifferently, "Then you'll just have to trust me."

If he had said that in another way, or another tone of voice, he must have known that I would trust him any time anywhere with my life. But it was as though, asking me to trust him, he was doing what he could to make sure I wouldn't.

I got out of the jeep. "Sometimes, Jonathan, that's a little difficult." I stared into his somber face and then turned and, leading Sedgewick, went into the school.

The barrier that Mrs. Gutierrez had drawn between us had stayed. Except when discussing school affairs we rarely talked. Nevertheless, school remained the part of the day that I enjoyed most. It was, I had come to believe, the one area where things worked, where there was cooperation instead of hostility. I loved the children, their bubbling good spirits, their pranks, their demonstrativeness. I had grown up with rather cold people around me. Mother was not given to rules of thumb, but once, when I was a child, being, in her own words, tiresomely affectionate, she did say, "All this hugging and kissing, darling, except, of course, when you're in love, is somehow very middle class." Since Mother was always in love with someone, I early learned the difference. But these children were enthusiastically affectionate with everyone, including Sedgewick, who was a huge success. Bringing him to school had proved an inspiration to everyone and his popularity instigated a whole series of letter, word and even number games in his honor:

A D O G sleeps on a M A T, he goes for a W A L K, on a L E A S H (or L E A D, as the English-oriented islanders called it). . . .

Or, "How many letter Es in Sedgewick?"

Or, "If Sedgewick walked two miles and met three dogs . . . ?"

He was patted, stroked and spoiled. I soon found that to be allowed to hold him on his leash was considered a high honor, and I used it unashamedly in a reward system. He became a prominent and important member of the school.

But even in school there were incidents to remind me of who and where I was. Sarah Jenkins and her two cohorts had kept to the strict line of civility laid out by Mrs. Gutierrez, but there were times I knew that only the teacher's authority kept in check the insolence and open revolt now simmering near the surface. Luckily for me, I didn't have much to do with them. They were the oldest in the school and were taught by Mrs. Gutierrez, so I stayed as clear of them as possible. It wasn't, however, always possible. One incident happened at the end of a school day as I was going back to the office behind the schoolroom. At the exact moment I passed Sarah, she got up. The aisle was too narrow for us both. One of us would have to yield right of way. I stepped back. "Go ahead," I said.

Over her face flashed a brief, fierce triumph. Then the flat, expressionless look returned. Similar episodes followed, sometimes instigated by Sarah's brother, William, sometimes by Francis Appleton, most often by Sarah. Nearly always they involved trials of face where one of us would have to give way: passing in the aisle between the desks, a foot carelessly stuck out and withdrawn slowly, without apology. Once, my handbag, kept in the office, was open on the floor, all the contents scattered. It could, conceivably, have been an accident, except that I knew the catch was hard to open. That was the trouble: They all could have been accidents.

Then something happened that could not have been an accident and it involved Sedgewick. By this time, what with being the class pet with children vying to hold or stroke him, his street-acquired caution and cowardice had receded. Nor did I keep my eye as firmly on him as I once had. So my back was turned one day when I heard a scratchy noise followed by Sedgewick's frantic and drawn-out yelping. There was a funny smell. I whirled around and saw Sedgewick cowering against the back wall and a little girl throwing away a match. The funny smell was the burning hair at the end of Sedgewick's stumpy tail. He was still yelping. Somewhere at the back of my mind I registered that the child, Augusta Jenkins, was Sarah's younger sister and that this was wholly atypical of what I knew of her: She was one of Sedgewick's most ardent fans. But of course I didn't think. I acted, or started to. Of its own accord my hand swung. If it had connected with little Augusta I would have knocked her straight out of the school into the bush outside. Fortunately, it didn't. My wrist was caught and held from behind.

I swung around expecting to see Mrs. Gutierrez and was astonished to find the handsome young Constable Richardson behind me. His tours of duty brought him often to the school and he would always stop and watch for a while. This time I hadn't even seen him.

Augusta screamed. There were other cries and screams. The curtain dividing the rooms was ripped open by Mrs. Gutierrez and, turning, I saw, taller than the other children, Sarah Jenkins. This time the look of triumph was even more vivid. Then a scowl replaced it as she saw my wrist held in Constable Richardson's massive hand.

"Go back to licking boots, Uncle Tom," she said softly.

"This was your idea, wasn't it, Sarah?" he said, releasing me.

She didn't say anything. He glanced at Augusta, down whose face tears poured. She was frantically patting the cowering Sedgewick saying all the time, "Poor white dog, poor white dog!"

Later, when the children had gone home and Sedgewick, anointed with some butter from the little school refrigerator and some tannic jelly from the first-aid box, had calmed down, Mrs. Gutierrez said to me, her voice as even as always, "I'm sorry about your dog, but never, *never*, under any circumstances whatever strike one of these children. I don't care what that child does."

I was still angry. "Not even for cruelty?"

She stared at me. "You speak of cruelty. Did you know that flogging used to be the standard punishment meted out to blacks by the white foremen who worked for the Kilgarens? For that reason, I, a black, would not strike a child here. For you, a white, it would be—disastrous. Don't you know," she added exasperatedly, "that that was the reason for the whole thing? Augusta Jenkins isn't cruel. Didn't you see her cry as she patted your dog? She has cats and a rabbit of her own, to say nothing of sharing two family dogs. By this time everyone on the island knows how devoted you are to your pet. Don't you recognize the act of an *agent provocateur?*"

"*Augusta?* At seven years old?"

Mrs. Gutierrez gave a wintry smile. "Not Augusta. Sarah. And to give the devil her due, no sophisticated radical from a world capital could have thought up anything more effective. It was a brilliant piece of political theatre. Any disapproval felt for cruelty to your dog would be swamped by the fury that you—a white teacher and a Kilgaren to boot—should strike a black child, a cane cutter's child."

"But why? Why me? I'm not a—a reactionary."

"That's why. In a way, it's a compliment. You were getting too popular. William and Sarah Jenkins are committed revolutionaries, like Seth Williams. They are bending every effort to make white equal evil in the minds of the as-yet-uncommitted blacks, those who are more sympathetic to Gervase Williams' integrationist viewpoint. Then you come along and the children like you and go home and tell their parents what a good teacher you are and what fun it is to have your dog as part of the class. One good slap across a black child's face could undo that, especially if it were over your dog. That could be made to read that to a white a dog is more important than a black human being. That's why I said it was brilliant. A true guerrilla uses the weapons at hand. *Now* do you understand?"

I felt sick at heart. Finally I said, "Did Constable Richardson know that. I mean—did he think something like that was going to happen?"

"Probably. Why do you think he stops in here from time to time?"

"Then he's not one of the militants?" I remembered my conversation with him. "He says he believes in self-determination."

"As all those of us do who are not fanatics at one extreme or the other," she said severely.

Jonathan didn't say much when I told him about it.

"Do you think I should leave Sedgewick up at the house after all?" I asked him.

"I guess it's six of one and a half dozen of another." He thought for a minute. "But I'd take him to school. At least they won't try that tack again. And you can keep your eye more on him."

There were other happenings that afterward, when it was all over, I could see made a pattern, but at the time were isolated events.

There was my meeting with Gervase Williams, leader of the black moderates, head of the island school system and brother of Seth. He was standing by the jeep one day talking to Jonathan when I came out of the school to go home for lunch.

"This is my sister Barbara," Jonathan said as I

walked up to the jeep. "Barbara, this is Gervase Williams."

I looked up at the tall, thin black with steel-rimmed glasses. Like Mrs. Gutierrez, he inspired me with considerable awe. "How do you do," I said rather shyly.

He smiled. "I hear you're a good teacher."

"From whom?"

"From Mrs. Gutierrez."

I was absurdly pleased. Furthermore, I was surprised, surprised enough to blurt out, "I didn't think she liked me."

"She likes you very much. She said you were a born teacher."

"Then why—" I was uncomfortably aware that Mrs. Gutierrez herself might come up behind me at any moment.

He asked the question for me. "Why doesn't she show it?"

I nodded.

He put one foot up on the jeep's fender. He had, I noticed, immensely long, thin legs. Unlike Jonathan, who was in his usual work uniform, Gervase was in dark trousers, white shirt, and tie. His hair was grizzled, his face tired, kind, and tough. "For a variety of reasons she's bending over backwards not to show favoritism. After all, when she took you she got a lot of criticism. There were several young black teachers here and in Jamaica who wanted that job."

"Then why did she give it to me? Because Jonathan made her?"

I became aware of an odd little silence. Then both men smiled. "I doubt," Gervase Williams said, "if anyone could make Louise Gutierrez do anything she didn't want to do."

"Then why? She didn't even know me."

"She had her reasons. I'm sure she considered them good."

I accepted the rebuff; obviously he didn't wish to discuss the matter further. "Did you hear about what happened with Augusta Jenkins?"

"Yes. I'm sorry about it. Has it affected the way you feel about the school and teaching there?"

I was about to give an automatic "no," when it occurred to me that it *had* affected the way I felt. It was hard to be on guard and spontaneous at the same time. "Yes," I said, and told him why.

"Do you want to stop?"

Equally clear was my answer to that. "No. I don't."

He smiled. "All right."

Jonathan and I drove back to the house shortly after that. There was something, an impression about that scene that was just beyond my conscious reach. It worried me until I finally stopped trying to run it to earth. If I leave it alone it will come back to me, I thought to myself. I was right, it did. But much later, when, in fact, it was almost too late.

There was the man in the crumpled gray suit.

He arrived one very hot afternoon before I was about to start Evelyn's afternoon coaching. I had just arisen from my siesta, where I had slept under the great ceiling fan, with the louvres shut, in defiance of the hundred plus heat outside. Even so, the heat had drained me, and a long, cool shower hadn't refreshed me that much. I was in the library, next to Jonathan's office, my favorite room in the house. A lot of the family portraits were there and, of course, several thousand books. To protect them the louvres were always kept pulled, and the room was (relatively speaking) cool. To my disgust Yolande was there, poking among the family papers that, bound and catalogued, occupied a set of shelves in one corner. It made me nervous to see her there. I wondered what she was digging up. She gave me her sweet smile and asked about Sedgewick, who had come in with me.

"Because," she said, "while at first I did not like him, I can see now why you do. He has a very winning personality."

Sedgewick, who has absolutely no discrimination, went over at the sound of her voice and put his front paws up on her lap. For a moment the smile froze. Yolande looked less than won by his winning personality.

I made a vow that before the wedding took place, Sedgewick and I would be off the island, or he'd shortly turn up on some islander's plate as *fricassée* of dog—a gift from the manor house. Besides, I reflected glumly, there would really be no place for me in any home run by Yolande.

It was after I got Sedgewick safely ensconced behind my chair that Hamish creaked in.

"Man to see you, Señorita," he said to Yolande.

"But who is it, Hamish?"

Hamish produced a grubby-looking card. "Esteban Garcia," he read, in an appalling accent.

Yolande's pretty mouth tightened. For a second the tycoon loomed like the reality behind the shadow of her pretty face.

She made a sound of annoyance and left the room. Mumbling to himself Hamish started out.

I got up. "Let me see that card, Hamish, please," I reached out.

He'd put it in his pocket, but he dove in again and got it.

The flowing copperplate legend read Esteban Garcia, then, in smaller letters down left, Perez, Ubiquo, Morales & Cie, with an address in Venezuela.

"Do you know who they are?" I asked Hamish.

"I dinna like him," he muttered, lapsing into the Doric and, while ignoring my question, answering the general tone of my inquiry.

I went out into the hall, but the door to the sitting room was closed. Risking being late for the coaching, I went into the smaller sitting room in the front of the house and waited. Sure enough, I heard the sitting room door open quietly and soft voices speak. I had a strong feeling that Yolande was trying to hustle her visitor out, but I was going to foil that. Boldly I marched into the hall and took a good look, ignoring Yolande's obvious displeasure. Mr. Garcia was a medium everything man: height, weight, hair and eye coloring. The only thing about him that made any kind of definite statement was his light gray suit. It looked stained and crumpled beyond belief, even in this climate. But if Yolande looked startled and irritated at my appearance, Mr. Garcia carried it off well, with a perfectly open, friendly smile.

"Who was he?" I asked her after she had shut the door behind him.

"An old friend of my father's. Just dropped in to wish me his best before the wedding.

"Why did his suit look as though he had slept in it?" Surely on old friend of Boss Arribe's would have managed to put on another suit, even if he had had to buy it, however expensive.

"It is the stupidest thing! He hired a car to come out here after he had landed in his private plane. But the car broke down, it was at night, he was in the middle of the cane fields, so he thought it was simply best to stay there until someone came by in the morning."

"I would have thought he would have had his suit pressed before calling. I've always heard that Spanish men are very fastidious."

"He would have, but he had to get back to his plane and didn't have the time."

A likely tale, I thought, and confided the whole thing to Jonathan that evening. What did I think—or hope—his reaction would be?

"Yes, I know," Jonathan said easily. "Yolande told me all about it. Who did you think it was, Skimp? The Black Hand?"

I felt rather stupid. Jonathan looked at me with amusement. "I hope he gives us a large wedding present," he said. "God knows he's rich enough."

"Doing what?"

"Drilling oil."

"Well if he's that rich he could have at least brought a change of suits."

"Now you sound like Yolande."

"Thanks a lot."

Slivers of ice entered Jonathan's voice. "You seem to forget she's about to be my wife."

"I'm not likely to."

There were two pluses that arose from our rather strained household. The first was that our food took, suddenly, a giant step towards improvement. Hamish had been many things to the Kilgaren family—butler, a sort of tropical gillie in the brief hunting season, general factotum and handyman. Only since Father died, with the family poor and the other servants defecting, had he become a cook, a role for which he had neither taste nor temperament.

He was constantly pleading for Jonathan to let him go out with a gun to shoot some fowl for the table, and Jonathan was constantly refusing. "Let's keep the birds alive," he said. Consequently, we ate, nine days out of ten, fish: boiled, without sauce, or fried in heavy fat. Accompanying this would be some watery, overcooked vegetable and gluey rice. Surrounded by a paradise of fruits and plants, Hamish had never overcome his deeply ingrained belief that such were undoubtedly heathen—and probably lethal. His idea of a perfect dessert, suitable for serving five nights out of seven, was rice pudding. The other two nights he served tapioca or semolina. I loathed all three.

"Couldn't we have some fresh fruit?" I asked indignantly one night after I arrived.

"You have my full permission to try to get Hamish to put it on the table," Jonathan said.

I shoved away the sticky rice pudding. "What's his prejudice against fruit?"

"As you may or may not remember, Father contracted amoebic dysentery about ten years before he died, and was never the same. Hamish blames that on the fruit."

"How blind can you be!"

"He's not all wrong. Father did get it from a papaya he ate one day when he was in the village. There was a vendor selling some from a tray. Father knew perfectly well he shouldn't have eaten it, not because the fruit was bad, but because it had been sliced open by the vendor's machete, which might well have been slaughtering a pig the day before. Anyway, within twenty-four hours he was very ill indeed. Twenty five years ago he would have died. Thanks to some new drugs he didn't. But Hamish never forgot. Hence the rice pudding."

"How can you eat it?"

"I'm not much of a gourmet."

It was true. He wasn't.

"It's not too different from the food we have at boarding school," Evelyn said approvingly. "If you're not going to eat your pudding, I will."

"I can believe it. Here."

Curiously, it was not Yolande who reorganized the cooking; I think she was probably restraining herself until after the wedding. It was Mother. At her first dinner she had looked at Hamish's offering and said, "You can't be serious!"

Jonathan said, "You have my permission to do what you like about the food within certain ground rules." He waited until Hamish left the dining room. Then he said, "You may not hurt Hamish's feelings in any way—and you can be sure that if you do I'll know about it. And you may not hire any other servant. Within those—er—guidelines you can do as you wish."

Mother eyed him thoughtfully, but said nothing.

The next night we had lightly sautéed fish with a delicious sauce, crisp snap beans, a little wild rice, and fruit. It was sumptuous.

"My congratulations!" Jonathan said, when Hamish had finally left the dining room with the last of the dishes. "How did you manage it?"

"With my own two fair hands, a skillet and some pans," Mother said grimly.

"I didn't know you were such a cook."

"How should you? With a kitchen staff of eight I never had to be. But rather than eat deep-fried sawdust and floating cabbage I'll bend my back to the stove."

"I wonder for how long?" Jonathan asked.

So did I.

But Mother surprised us both: She found Nemi, my old nurse. "She'll work for her board and room," Mother told Jonathan one day after lunch. "Of course that's slavery and peonage, but I don't suppose that bothers you."

"Does it bother you?" Jonathan asked.

Mother gave him a rather acid look.

"I mean," Jonathan said agreeably, "bother you enough not to take advantage of the situation?"

"Where did you find her?" I asked. "I thought she'd left for Jamaica. I tried to find her when I first arrived here."

"Apparently she's back."

"Sober?" Jonathan asked.

"I'll keep her sober enough to help me in the kitchen."

"All right. Where is she? I'll go down and get her."

I went with Jonathan when he drove down into the fields to a shack not far from the tree under which I had had my nap. As we neared the place, Jonathan steering the bucking jeep over ruts and gullies, the memory of my panic there filled me, even in that blazing sun, with a curious chill.

"What's the matter?" Jonathan asked abruptly. His radar was excellent.

"I was just remembering. . . ." My hand closed over Sedgewick's collar. He was sitting between us.

"You deserved what you got. Silly little wight," Jonathan said crossly.

We passed the tree and continued on. It was hot and still and the thick green of the forest was only a few yards off. Then a shack came into view and Jonathan pulled the jeep up near it.

"Stay here and don't get out. Understand?"

"What can—"

"Just do as I say for once, Barbara. Without argument."

"Yassah white boss capt'n," I muttered.

I waited perhaps five minutes, stroking Sedgewick's back. The wide brim of my straw hat shaded my face. Even so, my eyes squinted against the green of the forest shimmering in the heat. Nothing moved. There was no sound. Even the wind which blew over the island most of the time was still. Then, from deep within Sedgewick's throat, started a rumbling growl. Under my hand the hair on his spine grew prickly. I looked down in amazement. All the way down his back and across his neck the hair stood in a rigid streak. The chill I had felt before came back. It's hard to explain, because other than Sedgewick I saw nothing, heard nothing. Around me the cane didn't stir. The forest was a green wall. There was no movement, no sound. But at that moment I felt in mortal danger.

I tried to call out, but the muscles of my throat wouldn't work. Uttering a silent prayer I tried again.

"Jonathan," I finally got out through a dry mouth.

He appeared in the door of the shack. "What is it?"

"Sedgewick—" I started.

As swiftly as the sense of danger came, it went. One minute it was there, like Death standing behind me. The next minute it was gone. There was just the heat and the peace of a blazing still morning. Sedgewick, seeing Jonathan, forgot his alarm and wagged his stumpy tail. Jonathan, strolling over to the jeep, ran his hand down his back.

"What upset him? His fur is still spiky."

"I don't know."

Jonathan looked at me. "Your imagination has always worked overtime."

"And Sedgewick's?"

"Animals are sensitive. They can pick up panic."

"It wasn't my imagination."

"Then what was it?"

How could I explain? "It was just—"

At that moment Nemi came trundling out of her shack, carrying some things wrapped in a shawl and a cardboard suitcase.

"Nemi—" I cried joyously. Tumbling out of the jeep I ran toward her and hugged her. "I'm so glad to see you!"

"Me too, child. Me too." And her fat arms went around me.

Nemi is five feet square. She has Carib Indian blood showing in her narrow features, she's a creamy brown, and nobody knows how old she is. As usual, her eyes were a little red and she smelled of peppermint and rum. During my childhood she had been better to me than anyone else—except, in another way altogether, Jonathan—and I loved her devotedly. I looked at her carefully. Her black eyes shone with joy at seeing me, but she didn't really look well.

"Are you all right, Nemi? Have you been ill?"

"Yes, Skimp, I've been—poorly. But now, since Master Jonathan—"

Jonathan interrupted rudely. "Get in back, Skimp. I want Nemi to sit in front. It's easier riding. Hurry up!"

"Ever the gracious approach," I muttered. I had planned to sit in the back anyway.

"Lord, child. I don't mind sitting in the back. Just give me a hand."

"Jonathan is quite right. You're to sit in the front. I wasn't complaining about that, just about his bad manners."

She looked at him, and for a moment her face seemed almost to sag. Had he threatened her, frightened her? Jonathan was in so many ways still such an unknown quantity.

I climbed into the back with Sedgewick, and Jonathan heaved Nemi into the front.

"We all thought you were in Jamaica, Nemi," I said.

"Yes, Miss Skimp." (Suddenly she added a 'Miss.') "I haven't been well at all."

It was an odd reply.

"I hear your mother is here." She gave a sudden fat chuckle which almost made me homesick for my childhood. How she and I used to laugh together!

Nemi went on, "She want help in the kitchen. I can't see her cookin' every night for everybody. I surely can't."

Neither could I. And, obviously, neither could Mother. I wondered who had told her about Nemi's return, and what Nemi had been doing in Jamaica.

Later, from time to time, I'd try to find out. But beyond repeating that she had been "surely ill," a common island expression, I got nothing. Nemi was vague, elusive, and, when pushed beyond a certain point, claimed total loss of memory. She spent all her time in the kitchen slowly but beautifully preparing the food that Mother cooked. She also stayed slightly but consistently drunk. I thought, when she first arrived, that she and I would have great times talking together the way we used to in the nursery, when I was a child. But I was no longer a child, and she was no longer in the nursery, and that had made more of a difference than I had realized. I would often go out to the kitchen, and, if Nemi were alone, we would go over old times and I would hear her ripe chuckle break out as she shredded vegetables or prepared meat. But she would only talk about the days before the fire and would tell me nothing about herself since except that she had been "ill" and not able to do much work. By "ill" I read drunk. The kitchen was always now more or less redolent with the ripe smell of rum. But it didn't cut down on her efficiency or seem to incapacitate her. And except that she would become obviously and visibly distressed when I asked her questions that she didn't want to answer—"When did you leave the island, Nemi? Who did you work for in Jamaica? What exactly did you *do?*"—she seemed happy.

Mother was delighted. By this time she had also managed to finagle the services of Yolande's maid—no mean feat. So that by now she was more in the nature of a grand chef than a cook.

"Mother, do you really like to cook?" I asked her wonderingly.

"Yes, darling. Given the right conditions, I love it. Would I do it, let alone do it as well as this, if I didn't?"

"Then why don't I think of you doing it before? I don't even remember your doing it."

"Of course not. Either we've been houseguests or in a hotel or I've been busy with a love affair. It does occupy one's time, you know, conducting a successful love affair." She raised her eyes from her cookbook. "I do wish that you—Oh, never mind!"

"You wish I what?"

"Nothing. I promised Jonathan that I wouldn't appear to criticize you."

I brightened. "Oh? That was nice of him—to insist on that."

"However," Mother said, obviously not to be totally repressed, "I have given the matter a great deal of thought and I don't think you have the right temperament for successful love affairs."

"I'd never thought of it as a career."

"There's no need to be uppity. You know perfectly well what I mean. Nor do I think you'd make a really fine cook. The only profession that occurs to me for you, other than teaching, is to be a veterinarian."

"What's wrong with being a vet?"

"Nothing, I suppose. Terribly smelly, of course. And one so seldom meets them socially." She went back to her recipe. "I wonder, it says six eggs. Perhaps eight. . . ."

I reported this conversation to Jonathan in one of our increasingly rare conversations—somehow he just wasn't around much. He grinned, but didn't say anything. "Do you suppose Hamish minds, being superseded in the kitchen?"

"If he did I'd drive them all out, gourmet food or not. He's delighted. Of course, he thinks your mother's cuisine is the mark of the devil, an inducement to gluttony and sybaritic living. I notice, however, that he eats it."

"And what else does he do?"

"There's plenty for him, and six like him, to keep busy around the house."

It was true. I ran into Hamish now much more than I used to, fiddling around the empty rooms, rearranging slipcovers, dusting surfaces that hadn't seen a duster in years.

"What's all the cleaning for?" I asked Jonathan one evening as we were going upstairs to change before dinner. This was one night when the entire household was going to the club.

Jonathan gave me a strange look. "I should have thought the answer to that would leap to the mind. The wedding, of course."

My heart gave a queer, sick lurch. "The wedding—I thought. . . . When is it?"

"Soon. In about three weeks. Yolande and I have decided to give a party on Saturday to announce the date."

I suppose, until that moment, I hadn't really believed it would happen.

11

The next two days passed for me in a kind of numb fog. At some point I came out of it long enough to become aware that Mother was watching me.

"What's the matter with you, Barbara?" she said.

"Nothing."

I should have known she wouldn't accept that. Also that she had the habit of zeroing in. "Why should you care that Jonathan's marrying Yolande?"

"What makes you think I care?"

"You do." Her blue eyes, sharp and narrowed, were on me. "Don't worry. It's not going to turn out at all the way you think. Your interests will be taken care of."

The phrase rang familiar. Where had I heard it? Jonathan's words, weeks before, came back: *She's here to protect her child's interests.* But that child was Evelyn. I returned her look. "I thought you were here for Evelyn." It was the first time I had made any mention of him to her.

"His, too," she said. "But yours are more—immediate."

That wasn't what Jonathan had said. Without thinking, and forgetting caution, I started, "Jonathan—" and then stopped.

Mother said quickly, "Jonathan what?"

I tried to get out of it. "Jonathan said you—you were also concerned about—Evelyn's affairs."

"There's a lot about Jonathan you don't know," Mother said. "You've always had an idiotic tendency to adore him. In spite of every kind of ill treatment."

"What ill treatment?"

Mother's brows climbed. "I suppose, in view of your recent obsession, I should be glad that you had forgotten about your facial scars. It seems a shame to remind you that he was responsible for ruining your looks—or have you forgotten?"

I hadn't thought about my face for weeks. And the reason came through to me at that moment, unmistakable as a clap of thunder. Mother hadn't been there to remind me.

Old habits are powerful. I put my hands up to my face. I could almost see, with my mental eyes, the metamorphosis from Barbara the pretty back to Barbara the ugly. Then I remembered Jonathan, his hands on my shoulders, forcing me to look in the mirror and see—an unblemished face. I forced my hands down. "I won't let you do that to me. The scars are barely visible."

"Who told you that? Jonathan? I thought so. Not, of course, that your face isn't much better. But don't trust him, Barbara. Everything he does has a motive, and it's not to your interest."

"What possible motive are you talking about?"

Mother opened her bag, got out lipstick and mirror and started freshening up. "The oldest motive of all my dear: money. We're all sitting on a hoard."

"A hoard of what?"

But Yolande came in at that moment with lists and menus, and while she and Mother were talking, I got out.

Once I would have gone straight to Jonathan, if I could have found him. Now, a barrier had come down between us and, anyway, he was hardly ever at home these days. And when he was there was a walled-off air about him, a *noli me tangere* that kept everyone, and especially me, at arm's length. Even our rides to and from the school had been discontinued. Mrs. Gutierrez had declared a two weeks' vacation after the episode with Augusta.

"People forget," she said. "Especially children. When they return to the place where it happened they will remember, but not as sharply. The feeling will be shallower."

So now I saw Jonathan even less than usual.

It was during those mornings that, to get away from the pre-party and pre-wedding bustle, I re-explored the cluster of hills behind the house. But, as I climbed from one level to another, sitting, finally, beside the waterfall, I discovered something that bothered me very much: new paths that had not been there before. I felt my personal wilderness had been violated. I felt that even more when one day I came on a small hut, cunningly hidden behind some tall bushes and the lace work of a bamboo tree. Even then I probably wouldn't have seen it except that whoever had camouflaged it by painting it the exact green of the surrounding leaves and bushes had forgotten to paint the metal padlock. As I passed, a ray of the sun, slanting through a hole in the foliage, struck it.

"Here, Sedgewick, let's look."

It was small, rectangular, and windowless. But the roof, supported here and there by uprights, rose six inches above the walls, and down below, at ground level, there were flaps that could be pushed out to allow entry to some of the cooler air near the earth. It was a familiar form of island ventilation. Most often—certainly in the better bungalows—inside those flaps were nailed screens. Scorpions and snakes abounded on the island and without screens they would have easy access. Since on this shack the flaps were down tight, I couldn't tell whether they would have screens or not.

I rattled the door to see if it would open. But it was firmly closed.

Sometimes I climbed to the highest point and sat staring out to sea. From the peak I could scan the whole island and the ocean surrounding it. Barely visible on a good day were some of the other islands of the archipelago, some inhabited, some, like the nearest island, about five miles to the southwest, totally uninhabited. On a good day without haze I could see, dimly in the distance, Jamaica. I watched the fishing boats, the oil tankers and freighters all going about their business. Kilgaren Island was so positioned that almost all shipping in the Caribbean passed it in full view and I found it endlessly fascinating. I would sit there, following the course of the masts, the sails and the smokestacks, reciting to myself the verses written by someone else fascinated by ships and what they carried:

Quinquireme of Nineveh from distant Ophir
Rowing home to haven in sunny Palestine,
With a cargo of ivory,
And apes and peacocks,
Sandalwood, cedarwood, and sweet white wine.

and the second stanza which brought it even nearer:

Stately Spanish galleon coming from the Isthmus,
Dipping through the Tropics by the palm-green
  shores,
With a cargo of diamonds,
Emeralds, amethysts,
Topazes, and cinnamon, and gold moidores. . . .[*]

It was the kind of poem that was not in fashion but that I had always liked because it made me think of the island. Once I remember thinking, as I got up, preparatory to going down to the shaded cool of the waterfall, that there were more of those small, tug-like ships—commercial fishing boats most likely,

---

[*] *Cargoes*, by John Masefield

sporting a lot of complicated machinery—than usual. Personally, I preferred the rowboats and the sails. The march of technology had obviously come to the waters around Kilgaren.

There was another reason for my watching the ships, the sea, and the island beneath me, although I didn't articulate it even to myself. I was saying goodbye. Soon now I would leave. Because I knew I would not stay and watch Jonathan married to that sweet-and-sour man-eater, no matter how much he—and the island—needed the money. Whenever the thought of his marriage obtruded I pushed it away, as I pushed away Mother's deliberately (I was sure) disturbing hints.

If I could have drawn a sketch of myself at that moment it would have portrayed Barbara, girl ostrich, head in sand.

And then, the day of the party, with temporary servants running all over the house, Yolande said to me, "I want you to be a bridesmaid."

Since I was not going to be on the island for the wedding, I was certainly not going to be a bridesmaid. Playing for time while I thought of an acceptable excuse, I asked, "How come you're having it here instead of your own home? Shouldn't weddings always be from the bride's church?"

I realized then, looking at her, with her near-perfection of face and figure, why she escaped not only being a genuinely beautiful woman, but even, to me, a very real one. The real Yolande, driving and wilful, had been disciplined and schooled in the best

Spanish fashion to recede behind an acceptable madonna-face—surely the dullest of all female masks. If she had let go, let the true Yolande emerge from behind the front, she would have had a sort of animal magnificence—frightening, perhaps, but real. Now there was just the stultifying quality of fake sweetness.

"But there is extra *cachet* in having the ceremony on the island owned by the bridegroom, don't you think? *Vogue* and *Harper's Bazaar* think so. Their photographers are going to be here. It should be a grand occasion and a great—how do you say?—come-on for any resort plans Jonathan and I may have." (On my beach, on my hill, beside my waterfall.) "We will make it very chic, very expensive, very snob, very difficult to come to. Then everyone will want it." She looked so pleased.

I felt sick.

"Well?" Yolande said, watching me carefully. "Are you going to be my bridesmaid?"

"I can't." Then I blurted out, much sooner than I had intended, "I have to leave the island before then."

The carefully shaped eyebrows rose delicately. "Oh, why?"

Nothing vague would do. I had to have an iron-hard date. I opened my mouth. But before I could say anything, she said, "Nick will be here. From Rome. You remember Nick Caldwell, don't you, Barbara?"

The air went out of me. While mentally blasting

Mother for her chattering tongue, I gave Yolande full marks for shrewdness. What she didn't know was how much Nick had receded in my mind. Until now even I hadn't known it. I hadn't thought of him in weeks. I wasn't going to tell her that, but my deep dislike of being manipulated rose to my aid. "I'm sorry I will miss him, then. But I have to get back. I have a business appointment—for a job."

"You have a job. Here. I thought Jonathan hired you to teach the island children."

Her dismay was disconcerting. I couldn't believe she was sincere. Surely she wanted me out as much as I wanted to be out. "That will be over soon. I've accepted a job in the States."

"Oh? Where?"

"Appalachia." It was the first place I could think of.

"But I thought you were coming here to make enough money to go to Rome to see Nick. Now Nick is coming here. I invited him specially for you. As a surprise! You are not telling the truth. It is all because you do not like me."

I was really baffled now. Yolande disliked me as much as I did her. I could feel it. In a sense, war had been declared between us at first sight and I was sure we both knew it. Therefore I assumed that all this talk about being a bridesmaid was simply *pro forma*; she could hardly *not* ask me. But, astonishing as it might seem, her distress at my plan to return to the States was entirely authentic.

At that moment Jonathan walked in the house, his

shirt sticking to his back in the sodden heat. His curly hair was wet. His gray-green eyes looked pale in his dark face, burned by the sun. He must, I thought, have been involved in the digging and irrigating that was being carried out on the other end of the island just north of the village. At that moment it occurred to me that it was in this period, between crops, that even Father, who was hard-working, relaxed and played. This was usually the time (as I remembered it) that he visited the club, played cricket, shot, invited house guests from the States, Europe and other islands, and went to various parts of the Caribbean as a guest himself. There had always been a lot of social activity. Now, of course, there was a lack of servants and general unrest. Even so, Mother, Yolande, and Evelyn were frequently out, either at the club or at the houses of other members. Suddenly I thought: "Jonathan doesn't see those people any more. Whom does he see?"

While these thoughts chased each other through my mind, Yolande was telling Jonathan about my extraordinary refusal to be her bridesmaid and—worse—my intention not even to attend the wedding.

I had wanted to tell Jonathan this myself—not necessarily that I was gong to teach in Appalachia, which I had made up on the spur of the moment (though it was not a bad idea)—but that I wanted to leave the island. I had dreaded it. I had known he would be angry. I hadn't expected such a burst of rage. It was as though some long fuse had suddenly exploded. Not since I was a child had he talked to me like that. I stood there, numb, with his anger engulfing me, searing me, catching sentences here and there.

". . . aside from showing yourself to be spoiled, rude and self-centered, do you realize what an insult you're offering Yolande, who is shortly to be my wife and your sister? I offer Yolande my apologies for you, but that's not enough. You will also apologize. And besides all that, Barbara, I didn't go to all the trouble and expense to bring you here, have you trained by Mrs. Gutierrez, only to have you throw it up when plans don't go exactly according to your whim. I thought you were supposed to be some sort of an idealist. . . ."

His voice went on, his words biting and sarcastic. I remembered that voice from my childhood, from his younger, wilder days, when he drank and caroused and defied Father, and conducted blazing rows behind closed doors. Behind my pain and humilation and gathering anger something untouched by all this at the back of my mind was trying to tell me something. But I was in no condition to pay attention to it.

I knew in a minute I would cry, so I walked out of the room and went upstairs. Locking my door, I sat down on my bed, shaking out of sheer nervous reaction. I sat there, clamping my jaws together, trying to get hold of myself. Sedgewick scratched at the door and I got up to let him in. Animals know when you're upset. He curled up beside me on the bed, nuzzling me every now and then.

Perhaps it would have been better if I had let myself cry. I might then have become exhausted enough to take a fresh look at what had happened. If I had, I might have been able to discern the pattern that was shaping up behind it and stopped to listen to that small voice in the back of my mind. But, having always before been defeated in my battle with tears, I was determined not to lose this encounter. A psychologist might say I was silly: better to let it out. But not yielding was, for me, a growing up, a coping with reality that I had set myself. I had lost so many battles. I was determined not to lose this. Something very painful and very important was happening to me. And I had to let it happen.

After a while I unlocked the door, put Sedgewick's leash on him and went downstairs. It was siesta time. The servants had all gone to rest up. Moving as quietly as I could, I left the house and walked around to the garage. Jonathan's jeep was there, and so was the rather dowdy sedan in which we drove to parties. I knew where the keys were because I had seen Jonathan put them away. They hung on a hook at the side of the garage.

I had better explain here that, technically speaking, I couldn't drive. Nor had the New York State Department of Motor Vehicles issued me permission to do so. I had learned in an off-hand way from the brothers of friends I had stayed with. Even Nick had given me a lesson or two in exchange for his coaching. But as I had been sitting upstairs it occurred to me that, not driving, I had become virtually a prisoner of the house and the school. Unless Jonathan took me somewhere (other than a ramble through the hills behind the house), I didn't go. Distance itself was not so much the problem as the heat. Walking to, say, the village was an impossibility. I'd die of heat or sunstroke before I got there. Ergo, I went where Jonathan decreed I go. And that was all.

I backed the sedan out, trying to remember everything I had been taught. Fortunately, it was an American car with an automatic shift. This might be the scorn of all European car connoisseurs, but with me it was just fine.

"Fasten your seat belt," I told Sedgewick. A gigantic yawn split his mouth.

"Thanks for the confidence," I said.

It wasn't that I thought I was going to get away with a secret ride to the village, more precisely to the office of *The Challenge*. There was no such thing as a secret ride to the village. The cane cutters, slipping through the cane, treading in their soft boots down the narrow dirt paths that surrounded the cane and the forest, lived far more hidden lives than any of the white people who, by comparison, conducted their affairs on a stage. In the days when that stage was secure that might have been all right. But today that stage was rocking, and the total exposure was not only dangerous (sometimes) but even humiliating. Today might be a case in point. But I had to go.

After the first few nervous minutes, the drive went much better than I expected. I drove fairly slowly, keeping a sharp eye out, and rolled into the village at about two thirty in the afternoon. Something told me that Gilbert Palmer would not be taking a siesta.

The main street of the village was a curious cross between New England and the Caribbean. The houses were white frame, lending a New England look. But the palms, the outsized porches—even on the two office buildings—and the general atmosphere of languor was anything but New England. The village had always fought a losing war with the ambiance of *mañana*.

Parking a car was not something I felt I could cope with, so I was considerably relieved when it proved no problem. There was only one other car on the street. I eased up to the curb, took hold of Sedgewick's leash, and got out.

I was half right about Gilbert Palmer. He was in his office, paper in his typewriter. But, his head on his chest, he was asleep.

There was a bell on the counter near the door. I slammed it down and Gilbert jumped almost a foot in the air.

"Who is it?" he yelled. Then he saw me. "Oh, it's you! Do you have to make such a filthy racket?"

"I thought the cause of the people neither slumbered nor slept."

He stretched and got up. His hair looked even less combed than it had before, and his beard was shaggier. "The cause of the people was being thrashed out at a political rally last night, and I was up reporting it."

"Was it interesting?" I was wondering if it was

Seth and his revolutionaries when Gilbert's next words stopped me.

"Very. Especially since your esteemed brother, the Kilgaren of Kilgaren, graced it with his presence."

"Jonathan!"

"Yes. Jonathan. Surprise, surprise!"

I thought for a minute, stunned. "Was Seth Williams there?"

"He was. But he was the opposition. This was a meeting of what Seth dubbed, over and over again, *ad nauseam*, Uncle Toms, white lovers, etc., etc., that is, the black middle class that wants to take the island away from the Kilgarens and their moneyed friends and try and run it as an independent ounce-sized democracy. But they want Seth Williams as little as they want Jonathan Kilgaren. Their leader is the other Williams, Gervase. All very cosy and in the family."

I tried to imagine Jonathan at that meeting. Yet hadn't Hamish said he went to meetings? "Were they all blacks?"

"No. Your great and good friend the colonel was there, and Mr. Formby, one or two others. The rest were black. That is, they were ranging in shade from coal black to the light sun tan of your fellow teacher, Mrs. Gutierrez."

"What line was Jonathan taking?"

"He wasn't taking any. He was, I should say, casing the enemy lines. That's certainly what Colonel Fortescue was doing."

"And Mr. Formby?"

"The same. After all, their lives, their fortunes, and their sacred honor are tied up with the island, white or black."

I recognized the reference. "There's no need to be sarcastic."

"Why are you honoring me with this visit? I've almost called you half a dozen times."

"Then why didn't you?"

He stared moodily at me. "All I'd have to do is go up to your mansion, the royal palace, to pick you up once or twice, and how much trust would most of the people have for me then?"

"You mean your career is more important than I am?"

"You betcha!"

I grinned. I liked Gilbert Palmer.

"So," he said, "why are you here?"

"Gilbert, if I wanted to get off the island in a hurry, how would I do it?"

He scratched his beard. "There's a certain irony about you, a Kilgaren, asking me this, that I appreciate. You own every pier, every boat, every dock on this spitball of an island. Do you know what they used to do to runaway slaves at the beginning of the eighteenth century? When I say 'they,' I mean, by the way, the ruler of the island, the then Sir Jonathan."

"I don't want to hear. And do you think you could get your mind off politics one minute and answer my question?"

"Why do you want to know?"

Pointing out that it was none of his business wasn't going to get me anywhere. "Because I might want to leave in a hurry."

"Sit down," Gilbert said.

I leaned against one of the desks in his office. Outside the louvres, the street shimmered in the heat. A huge ceiling fan whirred. Even so, Gilbert got a limp-looking handkerchief out of his pocket and mopped his face and neck. Unlike Jonathan, his skin couldn't take the heat too well, and it looked splotched in places.

When he had put his handkerchief back in his pocket Gilbert pulled over a straight chair and sat astride it, backwards, his arms on the back. "Why might you want to leave in a hurry?"

"Is it important? I mean, do you have to know? It's a family affair."

"Any family affair, as you call it, if that family is named Kilgaren, belongs to the island and the people. Do you know what happened to the people when one of your noble ancestors developed a family problem with his wife? He went back to England for a year or two. His bailiff took to drink. Cholera broke out, and—"

"All right, Gilbert. Good heavens! You must have put in a four-year course studying the annals of the Kilgarens. I didn't know that much was down on paper. Where did you find it?"

He stared at me and then put back his head and roared with laughter. "You don't know the first thing about it, do you? There are no written records. They're all oral—songs, stories, legends, tales, sagas. All you have to do for a while is listen. Just listen. Take along a bottle of rum and a small drum for the child and listen. If they think you're remotely sympathetic—and they know I am—they'll talk and sing until you can't stop them. Every now and then I'd check on a story—look up a record here and there—and find it in the main entirely true. That's why I didn't call you or come to see you. If I had done that, my friends wouldn't have trusted me as much the next time. After all, I am white. That's a lot to overcome."

He continued to stare at me. "You don't know, do you, that there's a whole little nation here ready to declare itself. It's got its own language, its own culture, its own tales, its own history, its own myths. If the snobbish white bastards, your family in particular, had been willing to accept the black middle class, invite them to their homes, their precious club, then the whole revolution might never have happened. Because class is often stronger than race. But the stupid whites thought race more important than class. So they forced all the blacks into an unwilling solidarity. The middle-class blacks, especially the younger ones, finally joined the island black nation.

"But the whites don't have a nation. They have their little commerce, their small professional affairs, their boring, drunken evenings at the club. But they are basically English or American. They're not Islanders. Your brother knows that. He knows that far more than any other white on the island with the possible exception of his friend and ally, the colonel."

Before I even thought, I said, "Jonathan isn't friends and allies with Colonel Fortescue. I don't think he even likes him."

"He may not like him. But their interests are identical. And, Miss Kilgaren, for all your pretty face and sexy body, so could yours be with them. If I told you how to get off the island without anyone knowing, you might just go back and tell them. After all, I was fairly drunk that evening at the club when we danced. Anybody could see that I liked you. Sending you to vamp me and ask me leading questions is pretty obvious, isn't it?"

"*She's Olga Polovsky the beautiful spy. . . .* " I sang softly to myself. And then said, "Yes, so obvious, in fact, that Jonathan would never do it. But don't put yourself out." I got up, picked up Sedgewick's leash, and made for the door.

"Not so fast. Maybe I will help you."

I stopped and turned. "Why?"

"Maybe for a little kiss?"

"No."

"Too bad. All right. Explain this. People leave the island all the time. Half the cane cutters are in Cuba. Why do you have to come to me?"

"Because I'm not a cane cutter with an underground ready to hand. And I don't have any means of getting around, that's why. I stole Jonathan's car today to come here. Other than that he drives me everywhere."

"Ah so. So that's the way it is. Piece five hundred and eighty-two falls in place and the puzzle is complete."

"What piece, what puzzle? What are you talking about?"

Gilbert got up from his chair and walked around the office, his hands in his pockets. I watched him for a minute. "I asked you what you're talking about," I said.

He ignored me, continuing to walk round and round. Then he waved at me. "Sit down. I'll help you. But I've got to think."

I was baffled, irritated, and, in a curious way, frightened.

"Gilbert, please tell me what you're talking about. What puzzle? What do you mean?"

"Did you ever hear of a male-chauvinist-pig institution called the law of primogeniture?"

"Yes. Jonathan told me about it. It means that everything goes to the eldest son and females can't inherit."

"Precisely. Well, that governed the inheritance of this island. The Kilgarens could pass the island and the title only from father to eldest son. Legitimate son."

"So?"

Gilbert looked at me a minute. "I told you to sit down. I think you'd better."

My heart was beating like a hammer. I sat down. "Go *on!*"

"According to a story that is all over the island your father, on discovering that his first-born was not legitimate, petitioned the Crown to have the laws of title changed so that his daughter could inherit the island on condition that if she married, the family would retain the name. The title would be lost, of course, but the island would stay in the family. Are you with me?"

"Jonathan isn't legitimate?"

"No. Apparently the foxy Lady Margaret did a switch when her own child died."

My mind was scurrying around like a rabbit. Then his face rose up in my mind. "But he looks like Father. He has to be Father's son."

"I never said he wasn't. Oh yes! He's your father's son, all right. But not by Lady Margaret. By her maid."

After a numb minute I said, although I knew, "Who?"

"Mrs. Gutierrez. Which makes him something far worse than merely illegitimate. It makes him black."

I sat there in a daze while Gilbert talked. Not much of what he said came through. Finally he said, "It's no use talking to you now. You're simply not listening. However, there is something you have to be aware of. So listen to me! *LISTEN!*" When he was sure he had my attention he went on, "Kilgaren will do anything to keep you on this island. Do you understand?"

I remembered Jonathan's rage when he was told I wanted to leave. I nodded. "But why?"

"If the story is true—that your father tried to have you made heir—then the chances are the papers are here. If they are here they can be disposed of. That, of course, is not certain. You might have them in some bank vault in New York ready to produce at the right moment. But it's not as likely as it sounds. Possession is nine-tenths of the law. You could be sitting in New York till doomsday clutching the papers, but if the island were properly armed and protected, much good it would do you."

"But—I thought he was afraid of the revolution. Of the people here—Seth and the others, the moderates you were talking about."

"That also. Have you ever heard of mercenaries?"

"Of course."

"Well, your brother and his dear friend, the colonel, have a good-sized posse of them stashed away five miles south of the island on that hunk of so-called uninhabited rock. The arms are collected in shacks here and there. They—the mercenaries—could pour themselves into a few motor launches and be here, presto! Who could resist them?"

"Seth would."

"Which is why he must be put out of action."

I remembered what Jonathan had said about being able to take over the island any time he wanted. So that was the ace up his sleeve: mercenaries. "But why has he waited?"

"Well, a few years ago he wouldn't have. But there is now such a tiresome thing as world opinion. He doesn't need to have the British Navy descend on the island and then hand it over to the Islanders. To dispatch Seth would cause an outcry—unless it were done in what amounted to self defense—that is, to defend the so-called innocent people of the island from murder, rape and pillage."

"*Agents provocateurs*," I said, thinking of little Augusta. So two could play at that game!

"Exactly. So the timing has to be right."

"And when is the time?"

Gilbert looked at me for a minute. "That's what we're not sure of. But supposing he has, say, found the papers—then a wedding, a Kilgaren wedding, when the whole island is given a holiday, would be a good time, don't you think? Especially since once the knot is tied he can afford anything."

I returned his look. "You say 'we.' You're not an Islander. And you're white. As you yourself pointed out, a grave disadvantage. What's in it for you?"

"I like to see justice done."

"And stir up a little mischief?"

His eyes sparkled and he laughed. "Perhaps. Let's say I'm always happy to light fires under the Establishment, any time, anywhere. It's a sort of hobby."

My head was in a muddle. I couldn't put what he was saying with what he had told me about Jonathan's birth and make any sense of them. "Where does the whole birth and inheritance business come in?"

Gilbert slouched over to the window and looked through the slanted louvres.

"That johnnie is still over there in his parked car. I've been wondering this half hour if he's here to watch you or me."

"But he was there when I came in. How could he have been sent to watch me. Who knew where I was coming?"

"You have a point. On the other hand, where would you go? How many possible co-conspirators could you drum up on the island?"

"But I still don't understand. If what you say is true, and possession is nine tenths of the law, why is it essential for me to be here. Jonathan could just take it and keep it."

"Unless, as I say, you wanted to raise a great hue and cry against the fascist goings-on on the island that rightfully belongs to you. The European nations and the United States are not at all keen these days to have a neighbor or possession give Democracy a bad name. Outside the island you might not be able to take it over, but you could cause a lot of trouble. Sanctions, for example. Just like Rhodesia. Where would the island be if no one bought its sugar and no happy tourists would come here after all those resorts and rich playgrounds had been built?"

I hadn't thought of that. I sat there, while Gilbert

continued to look out the window. Finally I said, in a useless flare-up of old loyalty, "I don't believe Jonathan would do that."

"Now that's what I call heart-warming. Such sisterly loyalty. You little fool! Why do you think, after all this time, he should suddenly write and offer you a job here, out of the blue, a job that almost anyone would be more qualified to fill? He could force his mother to take you, and he could count on your falling for the idea of teaching the children of cane cutters. Such idealism! It was tailor made!"

"*She had her reasons. I'm sure she considered them good.*" Wasn't that what Gervase Williams said of Mrs. Guitierrez, when she took me before other applicants, and in the face of criticism?

It was at that moment that my belief in Jonathan crumbled. My initial astonishment that he should send for me and offer me the job, and my suspicions of his motives, had proved well founded and justified. I said numbly, "What on earth should I do?"

"Right at the moment I suggest you get out of here fast. Your brother hasn't showed up yet, but something tells me it won't be long before he does." Gilbert turned back. "I'm going to help you get off the island."

"What part does that play in your conquest of the world for the working classes?"

"None at all." He paused. "I don't seem to have made myself very clear. The only reason you're still alive is that your brother has not been able to locate those papers. He would like to get rid of them before he gets rid of you. If he reversed the process and they turned up after you had—er—departed, it might make things look awkward."

He was watching my face which, at that moment, told him he had hit the target. I remembered Jonathan's casual question about any papers I might have to put in the safe. Suddenly, that unexpected tenderness he showed that night in his study came back, and it was as though he was standing there. I felt torn in half, and I couldn't take any more.

"I have to go."

"There's going to be a party at your place tonight, isn't there?"

I nodded. I had forgotten about the party. At the moment the whole thing seemed hilariously incongruous.

"Needless to say, I haven't been invited, but I'll struggle into my black tie and go up there."

Wearily I got up. "It seems unlike you to have one."

"A black tie? Not a bit of it. A uniform for every occasion! Remember, you've invited me. Some time in the evening we'll go out for a stroll and a snuggle. If you want that flea-bitten hound to go too, you'd better have him handy. I'll take you down to a beach I know where there'll be a launch waiting. It will take you to Jamaica. After that you're on your own. Now go."

I half expected to see Jonathan's jeep looming up behind or ahead of me all the way back, but I encountered no one. It was lucky that I was such an amateur driver. My need to concentrate on what I was doing held at bay the thoughts and pictures that were crowding into my mind. The heat was stifling, only slightly better as we started to climb than when we drove alongside the fields. But the roof of Four Winds came into view too soon. I knew I could not go up there and face Mother, Yolande (Did they know what Jonathan planned? Were they part of it?), possibly even Jonathan. Not yet. Driving the car along a small dirt road that ran the width of the island just below the house, I started to climb the rocky road leading up behind to the hills. It was less a road than a path, and the jeep could have navigated it far better. I took the car as far as I could, then I got out.

I don't know what I meant to do; sit somewhere, I suppose, and try to sort out what had happened and who Jonathan was turning out to be and who I was. But, almost automatically, I kept on walking, Sedgewick's leash around my wrist. We walked for a long time. Up there the air was cooler, the shade so thick that the sun barely penetrated in small diamond flashes here and there. Without consciously planning it, my feet turned towards the waterfall, and after a long climb I pushed my way through some bushes and looked at the cascades of water dropping fifty feet into a pool. If I went any further up I'd leave the shade. I sat down on the moss and rock that edged the waterfall.

Sedgewick was pulling at the leash and acting generally in a very antsy way.

"All right," I said. It seemed a shame to keep him always tied up, particularly up here where I was quite sure we were alone. I let the leash go. He stood and shook himself, then went sniffing around the rocks, weeds, and trees, trailing the leash behind.

And then, because I couldn't not face it any more, I confronted what I had learned about Jonathan. I knew now that the reason I had once thought I hated him so much was because I had loved him so much. And had come to think he loved me.

I also realized something that seemed inconceivable when brought out in plain day. I was in love with him: my brother. The fact that he was not Lady Margaret's son was a relief more than anything else. The fact that he had a black strain was, on the whole, an advantage. That's where the future of the island lay.

But he had not loved me. He had kept me here to take any claim I might have on the island, and, if I did not escape, would most likely kill me.

Incest and murder: What a charming pair we were!

I put my head down on my knees, listening to the water pounding below. People were right, I thought hazily, to seek out the water when they needed solace. It had a rhythm, a beat just below the constant roar that was soothing, whether it was a waterfall or the tide coming in.

And that was the last thought I remember having.

12

I came to slowly, aware of two overwhelming facts: I had an appalling headache, so bad it was making me sick, and I was surrounded by total blackness. Panic hit me and I sat up and then immediately lay down again, fighting nausea.

I lay there for a while and then gingerly put a hand behind my head and felt a lump. Pain shot through me. Movement was agonizing and I passed out again.

The next time I woke up I felt slightly better, although I was still in total blackness. This time I was able to ascertain that I was lying on some kind of camp bed, and that the air was stiflingly hot.

My next thought was of Sedgewick, and I groaned. Poor pup! Somebody had coshed me on the head and put me here and heaven knows what they had done with him: Probably killed him and thrown his body down the waterfall or buried it under one of the huge trees. . . .

Waterfall. Until that moment I had forgotten that

that was where I had been. I lay still, trying to put my thoughts in some kind of scquence. What emerged finally was 1) Either somebody had been following me (most likely) or 2) I disturbed somebody who was doing something he didn't want known or somebody whose presence would, of itself, have been an alarm signal. Probably, in that case, he had taken care of Sedgewick before me, otherwise Sedgewick most certainly would have barked. But who and why were anybody's guess.

Gingerly, I sat up again. This time my stomach didn't rise with me. Getting off the bed, walking slowly, with my hands out, I finally made it to a wall and rested there for a second.

Unnumbered minutcs later after some trial and error I had made several discoveries. For one thing, the total blackness had, as my eyes got used to it, thinned. There were gray spots both near the ceiling and the floor that told me where I was: the green shack. But even though the flaps had been propped open a little to allow some air in, they were slanted down over the openings so that what little light showed could only be seen by contrast with the Stygian dark of the inside. Another discovery was that this shack had been used to store guns. I had seen the gun racks at Winds too often not to know what they were as I touched them. But the racks were empty. The floor was made of planks. Other than the racks and the bed, the only other article in the room was a chest, on which I cracked my shin. Feeling along the lid I found the hasp and staple and open padlock.

Sliding the lock away from the staple, I opened the chest. An oily smell greeted me, but the chest was empty.

After that I made my way back to the bed. Now that I had no further activity to distract me, I started to fight rising waves of panic. The temptation to run to the door and beat on it and yell was almost more than I could resist, but something, I don't know what, kept me from doing it. I don't know how long I could have withheld, but as I sat there I heard a sound. It came from outside the shack, then the noise of a key in the lock. Quickly I lay back on the bed in the position, as nearly as I could remember, in which I had been laid there, or at least in which I had waked, my face towards the door.

The door opened and there was a stream of light. Not to run into that light out of the horrible dark was a greater temptation than anything else. But I forced myself to lie still. A man—I knew it was a man from his stride and the way he placed his feet—came over to the bed and stood over me. I felt his hand on my wrist and barely prevented myself from snatching it away. Then there was another sound, and someone else came in the room.

"She seems all right." It was Colonel Fortescue. I realized when I heard his voice I had expected it to be Jonathan. While I was still reacting to this I got a real shock.

"You had no right to hit her on the head like that. You might have killed her." That was Mother. Just barely did I stop my eyelids from flying open.

"Don't be silly, my dear. I know enough to stun without hurting. Give me a little credit."

"There must have been some other way. You could have tried to think of some explanation."

"If you can tell me how I could have prevented her from going to Winds without telling her a lot more than is healthy for her to know, then you might have informed me sooner. It was your idea to get her away, just as it was your idea to bring her here to the island in the first place." (But hadn't Gilbert said it was Jonathan's?)

The colonel was ploughing on in his precise voice. It was odd that even in the midst of my growing terror I couldn't help registering the fact that while discussing disposing of me his voice was as meticulous and unemotional as though he was outlining the pros and cons of interoffice memos in triplicate. "You know perfectly well," he said, "that if she knew what was going to happen tonight she'd go and spill it all to Kilgaren. That's become abundantly clear in the past few weeks. That, by the way, was your miscalculation. You were so sure of her dislike of him! You must have been careless enough to let her know, somehow, that he had paid for her surgery."

"No, Frank, I didn't," Mother said wearily.

My heart gave an extra beat. *Jonnie*, I silently apologized, *how could I have believed that fairy story about money suddenly materializing from an estate long settled?*

". . . Well," the colonel was saying, "if she'd sat in that clearing by the fall much longer she couldn't help but know what was happening. I couldn't keep all those men silent for any length of time. Sooner or later they'd have to move."

Men? *Mercenaries?* I wondered.

"Well what are we going to do now? She's bound to wake up soon."

"That launch should be here shortly. As soon as I get the signal it's on its way we'll take her down to the beach."

"But will there be time? The party starts at seven. We *have* to be there. That was the whole point in having the party. If we're not there when the house is fired suspicion will fall on us—you especially, and the whole thing will fail—as it did before."

"That was hardly my fault. It was you who were supposed to drug Kilgaren's drink. You bungled it."

"Thank God it did fail! I didn't know Barbara was locked in the nursery. She nearly died in that fire, a little detail you've forgotten. As it was she was scarred."

"This time it won't fail. The men will see to that. Then I can announce martial law and take control of the island. I'll have every excuse. What else could I do?"

"And Jonathan?"

"He won't be around. At all. There isn't room for both of us. The men will take care of him. No, Evelyn will inherit. We can fix that. And he'll do what we say."

"What if Barbara wakes up on the way down to the beach or in the launch. She'll be terrified."

"I've already thought of that. I have an injection that should keep her out for at least eight hours."

"What kind of injection?" For the first time I heard real alarm in Mother's voice, which frightened me considerably.

He named a chemical I'd never heard of before. Evidently Mother had. "That's powerful. Are you sure you know what you're doing, Frank? Have you ever given it? You're not a doctor. You mustn't hurt her—seriously hurt her, I mean."

"My dear—this panic won't do! Now do you or do you not want to go on with this? You realize, don't you, that any second now she could come around, see us, or guess what we had done, tell Kilgaren, and then the whole game would be up."

And then Mother said, to me at the moment, a strange thing. "If only she had pursued on the way she was going, when she came onto the island, I mean."

"Yes but she didn't. Obviously Kilgaren managed to reactivate her old affection for him. Now you have to make up your mind once and for all. If you want the money, then we have to go on. And the decision, the final decision, must be made now. If you want to stop everything, we can pretend, when she wakes up, that we just found her. It would be difficult to prove otherwise, however suspicious she or Kilgaren might be. But you told me that without money Renaldo would leave you. How much do you want to hold him?"

I think it was then I believed everything that was

going on. I knew from personal experience how much Mother wanted Renaldo, and how much Renaldo wanted money. With that choice before her, Mother would give in, however much it might hurt somebody else.

Mother said, "Be careful, Frank. Don't give her any more than you have to."

I tensed my muscles, ready to sit up. Better to make a fight for it on my feet, even though revealing that I had been conscious would make a serious threat to the colonel. Mother, perhaps, I could maneuver or shame into helping me. Just as I was about to give the game away, though, Colonel Fortescue said, "Well, give me my bag."

"I left it in the car."

"I told you to bring it."

"I forgot."

"Of all the stupid—stay here and keep an eye on her."

"I'm coming down to see what you put in that syringe. I don't trust you, Frank."

Neither did I.

"Please yourself," he said. I don't know why, but that sent a shiver down my spine. In some way it confirmed the unpalatable fact that if he were going to put a lethal dose in that needle, then he would do it whether Mother was there or not. Since I didn't know what the stakes were, or what "money" they were talking about, I couldn't guess what he would do. And I didn't think that money, of itself, was what he was after.

He came back over to the bed, and felt my pulse again. Then he leaned over my face. It was hard not to recoil.

"Barbara," he said softly. "Barbara?"

Astonishingly, it was also hard not to respond.

"You've killed her!" Mother's voice was rising, as I had heard it so often before when she was excited or angry or not getting what she wanted.

"Of course I haven't killed her. If you don't believe me, come over here and feel her pulse. It's a little fast, but perfectly healthy. Now stay here while I go down and get the injection."

My heart sank.

"I said I'm coming with you."

With sickening relief I heard their steps going towards the door. I had one chance: that he leave the door open. I heard his steps arrive at the door and step down.

"Shut the door after you," he said.

Perhaps it was the tone of voice Mother didn't like. Perhaps, and I like to think this, she was giving me a chance. Whatever the reason, Mother disobeyed him. She left the door open.

As soon as their voices retreated I was at the door myself. I stood there, listening, trying to decide where they were. As I hesitated, two sounds came to me. One was the soft plunge of the waterfall where I intended to go. I had never told anyone about my hideaway behind the curtain of water. It would conceal me until I was safe. But the second sound held me where I was: Much nearer to me, in fact, somewhere not far from my feet, was a faint whimpering—Sedgewick.

"Sedgewick!" I whispered. "Where are you?"

He heard my voice. From the muffled, agonized cries I knew his muzzle had been tied. Poor Sedge! What a life! He would have been safer on the New York streets after all.

"Sedgewick!"

The sound came from under the shack somewhere. But I couldn't investigate. The voices of the colonel and Mother were sounding close again. It was too late now to run. And what would happen to Sedgewick? Would the colonel kill him in spite for my escape? I could easily imagine it. There was only one other thing to do and I went back and did it. I got into the chest. If he and Mother went looking for me I might have time to get Sedgewick loose and we could both get away. With any luck Sedgewick would run back to Winds.

The oily smell inside the chest was suffocating. It was only after I was down, lying on my back, that two things struck me: One was that I could suffocate, the other was that the colonel might take it into his head to secure the padlock. I lay sick with fear, praying silently.

There were footsteps, then, "My God! She *was* awake. She's gone!"

There was a sort of sob. Then Mother said, "Thank Heaven!"

Luckily for me, the chest was not made of solid

wood but of planks that in the heat and damp had warped. A little air filtered through the cracks. I lay there as the battle raged.

"I wonder if you'll be glad when you're standing in the dock listening to your daughter condemn you."

"I don't care. Not any more."

"It's a pity your maternal feelings didn't manifest themselves sooner. We'd never have got into this. Well you can kiss your Italian lover goodbye—that is, if you can get near enough to him. I shouldn't think he'd waste much time with a *poor* middle-aged woman."

As I said before, I'm not very fond of Mother. But at that moment I hoped I could one day, if I survived, push the colonel an extra foot toward the gallows on her behalf.

"You would have killed her, I know," Mother said. "I knew it when you went to get that hypodermic."

"Why should I kiss goodbye such a potential gold mine as Barbara?"

"Potential gold mine?"

"Yes. I could ransom her. I think Kilgaren would pay quite a lot to get her back." (My heart gave a queer jump. Would he? Then I remembered what Gilbert told me: Jonathan wanted me under his eye, but not for love. Just because the colonel meant to dispatch him did not make Jonathan innocent; thieves could fall out. In fact, they usually did.) The colonel was saying, "And it looks as if he's going to have a lot with which to pay."

"I couldn't risk it, Frank. You've gone too far,

committed yourself too deeply. If you felt threatened or cornered, you'd kill her, I know. And besides being her mother there's another reason I couldn't let you do it."

"And what is that?"

Mother told him.

"Yes," the colonel said. "I know."

He didn't look in the chest and he didn't padlock it. It was too much to hope that he wouldn't padlock the door, and of course he did.

After the door slammed and I heard the lock turn I counted slowly to three hundred. Then I opened the lid of the chest and got out. It did worlds for my morale. Somehow being alive and out of the chest made being locked up in a small shack less final. I walked around thinking, going over in my head everything I had observed about the hut.

There was still a dim light where the flaps both above and below had been left propped ajar. I put my hands next to the floor and felt the slight current of air. The vent was about a foot long and six inches high, and screening had been roughly nailed in front of it, undoubtedly to keep out snakes and scorpions.

Getting up, I pushed the chest to under the open flap below the roof and then stood on it. Up there there was no screening. But the edge of the roof came down, forming what amounted to an awning, but an inflexible awning that could not be moved. There was no way I could get out there, but while I was standing up there I could hear again the feeble whimperings that meant that Sedgewick was near and tied up. And there was something in those cries that made me afraid he wouldn't last much longer. My heart contracted. I tried to locate just where those sounds came from and decided they came from *below* the hut.

I didn't dare call out too loudly, but I whispered, "Sedgewick! Sedgewick!"

The cries stopped, then crescendoed. "It's all right, I'm coming," I said, hoping faith would supply the means, and that the sound of my voice would boost his morale.

I got down and crouched with my ear to the floor near the wall. It was a hot, dirty, splintery task but eventually I found a place where I could hear Sedgewick's cries quite clearly. It was near one of the flaps of the back wall. It must have been closed because I could feel no air. I ran my fingers around the edge of the screening and then felt the plank covering the floor move. It was a little loose. Following the plank back with my hands, I found it was about two feet long, at which point it joined another. As the weakest point, that should be the place I should work on.

I lost track of time, so I have no idea how much later it was that I was able to pull the board up away from the dirt floor. Keeping my mind off the likelihood of spiders and socrpions, I lifted the plank out. Underneath the plank was wire netting and underneath the netting was a hole from which muffled and weary whimpering was now coming.

There couldn't have been much air in that hole. Sedgewick must have been nearly played out. But the influx of (relatively) fresh air and perhaps smelling me revived him. His whimperings strengthened.

"Just hang on, Sedge," I told both of us. Obviously the netting was spread over all the dirt floor because trying to pull it did nothing but cut my fingers. There was nothing for it but to work loose other planks. As I tore and pulled and heaved my hands grew sticky from what I knew was my own blood from myriad cuts. My nails broke and tore. But pushing me with increasing urgency was the need to warn Jonathan. I had no idea what time it was. But I had to get to him before seven. No matter what he'd done, what he'd plotted, how he had used me, I had to get to him in time. The clarity of that was so overwhelming I didn't even stop to wonder at it, or at myself.

Eventually I pulled the wire clear. It had not been nailed to the walls anywhere, so once I came to the end of one section it slid out fairly easily. Sedgewick jumped up, and after I removed the twine from around his mouth we had an extremely emotional reunion. "Quiet! Quiet!" I said, hugging him.

After that, using the sharp end of one of the boards, I dug myself out of the shack by way of Sedgewick's hole.

It was dusk when I got out. "Now," I whispered. "We have to move!"

I had forgotten that the colonel would obviously leave one of his men on guard. After all, he knew I was roaming around somewhere. But I almost walked into the guard: a huge man standing, fortunately, with his back to me, a rifle in his hand.

I picked up Sedgewick, my hand over his muzzle. My sandals made no noise as I backtracked. This time I walked more carefully. It was as well I did. Because I saw the next guard only just before he would have seen me. They were all around. It would have to be the waterfall.

I got to the rocky edge without noise and without seeing anybody. One thing was in my favor: Near the fall the water made enough noise to deaden any ordinary sound.

I was taller and bigger than the last time I had slithered behind the water, but I had not been holding a dog. The drop, if I slipped, was fifty feet, with boulders beneath and all around the pool.

I knew, of course, that as far as my own safety was concerned, all I had to do was to stay put. In a few hours the guards would be down by the house and in the village and cane fields, helping the colonel establish his martial law. I could easily then get to the car and drive to Gilbert's office. He would hide me until he could get me to the boat.

But then Jonathan would be dead.

At the edge of the fall I picked Sedgewick up again and put my hand around his muzzle. I said a prayer. Then I walked into the first spray of water.

I have always maintained that mutts are more intelligent than highly bred dogs. Take Sedgewick: He lay shivering on my shoulders while I penetrated the first layers of water and got to the rock behind and walked along it. Of course, it could have been that he was paralyzed with fright, as indeed I almost was. At eight years old I had found it a lark. Now it seemed more a nightmare. Eventually I felt the rock slant in and followed it, and there was my cave, much smaller than I remembered it. I put the shivering Sedgewick down and tried to wipe him off with my hands. Then I took a firm hold of his leash (which, incongruously, he was still wearing). "We're going for a long crawl," I said.

There were two ways I could have gone from that shallow cave. One led up almost to the peak and emerged just under it. The other led down and gave out not too far from the house. There was just one problem about that: The path down, so narrow and low that at time I had to be on hands and knees, branched out several times. I devoutly hoped I remembered which branch led to the cave near the house. The others were dead ends filled with snakes, scorpions and bats, and, coming back from a dead end, it was sometimes hard to remember which was the main path and which another cul-de-sac.

There was another problem. Beyond the watery light of the cave the path was dark, far blacker than the hut I had just dug myself out of. But I had been a resourceful child. It had been great fun to outwit Jonathan. Praying that no one had disturbed what I had left, I put my hand high up to a shelf in the cave, hoping not to dislodge any bats. My fingers found what I was looking for: a box of matches, carefully wrapped in oilcloth, and some rolled-up balls of twine. I struck a match. The sides of the cave sprang into view. I put the other matches and the twine in my pocket and started forward.

That journey down, under those conditions, hurrying against time, was something I hope I never have to repeat. I was many inches taller and wider in the shoulders, among other places, than my eight-year-old self. I used the matches as sparingly as possible, each time committing to memory, before the flame burned to my fingers, the few yards immediately in front of me. I heard frequent scrabbling that did nothing for my peace of mind. I tried to summon my childhood indifference to various forms of animal and insect life. I muttered to myself,

> *All things bright and beautiful*
> *All creatures great and small . . .*

in a mind-over-matter attempt to remind myself that we were all—scorpions, snakes, centipedes—part of nature and not to be feared. It didn't work. I kept on unrolling the twine and it was just as well, because twice I had to back up. I bumped and cut my head. I heard Sedgewick give a yelp every now and then. Twice I fell and let the leash go. But he always came back.

"Why aren't you Rin-tin-tin or Lassie or some hero dog?" I said to him once, when he had come back and waited for me to get up, helpfully licking my face. "By this time you would have found the marshal's posse and come and rescued me. . . ."

Eventually I felt a current of air. The passage suddenly got wider and higher. I emerged into a shallow cave and pushed aside the bushes covering it.

It was already dark, or would have been if flames hadn't lit up the grounds of the burning Four Winds and the sky above it.

13

I will never forget the sight. Nor will I forget the fear that clamped down on my whole body, gripping me in remembered horror. Sedgewick, released now, stayed close by me as we ran towards the house, where people were huddled and the flames roared like an angry god.

Fire is a terrible thing, especially to anyone who has ever been trapped by it. I could almost hear my child's voice screaming in terror, fists beating against the door.

"Are you all right, Miss Kilgaren?" I looked up. It was Constable Richardson, looking incredibly competent and kind, even in that devilish light.

"Jonathan?" I gasped.

He hesitated. "We can't find him. He called in the alarm. We've been getting the others out. The firemen are looking for him now."

My men will take care of him. "They were going to kill him," I cried.

He took hold of my arm. "Who, Miss Kilgaren? The colonel was trying to take over and declare martial law, backed by a lot of guards I've never seen before. I think he thought the rest of the island police force would join him. Is he the one you're talking about? Who was going to kill Sir Jonathan?"

"Is everybody safe—besides Jonathan?"

"Yes. People are trying to rescue some of the things now, the paintings."

"Oh, never mind those. Jonathan's going to be killed if he's not dead already."

"By whom?" He shook my arm. "You've got to tell me."

"I don't have time to explain everything." But I stumbled out the bare bones of the story.

Richardson said, "We thought at first, when he didn't appear and we couldn't locate him, that he might have gone to the other end of the island to rally the island militia."

"Is there some?"

"Oh, yes. Sir Jonathan, he's been expecting this. From Seth and those wild men on one side, and the colonel on the other."

"Where is the colonel?" I asked.

"Over there." Richardson pointed. "He's raving. Out of his mind."

I started to run to where Colonel Fortescue was standing between two military-looking blacks. It was then I noticed the faces of all the watchers. There was a small group of white women—wives mostly, in their evening dresses for the party. I knew their husbands were part of the volunteer fire-fighting force. Some of the women, in the best English tradition, had set up a table and were giving out coffee or tea to the firemen. Where they had got it, I didn't know; possibly from our kitchens, which were away from the worst of the flames. Others were just standing. I didn't see Mother or Yolande or Evelyn. Hamish, yelling "Ye black scoundrel, let me go look for the master," was held by an enormous young black policeman. Tears were running down the old servant's face.

But it was the blacks who caught my eye. More than half the island must have been there, watching. As I saw their faces reflected in the writhing flames, I realized that to some of them at least, probably all, what was burning was the symbol of everything that had owned and oppressed them, even when it was not overtly unkind. They're glad, I thought, even those who are are not with Seth are glad. I couldn't blame them.

At that moment Gilbert Palmer ran up to me. "Where the hell have you been? The boat's ready, if you want to come now."

"I can't. Jonathan's in there."

"After all that I've told you about him! You're still going to sit around to see if they rescue him. Better for everybody if they don't."

I wheeled on him. "Don't ever speak to me again, or come anywhere near me. Jonathan, at his worst, is worth fifty of you."

"All right, don't get shirty. But I can tell you that

the fair Yolande lost no time in getting to her yacht, taking Evelyn with her. She tried to take your mother, too. But she wouldn't leave."

I pushed him away and ran towards the colonel. "Where is he? Where's Jonathan?" I yelled above the sound of the fire and the firemen.

He was staring up at the house, a strange, wild look on his formerly precise face. "It didn't work. After all the planning, it didn't work."

I took hold of his arm and shook him. "Where is Jonathan? You were going to have him killed. Where is he?"

"He betrayed us. Bloody nigger." His eyes focussed on me and I saw what Richardson meant when he said, "raving!"

Fortescue went on in the same mad way. "It was all her fault, you know. Lady Margaret. You'd think with a background like hers she'd have known better. But she got stuffed with radical nonsense. When she couldn't have children she put a—"

I beat upon his chest. "Colonel Fortescue! Listen to me! What did you do with Jonathan? Tell me!"

"He's in the house, Barbara." It was Mother. I hadn't seen her, but she was standing behind the colonel in her white satin ball gown, now filthy with soot. Beside her stood Nemi.

"*Where* in the house?"

"I already told the firemen. They're trying to get into his bedroom. The fire broke out while he was still dressing. But he was dead, Barbara, before the fire."

"Dead? Who killed him?"

"Frank . . . Colonel Fortescue . . . You see, before dinner Jonathan told Frank that he knew what he was trying to do and that his men were surrounded. He also told him that he intended to give the island to the people. And Frank . . . well, he went round the bend. Just like that. He adored your father."

"*My* father? You mean Jonathan's father. The last, real legitimate Sir Jonathan. My father is this murdering lunatic, Colonel Fortescue."

"So you heard."

At that moment a blackened fireman in whom I barely recognized the village chemist came up and said, "I'm sorry, but we got into Sir Jonathan's bedroom and he's not there."

I turned to the colonel. "Where *is* he?"

The colonel spoke, suddenly sounding quite rational. "It was just like the last time. I shot at him, but he was running down the hall. He seemed to think that Barbara had come back and was locked in her room. I fired after him. I'm quite certain I hit him. But this time the fire will get him. You'll see, Sylvia." The words were insane but he sounded like his old self.

Mother shuddered and put her hands up to her face.

I was running towards the southeast wing before I knew what I was doing. There were shouts behind me. But I ran on. Not for nothing had I climbed every tree on the grounds. If the tree were still standing, if I could just get up to the balcony. . . .

It would be nice to report that, selfless in my desire to save Jonathan, I had forgotten my horror of fire and the memory of what it had done to my face. I didn't. Not for one minute of that ghastly climb up the huge live oak, its leaves almost seared off in the heat. It was as though I was living through it again. I had one thing going for me. The wind was blowing away from the tree and away from that end of the house.

I heard the wheels of one of the ladders behind me. Jonathan's bedroom was in the other wing and they had been concentrating all their equipment there.

Somehow I got up the tree, level with the balcony of my bedroom. The smoke was blowing away. The flames crackled, but not immediately in front of me. I don't think I have ever felt so frightened in my life. All I could remember was something I had once read somewhere: When fear is engulfing you, all you can do is to plunge into the middle of it and hope you come out the other side.

The glass of the French windows had long since cracked. I kicked the door open. The room itself was not on fire—yet. I ran to the door, but it had jammed. I went back into the bathroom, turned on the water and soaked a towel, put it around my face and went into Evelyn's room. The flames were licking around the baseboard and there were unpleasant cracks in the ceiling. Then I went to the door and pulled it open.

The hall was a furnace, the flames only feet away, the air dense with smoke. Jonathan was stretched across the hall. There was blood on the back of his shirt. One hand was outstretched to my door.

Jonathan is a big man. I don't know where I got the strength to move him as fast as I did. But, choking and gagging even with the towel around my face, I dragged him into Evelyn's room and across to the bathroom as the ceiling crashed behind us. As I pulled him into my room I saw the world's most welcome sight: the sooty and streaked face of a fireman coming through the window. Then I fainted.

"I had known for a while what Fortescue was up to," Jonathan said. "It was just a question of finding out when. He almost fooled me there."

"Couldn't you have stopped him?"

"There was no real evidence. I had to depend on catching him red-handed."

Jonathan and I were sitting in his study which, with two small downstairs rooms and one washroom, was about all that was habitable of what was left of Winds. We had moved into the tiny hotel in the village, but had come up here to sort out what papers were left. The colonel's bullet had grazed Jonathan's side, and the fire had scorched him down the other side. With burns and bandages and blisters he wasn't very comfortable but, as he was inclined to say when people asked him how he was, he'd survive. Hamish was at the hotel with us. Mother had returned to Rome and Evelyn had gone back to England.

"Is it true," I asked, picking some papers off the floor.

"Is what true?"

"That—that Mrs. Gutierrez is your mother, and not Lady Margaret?"

Jonathan eased his sore leg. "Quite true. Father unloaded that tidbit of information at the peak of one of our battles. Do you remember our fights?"

I remembered. They lay like a storm over the meals and blew through the house, leaving harshness, anger and sometimes bullying in their wake. "Yes. I remember."

Jonathan gave me his smile that now, thanks to some blistered skin, was more one-sided than ever.

"He was the last of the old regime. He believed in the feudalistic life. To be fair, he was more generous to most of the people who worked for him than employers on other islands who hired free labor. But to him the island was as much a part of him as his name. I was younger and had lived more among the people since Mother—or perhaps I should say Lady Margaret—died. I knew it couldn't go on and shouldn't. That was usually what our fights were about. One night, when I accused him of making Louis XIV look like a democrat, he told me that if I didn't mind my manners he would make public what he had learned about my birth, which would, in effect, disinherit me. That was when he threatened to have you made the heir subject to certain conditions, such as your husband taking the name."

"Why didn't he anyway—make the whole thing public if he had all that feudal pride?"

"Because I think his male pride was even stronger. He didn't want to admit publicly that he had been made a fool of."

"And anyway, he wasn't my father." It was an effort to say that. "At least your real mother is *nice*," I said bitterly. "How would you like to have a flaming lunatic bigot for a parent?"

"You know, Skimp. He wasn't that bad when I first knew him. It isn't fashionable to talk about war records these days, but he had an honorable one, and that included being among those who helped liberate some of the concentration camps. He didn't start life as a lunatic bigot. He had been in the colonial police in Africa and then came here with Father. I think he somehow got his bitterness over a changing world and devotion to the family and its supposed traditions all mixed up together. He was a good chief of police, you know. He never abused his power. No Islander ever accused him of bullying tactics. It was just that this was the last stronghold of things as they used to be, and he got an *idée fixe* on the subject."

"Who told your father about . . . about your not being Lady Margaret's son?"

"I'm afraid your mother did that. She produced it when he was being feudal and difficult about something she wanted to do." Jonathan glanced at me. "Father wasn't an easy man to live with, and he got more difficult as he got older and his health failed."

"And who told Mother?"

"Colonel Fortescue."

I stared back at Jonathan. "That seems strange, doesn't it?"

"Even stranger is how he knew. Lady Margaret told him."

"But why?"

"I'm not sure. I don't know. But I'd bet it was to make him uncomfortable. She knew it would drive a wedge right down the middle of his loyalty. Should he tell my father, whom he revered, the truth? Or should he stand aside and let a partly black bastard inherit the family name and honors?"

"But what an extraordinary thing for her to do? She was supposed to be such an idealist!"

"Yes. And to make sure her ideals worked out the way she thought they should, she was just as arrogant and, as I once said to you, manipulative as the rest of her class. Mrs. Gutierrez—my mother; it still doesn't seem quite right to say that—tells me that once Lady Margaret discovered that she, the maid, was pregnant by my father, the master of the house, she all but adopted her. Perhaps she suspected, after all those barren years, or perhaps from something one of the New York doctors had told her, that her own child might not live. I don't know. But when her son died, what with the golden opportunity of Father being away, there was no stopping her."

"And Mrs. Gutierrez didn't object?"

"Why should she? Her son would be brought up to be master of the island, and she herself would receive training and education to come back and help her people. She was intelligent and ambitious and Lady Margaret obviously knew it."

"How do you feel about her . . . Mrs. Gutierrez?" I asked awkwardly.

"The same as I have always felt: respect and regard." He smiled. "It's a little late for me to develop filial sentiments."

"Is that why she took me on? Because you wanted me there?"

"Oh, no. She's an ardent integrationist. I wouldn't have attempted to force her about that against her will."

I thought for a while and then said, "So Lady Margaret was behind everything?"

"All roads lead back to her. Including, by the way, a small farm I own in England, left to me in her will 'in case,' she had it worded, 'my fortunes didn't work out as she had planned.'"

"Do you intend to go there? Or stay here?"

Jonathan shifted his leg again. "I don't see any future in being the only white—" he grinned, "relatively white—family here. But if I can persuade some of the other white families to stay so we can have a real, working, truly assimilated democracy, then I will stay. After all, my family took enough out of the island. I'd like to try to give some back."

There was a question I had been nerving myself to ask. "What about Yolande?"

"Well, what about her? I've never seen anyone leave so fast after she discovered the true and grisly facts of my parentage. I think it was the loss of title as much as anything else. Being illegitimate I become plain Mr. Kilgaren. I may have to make the name legal by deed poll or whatever, but I've been used to it too long to change that."

"Was that, by the way, what you meant when you told me you had an ace in the hole? The fact that you share a black strain with the other Islanders?"

"Yes. Although I'm not sure how much, in the long run, it will count. The fact that I'm still a Kilgaren may heavily outweigh it."

"Will it be unpopular with the Islanders? I mean, your keeping the name of the island?"

"No. They're talking of changing the name of the island back to its original Indian name—Nêmicha."

"So everything about the Kilgarens has gone, or is going—first Kilgaren's Castle, then the island. But what a pillar of self-importance our—sorry, your—noble ancestor must have been: the original Sir Jonathan!"

Jonathan grinned. "All founders of dynasties like to leave their stamp."

"Still—" I looked at him. "I'm glad you're keeping the name. After all, a lot of island history is wrapped up in it." I reverted to our original subject. "Did you mind Yolande's leaving?"

"Not in the least. I was never in love with her, Skimp, you should know that, nor she with me. Yolande was a collector. She wanted to acquire me—and my title—much as she wanted the villa she has in St. Tropez, her current yacht out there, and her collection of jewels. And her father wanted to collect the island and the off-shore rights. I went along with the whole thing to take everybody's attention away from you. I didn't know whether those stories about Father's trying to make you his heir were true or not. I didn't think they were. But if true, you were in considerable danger. That's why I manufactured that job to bring you here where I could keep an eye on you. That's why I asked you about any papers. That was the reason for the—er—amorous charade you stumbled on in the garden. Convincing you, for your own protection, was as important as convincing everyone else. That's why I let the pomp and frou-frou of this entirely bogus wedding scheme go on. And that, my dear, is why I blew my lid when you threatened to leave. I'm sorry about that, by the way. I was tired and scared for you, and I realized immediately afterward that I'd probably done what would most drive you away." He paused. "Do you remember that man who came to call on Yolande?"

"In the crumpled gray suit?"

"Yes. As a matter of fact, Yolande told you the truth—as far as it went. He *was* a friend of her father's. But your instincts about him were right. He was also Arribe's business associate and he wanted to make sure that everything was shipshape and the wedding was going to take place. His company owns those spurious little fishing boats that have been cruising around so industriously lately, investigating rumors of oil under these coastal waters. If you were indeed the heir, and there was oil, you would be a very rich girl and, before too long, I was afraid, a very dead girl. So I spent a lot of time and noise putting on the appearance of being the Kilgaren of Kilgaren to squash any speculations about your inheriting it." Jonathan said reflectively, "We discovered a lot about Senior Garcia when he was stuck in the cane."

"I suppose you arranged that."

He grinned. "What makes you say that?"

I grinned back and then said, a little sadly, "And, of course, if it had been true, that I was the heir, Mother would get some money, so she could hang onto Renaldo. That was the hoard she was talking about. And that's what made her come back, wasn't it?"

"Yes. Although she got wind of something earlier, which was why she was so amazingly cooperative about sending you here in the first place. Do you realize, Skimp, how fast the glamorous Renaldo's attention would have switched if he caught even the slightest whiff of rumor that you might be heir to an oil field?"

It didn't take me long to appreciate that. "I see," I said.

"I thought you would."

"So between hoping that I might inherit, or that she could manage to make Evelyn an heir, she was hedging her bets."

"I'm afraid so."

All this time Sedgewick had been snoring in a camp chair. The heat had been intense, and there were no ceiling fans, just a burned-out window with flies and mosquitos coming in. Something must have bitten him because he sat up with a yelp and started frantically biting his leg.

"You know," I said, "with all Sedgewick's been through he probably looks upon life in New York as a pastoral episode." I remembered my walk through the jungle. "That was my loving father who cut Sedgewick's leash and took a pot shot at me, wasn't it?"

"Yes. He was trying to warn you away from the cache of rifles. Richardson and I and one or two others raided and captured it right after you told me."

"Is that what you've been doing while you've been away so much? Training the militia?"

"And setting up a constitution and having town meetings."

"What's going to happen to . . . to the colonel?"

"He's on his way back to England to a hospital. We don't have any facilities to take care of him here."

"And Evelyn? What's going to happen to him?"

Jonathan sighed. "He's going to sit for that exam and, if he passes it, return to his school. If he doesn't, I'll just have to try to find another school for him—one that he'll accept—and that will accept him. We had a talk before Hamish put him on the plane. I offered to let him stay, but he doesn't want to. He's very bitter, Skimp, and I don't blame him. It's very much my fault. I should have taken more responsibility for him much earlier on. I'll do what I can now to make it up to him, but I'm not sure I'll succeed. One good that's come out of this is that he's become attached to your mother, Sylvia. He may go to Rome to visit her. Perhaps they can console one another—I have a feeling that Renaldo is shortly to become a past episode."

"Did Evelyn . . . did he know . . . about your being Mrs. Gutierrez' son?"

"Yes. You remember that leather book you saw him reading?"

I nodded.

"That was a diary kept by Lady Margaret and secreted in one of the myriad drawers in the huge headboard of her bed—the bed Evelyn was sleeping in. It never occurred to me to go through those drawers, but of course, Evelyn did. Any boy would. When you mentioned the book I thought at first it must be a diary he was keeping. Then I remembered that I had seen his diary—and it was a bright red notebook. So I went up to his room, and the obviousness of that monstrous bedstead struck me. I opened up one drawer after another until I found the diary." (Those, I thought, were what those knobs were: drawers.) "So," Jonathan said, shifting his leg again, "I had it out with Evelyn. He wasn't happy about me or the island to begin with. I'm afraid that discovering that some of my remote ancestors—and therefore his—were African slaves supplied the *coup de grâce*. It was after that that he became so thick with the colonel."

"Maybe," I said slowly, "that was why he hated me."

One of Jonathan's eyebrows went up. "Meaning?"

My hands strayed to my face in an old gesture. "You hate other people most when you hate yourself—I should know."

"Surely, Skimp, you're over that!"

"Yes. Thanks to you!" I looked at him. "I mean that. Mother spilled that up at the hut: That you'd paid for my plastic surgery."

He grinned a little sheepishly. "I just didn't want it on my conscience."

I was silent for a bit and then asked, "And where are Seth and his gang?"

"In Cuba. Permanently, I hope. They made an abortive try when the house was fired. But the police and militia outflanked and out-fought them."

"And Gervase?"

"I wouldn't be at all surprised if, at some time in the not-too-distant future, we shouldn't be addressing him as Prime Minister.

I remembered then that impression I had been chasing down as I saw the two of them—Jonathan and Gervase—together. It was one of equality—something I had never seen between a white and black Islander. No wonder I hadn't recognized it. If I had, I wouldn't have been so bowled over by Palmer's interpretation of Jonathan's motives. I mightn't, I thought with a pang, have been so ready to misjudge Jonathan. I looked at his burned and peeling face and found his gray-green eyes steadily regarding me. My heart gave an absurd little flutter.

I said a little breathlessly. "Who set fire to the house? The colonel?"

"Yes. Though I think it was going to be blamed on Nemi, as they tried to blame her for the last fire. Which was one reason she was brought back. But Hamish caught the colonel himself with the matches and the gasoline. Unluckily, the wind was wrong and we couldn't stop it."

"You mean they tried to blame poor old Nemi for the fire twelve years ago?"

"Yes. After they tried and failed to blame it on me—I was at someone's house all that evening. So they put it on Nemi who was known to drink, and she was too frightened to say anything. Then the colonel arranged a job in Jamaica for her. She hated it there but was afraid to come back until your mother sent for her a few weeks ago."

"But why did he want the fire the first time?"

"I think what Lady Margaret had told him about me had been seething in him. He couldn't bear the thought of me inheriting. If he could have got rid of me, either he could have persuaded Father to make you heir, or he might have talked him into handing over the government of the island to him."

At that moment there was sound I hadn't heard in a long time: rain.

Sedgewick sat up and barked.

"It's raining," I said. "The rainy season's begun."

Jonathan stood, a little stiffly. "Hallelujah and

amen! We'll have a new sugar crop ready for cutting soon." He looked down at me and said awkwardly, "Well, Skimp, are you still feeling sibling-ish?"

This was a point I had grasped with joy the moment I learned of it that day in the shack. I didn't like being Colonel Fortescue's daughter. But that was more than made up for by the fact that Jonathan and I were not even half-sibling. "We're not related at all, are we?"

"Not at all." He limped over to me and grasped my arms. "How does that sit with you—one way and another?"

I put my hand up to his face. "Have you always known we were not related?" I asked.

"Since long before you came back. Yes."

"Did Mother tell you?"

He nodded. "Yes."

"Did you love her, Jonnie?"

He drew me to him. "No, Skimp. Perhaps it would be better, or would sound better, if I had. But it was when Father and I were battling and he had just told me about my own birth. I was sore and angry and we—your mother and I—were both in London and—it happened."

"Then, if you knew, why did you look so unhappy the night you kissed me in here?"

"I thought you were still in love with Nick Caldwell and merely displaying—er—sisterly affection."

"That was very silly," I said, and kissed him.

Jonathan took a breath and tightened his arm.

"Don't do that, Skimp, unless you mean it. I'm not your brother and I haven't the faintest intention of behaving like one. I love you very much and not at all in a fraternal way."

I kissed him again. "I'm delighted to hear it."

After a very satisfying interlude I said, idiotically, "I think I've always loved you, Jonnie. But when did you first love me—*fall* in love with me?"

"The day you arrived, a few weeks ago."

"What was it about me?" I asked, beginning to preen myself.

He looked down at me with the old glint of amusement. "I'd like to say it was your beauty, charm, and visible intelligence."

I straightened. "But it wasn't?"

"No. I'm afraid not, though you possess all those admirable qualities in great abundance."

"Something tells me I'm going to be sorry I asked."

He grinned. "You want to know what it was? You and your mangy hound—sorry Sedgewick! I've never seen two creatures more forlorn and more gallant. Daniel and friend, about to encounter the lions!" He looked at me for a minute. "There's just one thing that bothers me a little. I'm much older than you, Skimp. Do you think you may have a father complex?"

"It beats incest," I said.

He laughed and pulled me back in his arms and kissed me.